REAPING

PEACEKEEPER'S HARMONY - BOOK 2

MAGGIE M LILY

This is a work of fiction. Names, characters, events, and incidents are the products of the author's imagination. Any resemblance to actual persons, living or dead, or actual events is purely coincidental. Certain long-standing institutions, agencies, and public offices are mentioned, but the characters and situations involved are wholly imaginary.

Cover design by Melony Paradise of Paradise Cover Design

For my kiddo—thanks for all the kisses blown through the office door, Cal.

I love you too.

1

A character index can be found at the back of this novel.

"*Because I love her. Because I don't like being apart from her.*"

The thought ran wildly through my mind as I waited for death. I knew I was dying; my head had been sliced off. There was no surviving that kind of nonsense.

In those moments before death, I held on to thoughts of Sianna, wanting the memory of her laughter to accompany me on that final, lonely journey.

Say what you will. Everyone dies alone, save for the love they've carried through life.

I could see her smile, hear her laughter, taste her mouth. We didn't get enough time together. My parents, my siblings, my family, my friends… my music. It was all there, making a whirlpool of memories in my fading mind. But mostly, I thought of Sianna.

Try as I might, I couldn't block out the annoying slices of

reality slamming into my brain. I was clinging to morose thoughts of dying before my time, leaving my only love too soon.

But fucking Sam wouldn't stop yelling something.

Then William smacked me.

I could hear Talise and Adaline crying.

It was putting a real damper on my "I'll love you forever even though I just met you" Shakespearean tragedy vibe.

I sighed.

Wait, did I actually sigh? I wondered.

"Yeah, dumb ass. You're not dead," Other-me said.

I would never admit to having an Other-Luke—a sentient, opinionated mental projection of my power. Never. I would never hear the end of it if I owned up to it now.

Once upon a time, my brother, Sam, had asked if I had an Other-Luke. Of course, I'd outright denied it and looked at him like he was absurd. At the time, I'd known it'd hurt his feelings. It'd made him feel like an even more isolated freak-show.

I hadn't lied about Other-Luke on purpose. I just hadn't realized my power had a personality.

Also, Sam was an absurd freak show. I hadn't caused that to be true. It was a fact of life.

"You're going to start waking up soon," Other-me continued. "We should finish our talk. Here's the long and the short of it: stop being a whiny asshole. You have the power to control peace in the world. That power does not limit your ability to feel or attract other emotions. So, quit blaming your power—quit blaming me—because you're scared of rejection.

"It's time to grow up, Luke. You have real work to do. Unfortunately, there are people in this world who will suffer and die without your help. I know you don't want that to happen. I know it hurts you to consider that possibility.

"So, stop being a coward. Stop trying to pretend like your power is something separate from you. I *am* you. If you continue trying to keep me separate, trying to keep me balanced without actively engaging and directing me, you're not going to make it in this world. And the world will suffer for your failure.

"You're strong. Between your family circle, your extended Harbor circle, and now your role as Peacekeeper with the beast affinities, you are easily the most powerful embodiment of peace to ever exist. Trust me. As that raw power, I know. I have *never* had the reach I do with you. Own it. The world needs this kind of mojo. Stand equal to Addy and Sam. Raise the rest of your circle's threshold and make a better world."

There was quiet between us for a moment.

"Um," I started.

"That's all I've got," Other-me snapped. "I don't do pep talks. Get your shit together and do the job. Quit being such a self-pitying shithead. Your life is great. Grab it by the horns, and let's do this."

"How? How do I reconcile the two parts? How do I combine you and me into one whole?" I asked.

I'd just spent what felt like hours telling this Other-me about how I met and fell in love with a shifter. In reality, it had probably only been a minute or two, but whatever. Now that I knew Other-me was there, I needed to know how to fix it so there was only one me.

"You don't get it, man. We *are* one whole person. You—Luke—are a person and also the power that makes up my awareness. You just need to accept it. Stop wussing out when things get interesting. Don't be scared of—"

"—WOULD be dead. It's not how I interpreted it."

Candy. I could hear my ex-girlfriend's voice. I couldn't open my eyes, but I could hear her.

And I could feel the energy. I could feel my family around me, radiating exhaustion and grief. I could feel Sianna next to me and feel her energy cycling through me.

Candy's brother, Charlie, was there along with one of the shifter elders, Edgar. I could feel Charlie's wife, Eleanor. My brothers too. But I knew Sianna was next to me, hanging onto my hand.

Sianna. My love. I knew there was a gold bond of love tying me to her. I was hers, and I would be hers for as long as she'd have me. I'd allowed that bond to come into existence.

I also knew there was no bond going from her to me. At first glance, someone looking at the bonds would assume my love was unrequited. But she sat next to me, holding on for dear life.

There was hope yet.

Candy was still talking.

"—and Luke almost died."

Her voice broke on the last words. I knew she was crying. I tried to offer her my peaceful energy. It wasn't working.

She sniffled. "It doesn't matter. I was wrong. If I have to pay for that with my life, so be it. If it costs me my dignity, that's fine too. Call me whatever you want."

I felt her sorrow and shame, her regret and sense of responsibility for my injuries.

I let fly another internal sigh. I didn't want to feel bad for her. From a purely objective point of view, she had betrayed me.

Nathaniel, the leader of all beast affinities—more commonly

called shifters, but they hated being called that—had set me up. He viewed my Peacekeeper abilities as a threat to his leadership. He assumed I couldn't be Peacekeeper while also being part of an empowered circle.

Somehow, he'd known I stood circles with my family. He'd played his cards so Candy had ended up confirming it in front of roughly a thousand people, all of whom might have taken offense to my dual peace duties.

I could be Peacekeeper to the beast affinities or Lord Peace to the empowered circles. Not both. Except, I *was* both. I seemed to be the first embodiment of Peace that could fill both roles.

Nathaniel hadn't realized it when he'd set me up. Poor Candy thought she'd found a way to "rescue" me from being torn to pieces by an angry mob. So, she'd snitched on me.

I didn't blame her for confirming something the beastly Overlord had already known. I wouldn't have wanted her to die over something so foolish. He'd already known I stood circles. It didn't matter that she'd confirmed it.

"Call you friend," I croaked, struggling to make my voice work. I didn't sound like myself anymore. I wondered if my vocal cords were ruined when my neck was sliced.

I tried to open my eyes and talk to my family. I wanted them to know I'd be okay, that I was healing faster than imaginable.

No dice. Those systems weren't online yet.

Sianna squeezed my hand, her grip so tight it was almost painful. I tried to offer her peace.

It didn't work that time either.

I would just rest a little more. I faded back out, wondering if I could talk with Other-me again.

No such luck.

I heard voices murmuring around me but couldn't make out the words. I wiggled my fingers against Sianna's hand, startling her. I smiled to myself. Very little caught her by surprise.

I was just starting to fade back out again, back to night-night land, when I felt it.

The energy rolled toward me, a wild offering of devotion and support. Shifters were coming. Fifty. One hundred. More than that. The waves of energy surfing into me just kept coming, pulling my own energy forward and waking my mind.

My children are coming home to me, I thought.

I tried to shake my head. I didn't have kids. *What the fuck?*

I couldn't shake my head. But of course, that was to be expected, given someone tried to chop it off a few hours ago.

My children will keep me safe, the energy whispered through my mind.

Oh, holy crap. I shivered with the realization of what was happening.

Earlier in the night, a thousand shifters had greeted me with a gift of their raw life energy. I'd accepted that gift. I'd welcomed it. I'd responded in kind.

I had begun the process or ceremony necessary to become the Peacekeeper for all beast affinities. It was official. I was Peacekeeper. There was no going back.

Now, the energy kept coming, reviving me. I could feel the people, my people, hovering at a distance, likely beyond the gated walls of my family's compound.

I felt one person cross the wards that kept unwelcome energy away. I felt him park his car at the curb and walk toward the correct house without hesitation.

I could feel his excitement. He would be the envoy to the Peacekeeper.

I felt his joy. There was a Peacekeeper to help those with beast affinities survive.

I felt his terror.

I felt his sorrow.

I was Peacekeeper now, no longer his best friend's kid brother.

I was Peacekeeper, sacred and beloved, but also endangered and hunted.

I felt Gary skip up the steps of Sam's house.

"Greetings, Peacekeeper," his voice rang through my mind. *"I'm glad you're still with us."*

As he rang the doorbell, he shoved a giant wave of healing energy through the house, directly to me. *"A gift from your fans, Luke. Tell them to open the door. Nathaniel doesn't know where to find you yet, but we don't have much time."*

"It's for me," I said, eyes half open as I tried to climb to my feet.

2

"It's the fox," Sianna announced, stopping me from trying to stand. "There are other affinities as well. They wait beyond the walls to lend aid. I believe they are mostly yours, Edgar. Stay Luke. Don't get up. You are healing but not ready to move on your own yet."

"Gary?" Adrian asked, climbing to his feet to let his best friend inside the house.

Resting my head back on the couch, I closed my eyes again. I'd be better after sleep.

"No sleep," Gary said, clapping his hands. "We have to get him..." His voice trailed off as his eyes landed on Candy.

"Why is she here?" That startled me fully awake. I'd never heard Gary sound so cold and unwelcoming.

"He already knew," Sam replied. "Nathaniel already knew. She confirmed it rather than die."

"Yeah, she needs to go," Gary said without hesitation. "And so do we. There's not much time before he finds this little hidey-hole of yours. The wards, guns, and walls won't keep beast affinities out. We need to run and hide to buy some time."

"Where is he? What is he doing?" Edgar asked, eyeing Gary. "And how do you fit here, fox? What have you brought to this place?"

Gary bowed his head in a sign of respect. "Edgar. I don't think he knows you're here. There's madness in the arena right now. I don't think Nathaniel realizes you're not there."

"Answer my questions." Edgar's voice cut with authority. He wasn't used to being ignored.

"Apologies, sir," Gary said quickly. "No slight intended. I am a lifelong friend of the family. I've known Luke since the day he was born. I'm here, as are the others, at the Walker's request. My family knows of this place and are welcome here. Deanna and Joe and their line, as well as some of the other families, have followed to lend strength. They're nearby, but they won't come closer unless we send for them.

"Nate is trying to gain control of the arena. He knows Sianna and the Peacekeeper are gone, but not where they went. I don't think he even knows how they left. Elias and Jordan are dead, decapitated by the Huntress and finished by Daniel." He nodded to Sianna, seeming to congratulate her on a job well done.

Sianna exhaled hard. I felt her shiver with relief.

"We have a short gap of time to disappear. The Trellis family has hidden the compound well, but it won't take them long to come knocking. So, let's get our 'go' on, Sam." Gary clapped his hands in my brother's face.

"We should gather the others," Sam muttered, not entirely focused on the present.

"Oh, man. I hate it when you do that in front of me," Gary

whined. "Can you go somewhere else and do your time thing? It weirds me out."

Edgar made a choking sound, trying to find words. His eyes were huge, staring in fear at my middle brother.

Sam, as the Walker, came from a long line of petty assholes who would destroy entire civilizations if you looked at them funny. Sam wasn't quite that harsh, though.

"Sam!" Will barked, delivering a smack upside Sam's head for good measure. "We need to go? I should wake Pip?"

Snapping back to the present, Sam shook his head. "Shower first. You'll scare her if you wake her up while you're covered in Luke's blood. We have at least two hours. Send the guards away, William. Their guns are useless. The shifters will come through here looking for fresh trails, find none, and leave. They fear me, and they adore Luke. They don't want to upset either of us. The guards would confuse things and get hurt. Let the beast affinities who come to inspect do their thing. They'll leave our stuff undisturbed."

William nodded, already moving toward the bathroom. Adrian was also on his feet, headed upstairs.

"I'll go get them clothes," Sam said, gone before the words registered.

Edgar jumped in surprise.

"For fuck's sake, he really is the Walker," Gary muttered.

"You doubted?" Micah asked.

Gary made a so-so gesture with his head. "I hoped not. He was a weird kid, but sweet. When I had an idea of what he was, I started taking stuff he liked from him, just to see what he'd do. He knew I did it too. Didn't say anything; didn't do anything either.

"Except for one time. He had this *Star Wars* poster. I knew he really liked it, so I took it. The next time I saw him, he asked why I took it—not if I took it, *why* I took it. I told him I wanted it, that I liked it more than he did. He shrugged, told me happy early birthday, and went about his day. I stopped touching his stuff after that. I thought maybe he had weird energy. Walkers of legend would have smited me for my insolence. Smited me? Smote me? Anyway, they wouldn't have taken it well."

"You've known what they are? What they all are?" Micah asked. "From when you were young?"

"No. Well. No. I didn't know about Adrian's shit until middle school. I didn't know about Will's shit until he came back from the military. I thought Noah was just horny. Someone said I was missing more than half of their Names." Gary shrugged. "I don't care. Hank and Darla are second parents to me. I grew up with them. So, I didn't really think about it much. I mean, I knew I was going to make a lot of money with Sam. I knew he could touch time. But I would have taken that job even if it wasn't a safe bet. I spend all day hanging out with my second family, my little brothers. We talk shit, play pool, and make cool stuff. It's a fun job."

Garry shrugged. "At least I did. That might be over now. But I will say, I had no idea about Jen. I almost shit myself tonight. Jen as Queen of the Mind? I thought that was a joke right up until she projected words directly into my brain telling me to get out, that everything was about to go sideways."

Sam gave a bark of laughter as he reappeared. "She scared us at first too."

"Did you know who she was when you hired her?" Gary asked. "I literally had no idea."

"No," Sam admitted. "What's the plan, Gary? Where do we

need to run to? What are we running from? Why are we running?"

"We need him healed," Edgar answered before Gary could make a sound. "He can't face Nate weakened like this. He's not even conscious."

"Yes, he is," Sianna disagreed. "In and out. Enough to know what is going on." Her eyes cut to Talise. "I think he is dehydrated and low on fuel."

Without a word, Talise took my other hand. I felt her water energy wash through me and felt her terror. I offered her my peaceful energy. I knew it worked that time because she exhaled.

"Addy," Talise muttered. "I can't make water appear in his body, only better circulate what's there. And I think there's some internal bleeding. I can't get that fluid to move like it should."

A gentle hand touched my cheek. I turned my neck the smallest of fractions to kiss Adaline's hand.

"Thank you," I mumbled.

Her terror and remorse rolled through both Talise and me. "I couldn't save you, Luke. I couldn't make things close fast enough. Charlie helped, but Sianna and the man saved you. I'm going to get you some water, and then you pull enough energy from me to drink it."

Gary snorted, actually laughing. "Adaline, there's no shortage of energy. Get the water. He'll drink it."

He was right, of course. Raw energy circled me, waiting for me to give it a task.

"How do I...?" I croaked. But before I could ask for directions, the energy washed into me, eager to get to work. Just thinking about it, just trying to touch it, opened a gateway into me. "Oh."

Edgar nodded. "We can force energy into you. Touch makes that easier. It's easier still if you welcome it."

I sat straighter as Adaline handed me a large glass of water. "Bleh. It's warm."

"Drink it," she demanded. "Your system has enough to do without bringing fluids up to temperature."

I chugged it as directed, and then the second and third glass she brought me too.

"One more," Talise murmured to Addy, her hand still on my arm.

"I'm going to float away," I complained, already sounding more like myself.

Adaline rolled her eyes as she turned to fetch more water.

"I'll get Pip and the parents," Will said, passing through the room on the way to the front door."

"Everyone else is on the move and knows what to expect. I'm headed to help Lucy and Linda with Ree. It'd be good if we could get Luke showered before Mom shows up," Adrian said, following William out the door.

"I will get Mama, Da, Jess, and her family," Adaline muttered, handing me another glass of water before disappearing.

"Holy shit," Gary breathed. "She does it, too?"

"Why did she go?" Sam asked, sounding panicked. "She should have stayed and sent me. I can't do the healing stuff!"

"It's fine, Sam," Tali muttered, now holding both my hands. "The wound itself is healing without her help. I'm just making things move faster to replace the blood he lost."

"Since when do you do this?" I asked, almost smiling at Talise. She was too focused to notice.

"Addy's been teaching me. I have life energy like she and Ava do. I can heal things directly. I just don't have as much practice. This is as much about water management as it is about healing, though."

"I agree on the shower," Sam muttered.

I looked down at myself. My shirt was ripped open and covered in dried blood. My pants were in tatters. I had no idea what had happened to my shoes. "Get me some clothes?" I asked.

"Already done," Sam replied. "They're waiting for us upstairs. When Tali's done, I'll take you and Sianna up there. You'll need help. Stairs are beyond you right now."

"I can't believe I'm about to say this, but I don't feel terrible," I admitted.

Everyone in the room glared at me.

"Okay, I'll just be quiet."

HALF AN HOUR LATER, my entire family was gathered in Sam's living room. Those who'd gotten muddy or bloody were clean. Those who'd remained ignorant of Sam's many plans were caught up.

My mother wouldn't even look at me. Her anger radiated from her and circulated the room. I knew I wasn't the only one feeling it. I could tell from the lack of eye contact.

I had to explain. "Ma, I had to—"

"Shut up," my mom growled. "You are on my shit list, along with number five."

"Me?" Sam asked, horrified. He dropped the backpack he was carrying in surprise.

"I told you he was not going to that thing! How *dare* you ignore me?"

"He's alive because—"

"I don't want to hear it right now!" Darla yelled over him.

"Let her be angry," my dad murmured. He stared at me, stoic and lost in thought, occasionally wiping his eyes.

"Where are we going?" I asked. "Why are we running?"

"Oh. Yeah," Sam said, shaking his head as he picked up his bag. "Yeah, we should go. You'll sleep for a few days. But, Gary, I don't think he needs the giant wave of energy. You should send those people home. And we need you to go home too. Play decoy."

"They know my scent, Sam," Gary muttered. "I'll dodge as best I can, but—"

"No, don't dodge," Sam cut in. "You misunderstand me. Go tell them you know Luke. Tell them everything you know about us. Spill the beans. Give them all the details on all of us. Everything you can think of, tell them."

Gary frowned. "What?"

"I'm serious," Sam said, taking in the glares from around the room. "That Overlord dude is nuts, but it's just him and his circle of confidants and supporters. We need as much information, as much truth, about *who* we are spread around. So, tell the ferret guy to start talking. The people that were in that church too."

"I'll go with you," Candy muttered.

Sianna snorted. "Of course, you will."

Sam glared at Sianna. "Stop it. I know why you're upset. I

know why you don't like her. You wouldn't have a Peacekeeper right now if things hadn't happened the way they did."

Sianna dropped her eyes, not responding.

"I'll go," Candy said again. "Gary, if you'll let me ride with you, I'll go."

"You need to stay with us, Candy," Sam said. "I'm sorry. I know you don't want to, but you must stay with us. He'll try to blame the Peacekeeper attack on you. If you go back, you'll be his sacrificial lamb to the enraged population of beast affinities."

Candy shrugged, eyes still on the floor. "Nathaniel? He can try. Maybe it'll work. But I don't think so."

"You'll stay with us," Sam said again, tone firm but kind. "You and Jen, Charlie and Ellie, will all come with us. Your parents will stay where they are. They're not in danger and will speak to what happened to you and Charlie. They need to tell their story. We need the politics of that to play out before we resurface."

"And me?" Edgar asked. "Why did you bring me here, Walker? You didn't need me to heal him. Sianna and Charlie could have done it without me."

Sam stared at him. "I didn't need you to heal him. But I needed you to see who we are. We are not like our predecessors. You are welcome to come with us, or you may go. But fair warning: your little brother is not long for this world. If you work against us, it will not end well for you. And that would be a great loss for your people."

Edgar shook his head. "I won't interfere with this justice. I'd kill him myself if I got the chance, and he knows it. He does not trust me to get that close now that I'm back to myself."

Sam snorted. "With good reason."

Edgar lifted his eyebrows.

"I haven't looked, but I will," Sam promised. He seemed to be warning Edgar of something that no one else could follow. "I'll answer her questions if you don't. Stay or go; it's up to you."

"Answer questions about what?" I asked, feeling Sianna go stiff next to me on the couch.

Sam shook his head. "Later. He will answer on his own, I think. So, what's it going to be, Edgar?"

"Peacekeeper?" Edgar asked, awaiting my preference.

"Walker, is his life at risk if he goes?" Sianna asked Sam, her voice soft with worry.

"His life is at risk either way," Sam said with a shrug. "There's no difference in survival probability if he stays or goes."

"If I go with him?" she asked.

"No," Sam, Edgar, Charlie, and I said at the same time.

"If I go, I can speak to what happened," she said quietly. "I can form a group of those who would support the Peacekeeper."

Sam shook his head. "If we do this right, they will all support him without war among the affinities. Please stay with us."

"Charlie is here," she said, not looking at me. "Charlie can protect and give him energy."

Sam shook his head, shooting me a look.

"Please don't go," I breathed, squeezing her fingers.

She still didn't look at me, but she nodded. "If my father is killed, my eldest brother will be named Overlord. He is sane. But in many ways, he is worse."

Edgar shook his head. "I'll go. Charlie will be the next Overlord."

Charlie groaned unhappily. "For the six thousandth time, I will not."

"Sianna will be the next Overlord." Sam nodded to himself. "That works best."

Edgar sighed, his glance at Sianna filled with love. "I wish it could be so, Walker. She should be next. But our people won't allow it. They've proven it in the past. A woman cannot be Overlord."

Sam raised his eyebrows, showing his little smile. There was an invitation to place a bet in the look. "Sianna will be the next Overlord. Those are the best futures. Failing that, Charlie. Any other future leads to the extinction of all beast affinities."

That surprised Edgar. "How so? Nate Jr. is not a leader, but he would not cause the end of our people. Daniel does not have the raw power, but even he could stand as Overlord if it had to be so."

"No, the younger one won't do it. Daniel? Candy's one is Daniel? No. In the futures where it's forced upon him, he opts for death. The other lords end similarly. It's Sianna, Charlie, or death. And you can tell them I said so." Sam glared at Edgar.

"I do not understand how my eldest brother becoming Overlord brings death, Walker," Sianna mumbled.

"He doesn't bring death, Sianna. I do. As Overlord, he'll try to take you as his mate. It leads to a battle in which you die. Then we come full circle with Luke's death and me playing exterminator."

Sam said the words so casually, so lightly, Gary couldn't help but laugh.

"I know he's serious, but he's so fucking 'oh well' about it," Gary sputtered, still laughing.

"Time's ticking," Sam said, tapping his wrist. "Go, Gary.

Take Edgar with you. We'll see you in four days. We're leaving our cell phones here. Tell them not to bother tracing us like that."

Gary stood, hugged Darla, shook Hank's hand, and then, in step with Edgar, left without another word.

3

"Lake house?" Adaline asked.

Darla scrunched up her face. "It's even colder there. If we're going on vacation, can we go somewhere warm?"

A heartbeat later, they were standing in the center of a large living room with a view of the moonlit desert.

Sam put his bag on the ground, sighing with relief. "I hate doing that without touching everyone. I have to go get Jen and the dogs, but we're here."

"Where are we? You don't own a desert house." Hank's eyes were slits.

"Well, I do. I just didn't *tell* you I own a desert house. There's nothing but desert around this house for a hundred miles in any direction," Sam replied, not making eye contact with our dad. "It's our safe house."

"When did you acquire this property?" Hank asked, voice chilly.

Sam's property buying tendencies were a particularly sore spot. The wastefulness of houses sitting empty bothered my dad.

"Eight years ago," Sam admitted. "Right after we built the lake house, I built this house. There's not even a driveway. There was a path when the house was built, but nature reclaimed it years ago. So, it's on maps and stuff, but it's not directly tied to my name.

"It was built as a company retreat and event center and is owned by a holding company of a holding company. Everyone that knows it's here thinks the company that built it went out of business.

"There's enough food and water here to last a while. Addy and I can go get anything we need. No one can follow us when we Walk. There are no markers here. I checked after Micah and Jen showed us how to use markers to jump through space on Saturday.

"We can take the dust covers off the furniture. It's new. I have extra filters for the HVAC system, but I don't know how to change them. The house needs a good dusting. It's been empty for years. But it's fine."

"We have a safe house?" Hank asked, dumbfounded.

Sam nodded.

"Where are we?" William asked.

Sam shook his head. "I'm not telling. I don't want anyone to know about this place."

"I'll draw you a picture, Reap. We're in Nevada," Hennessy muttered.

Sam's eyes narrowed in anger.

"You think you're going to hide shit from me? Fuck you," Hennessy retorted with a dismissive head shake.

"Samuel," Hank began, voice tight, "how many homes do you own like this?"

"Like this one? Just this one and the lake house."

"No, Sam. I don't mean the layout, though this is very similar to the lake house—"

"It's the same. It's the exact same house plan," Sam interjected.

"How many safe houses do you own, son?"

Sam hesitated, fidgeting with his bag handle. "I won't answer that."

"Samuel," Darla chided.

"Eight around the world," Hennessy muttered. "They are *very* well hidden."

"We need them," Sam blurted. "I didn't build any that we might not need. They have a purpose. Just leave it be."

"What's in the bag, Sam?" Ethan asked, voice resigned.

As far as I could tell, it was the first time Ethan had spoken to Sam since Monday.

Sam bit his lip. "I didn't want to pull the hate out of Micah—"

Ethan held up his hand in a stop gesture. "I don't give a flying fuck why you did what you did. It's done. I'm not okay with it. I asked you a question. What's in the bag?"

Sam stared at his backpack, lost.

"Notes, Ethan. Some of his notebooks," Adaline supplied, voice subdued. "The ones he thinks are most important. He demanded hate from Micah to help Luke. It did no permanent damage. Sam would sacrifice almost everything for you. Don't do this."

"I know, Adaline," Ethan replied, sighing. "Micah's been telling me off about it all week. But, again, it's done. I don't have to be happy about it. Why do you have notebooks, Sam?"

"He keeps notes," Jake said. "He told me that a while back. He keeps notes about details he finds in different futures."

"There's a vault in our house filled with them. It's fire-safe and secure, warded against everything imaginable," Adaline added.

"People are going to go through our houses. They won't hurt anything for fear of upsetting Luke. But they hate me on general principle. If they find a way into the vault, I don't want them to have these," Sam muttered, touching the bag gently.

He walked toward the bedroom that would be his at the lake house without another word, eyes on his feet the whole way.

"I'll go get Jen and the puppies," Adaline said, still scowling at Ethan as she disappeared.

"I love how I'm the designated asshole in this," Ethan muttered to himself.

Beth snorted. I could feel her glaring at the back of my head from where she stood behind the couch. "You're not the asshole in this, Ethan. You didn't get your head lopped off. You didn't put yourself in danger even *after* the guy that walks through time told you it was going to happen."

"There were—" I started.

"Yeah, I know. Babies and kids stuck and blah blah blah. Adaline would have helped them, and you know it. You did this for the power," Beth snapped, headed out of the room to her would-be bedroom.

"He even has the same fucking furniture in this house!" she yelled a second later.

"She thinks I did this for power?" I asked, looking around at my remaining family, confused.

As my mom blinked her eyes, tears dripped down her face. "Why did you do this? He told you what was going to happen. He spent all week telling you what was going to happen. Why do this?"

"I had to," I whispered, blinking quickly to avoid my own tears. "I had to, Mom. He told me about the danger but said they'd all die out if I didn't do it."

Darla sighed, bending to touch her forehead to mine before kissing it. "I don't care. They should have been left to die out. The world would have been better off without that kind of hate and misogyny."

"Mom," I started, unable to ignore my internal triggers any longer.

"No, honey. Never mind. Let's call it done for the night. Get some sleep."

One by one, my family disappeared in the direction of their bedrooms without another word spoken.

"Wow," I muttered. "I didn't think they'd be mad."

Sianna didn't respond, just sat next to me, rigid and uncomfortable. I couldn't read her emotions at all, so I knew she was working hard to focus on nothing.

"You're angry, too?" I asked.

"Sleep," she said, standing up, then leaning down to pull me to my feet.

"Sianna?"

"You need to rest."

A wave of fear washed through me as I read one single emotion from her: resentment. I froze, trying to think of something to say.

"You must heal, Peacekeeper."

My fear flipped to anger readily enough. "Fucking *Peacekeeper?* Are you kidding me?"

"Have you looked at yourself?" she asked suddenly. "Did you look in the mirror earlier?"

"No," I admitted. "I knew it wasn't going to be great, so I didn't bother with it."

She nodded, seeming to hesitate. "Before you get too angry with your loved ones, realize they've faced the damage you avoided looking at."

That shut my anger down. I could almost hear Other-Luke calling me a coward again.

"Luke is dear to me. He is a friend. Peacekeeper is Peacekeeper—not so personal. Let me have that space while I have to see you like this."

"I'm sorry," I muttered. "I didn't think about it in those terms."

"I failed you," she responded, almost choking as she tried to breathe deeply, eyes on the ground.

"You—" Her finger over my lips stopped my words.

"Your mother is right. Rest now. Where is your room here?"

4

I don't remember much from Thursday. There was some sort of sunshade on my bedroom window that kept the light at bay while I slept off my injuries.

My mother brought me a trough of scrambled eggs that morning. When I stared at her, bleary-eyed and intimidated by the portion size, she shrugged. "Adrian and Adaline both agree your body needs protein. It's either this or protein drinks. I'm not even sure this will get you out of drinking nasty shakes. We're mad at you. No one's going to fetch you the good stuff."

"Even Sam's mad at me?" I asked, surprised. I thought he was on my side.

"Well, no. But we're all mad at him too, so he's hiding."

"Mom, why do you ping my affinity senses? It's faint, but it's there." I blurted the question quickly before she could avoid me again.

She scowled at me.

"I can feel it," I muttered. My brain said to let it go. Darla's scowls were fierce. But it would aggravate the crap out of me if I didn't know what was going on.

She blew out a sigh, still scowling. "Eat."

I picked up my fork, shoveling food in my mouth without looking at it, eyes glued to my mom.

"My family, my dad in particular, had this thing about being able to talk to coyotes. He'd get drunk and babble on about beast masters and lords. I thought he was full of shit, confusing movies with reality in his drunken stupor. The few times I saw him near one, the coyote didn't seem impressed. The whole thing was ridiculous.

"He and my brothers were overbearing and possessive in the extreme. My mother was meek as a mouse. I was out of that house the first day I could legally leave. I climbed out my window before daybreak and never looked back. You know that."

I nodded, still staring.

She shrugged again. "I thought it was all a giant pile of horse shit right up until I saw Charlie boss Roscoe around."

"You didn't tell us then?" I'd meant it as a statement, but it sounded more like a question.

She laughed. "What would I tell you? Maybe the grandfather you didn't know had a coyote thing going on, or maybe he was just a nasty, weird drunk?

"If I'm tweaking your senses now, I guess we know. But now that I think about it, he had a coyote thing going on while also being a nasty drunk. Those things aren't mutually exclusive. Drink the juice too, Lucas."

I dropped my gaze to the platter in my lap. I'd eaten all the eggs in the three minutes my mother had been talking. I chugged the quart of orange juice and then what felt like a half-gallon of water. By the time I was done, I risked tipping over, unsure if it was from the fluids or the fatigue.

I woke up a few hours later for Sam to help me to the bathroom. Then I was out again.

Adaline brought me lunch.

"I can get up," I mumbled, staring at the bowl of protein-packed salad-like food, including beans and more eggs. "Though, I get the feeling I'm in here by myself because no one wants to smell my ass after this."

She didn't even smile.

"Adaline." I sighed. "I'm sorry. I had to. It had to be done."

"You would have died," she whispered, her horror and remorse pouring into me. "I couldn't fix it fast enough. There was too much damage. I thought you were going to die. It was Sam's vision. Did he tell you that? I saw it. I knew it was coming, and I still couldn't fix it. You are *mine*. Peace belongs to me. And I couldn't save you."

My mouth hung open. I had no idea what to say to make this better.

"We will lose pillars over time. The pillars will dwindle before Sam and I lose our places. I cannot fathom losing any of you. I would sacrifice a lot to keep you all with me. I think maybe I'm not meant to hold the position I do."

Holy fuck! Holy fuck! What the fuck do I say to this? I had no words, so I offered my peaceful energy, hoping to clear her thoughts.

"Sam was willing to lose you in the gamble. He didn't want to, but he was willing to risk your life for the well-being of many others. Many, many innocent lives. I feel the beast affinities. I know how many there are. I wasn't willing to risk you." She blinked hard, tears dripping down her cheeks.

"I don't think I can lose my pillars and keep my sanity. Perhaps this is why the former mistresses didn't hold their power completely? Or maybe this is why the Walkers give way to madness?"

"This is why there are two," Sam said, walking out of the ensuite bathroom. "This is why we are a pair. We balance, love." His arms wrapped around Adaline, holding her steady as she sobbed.

I raised my eyebrows. "Just hanging out in my bathroom?"

He pulled a face at me. "I knew you wouldn't have good words for her. Eat."

I didn't need to be told twice. I scarfed the food down while Sam and Addy had a whispered conversation filled with many hugs.

I wasn't going to be envious of that kind of togetherness. I wasn't. I refused. Sam and Adaline faced terrible things; they needed each other.

My own peaceful energy rolled around me as I drifted back to sleep. If someone tried to wake me for dinner, I didn't remember.

I WOKE up before the sun on Friday morning. The bedside clock said it was a few minutes after five. I climbed out of bed on my own and shuffled my way to the bathroom.

That was the first and only time I looked at myself in the mirror while healing. Two days removed from the injury, the wound around my neck was a wide, red jagged scar with deep blue and purple bruising around it. My eyes were sunken, and my skin was grey.

Holy shit. I almost died.

I staggered, almost falling. If there had been anything in my stomach at that point, I would have puked. I was shivering with cold sweats, running my wrists under cool water when Sianna came in carrying a pile of fresh clothes.

She touched my arm in passing, helping my energy to cycle and steady. "Take a shower. You will feel better. Mistress Life and Lady Water want to see if they can use the energy Charlie and I create."

Then she was gone again.

My stomach dropped.

I had the distinct impression I was in the doghouse, though I had no idea why Sianna would be angry with me. I'd done everything I could to help her and her people.

Showered and dressed, I was out of the bathroom before the mirror defogged. I was a little wobbly but able to move without assistance.

When I made it out to the great room, Sianna, Adaline, and Talise were sitting at the dining room table in silence, facing the hallway I had just exited. They were obviously waiting for me. In complete silence.

I looked around guiltily.

"Hi?" I asked.

"Sit," Sianna said without preamble, pushing the chair across from her out with her foot.

"How… how is everyone this morning?" I asked, moving to take the chair.

Talise reached for my hand, jerking it across the table none too gently.

I sighed. "How long is everyone going to be mad at me?"

The three women served me identical glares.

"Okay," I muttered, focusing on the wood grain of the table in front of me.

"He's hydrated enough for this," Tali said, throwing my hand back down.

Sianna and Adaline shared a look. Then, stretching across the table, Sianna took my left hand while Adaline took my right.

"Do it," Sianna muttered to Adaline.

"I am. Nothing's happening."

"I told you it would not work," Sianna said. "It will take time to heal—"

"Try it the other way," Addy interrupted. "You direct while I pull it from the circle."

"I do not know how to do that." Sianna shifted uncomfortably.

"Like you do when you heal him. Like that," Adaline offered, nodding.

I bit back a smile. Neither Adaline nor Sianna were great about communicating with words. Talise was marginally better. I wondered how long it would be before they gave up and moved on to sharing thoughts.

I laughed out loud, thinking about the potential conversations they'd have.

The glares returned.

Oops. I swallowed my laughter and tried to appear serious and contrite again.

"I do not direct it," Sianna countered. "I offer it. His body takes it."

"Yes," Adaline said, nodding. "Let's try that."

I felt Sianna's energy wash through me, causing me to sigh in relief. Somehow, I rarely realized I felt terrible until she made it better.

"I do not have any more..." Her words trailed off as more energy slammed into me. Rather than the cool wash of Sianna's power, this was warmer, almost uncomfortable.

Even as the power was flowing, Talise smacked me upside the head. With vigor. She was pissed.

"Why are you so fucking stubborn?" she whisper-growled. "Why can't you just pull energy from the circle yourself? Why do we have to do everything for you?"

She slammed her chair against the table and stomped off to stand on the patio alone.

I looked between Adaline and Sianna, confused.

"The energy is working. The wound is improving," Sianna murmured, not meeting my eyes, even though she still held my hand.

There was a softness in Addy's eyes. She wasn't as angry now. "We couldn't seem to help you yesterday. Sianna and Charlie can heal in small waves, but not like I can. And your body wasn't accepting my help easily."

"You should have woken me yesterday. Maybe if I was awake...." My words trailed off at Adaline's head shake.

"The energy just ran through you," Adaline explained. "It passed through you like there was nothing wrong. It didn't recognize the wound as an injury to heal. I've never known that to happen before."

"Well, it's not pretty, but it's scarred over now..." I stopped again as the head shake resumed.

"It's almost gone now. The bruising is gone, and the scar is almost healed."

Sianna made an unhappy sound. "My energy does not heal for vanity like this. It does not remove scars as such. Beast affinities with healing energy, like Charlie and me, use the power to transform. The transformation itself heals and removes the marks. But you do not transform."

"So, the circle energy didn't find anything to heal, and the affinity energy doesn't do this kind of healing. I'd be stuck with the scar if you hadn't figured this out?" I summarized.

Adaline nodded, eyes sad.

"Addy, it is not your fault. I had to go. I have to do this," I said, picking up our conversation from yesterday.

"It is not your fault," Sianna agreed. "It is my fault."

I groaned. "Please stop. It's not your fault either. You didn't try to chop off my head. I'm alive because of you."

She shook her head. "I should have known. I should not have trusted where I did."

"Edgar? The only person you seemed to trust was Edgar, and he did me a solid, so I think we're fine, Sianna."

"I should have known when I saw their swords on the ground. I should have known and forced you out of there."

I stared at her, lost. "Please don't do this."

She lifted her eyebrows.

"I can't do this, Sianna. It's not your fault I got hurt. It's your fault I *survived.* I saw the wound this morning. I almost died. I get it. Sam told me. He told all of us. Even knowing what was likely, I still walked into that arena. I don't think there's anything we could have done better or differently."

She met my eyes, frowning. "I was your guard and protector, Luke. I utterly failed. By rights, my life is forfeit—yours to destroy."

"I love you," I murmured, realizing I had not said the words previously.

Her eyes lit with rage. Then, yanking her hand back, she stomped off to join Tali on the patio outside.

I sighed at Adaline.

"She is not used to that," Addy murmured, trying not to laugh. "There is love for you too. It's why she blames herself."

I nodded.

"No binding," Addy noted.

I nodded again. "I don't believe there will be one. It would cost her dearly."

Adaline nodded. They must have discussed this.

"How do you feel?" she asked.

"Better. It doesn't hurt to move my neck now. Hungry. Thirsty," I said, smiling. "How are you?"

"Much better. Easier to look at you now." Her eyes filled with tears.

"Not you too," I grumped, climbing to my feet in search of breakfast. "Pancakes?"

She nodded again. "The others will be awake soon. It's almost seven."

"On a scale from one to ten, how mad is Talise?" I asked casually. Truth be told, I was worried. Tali and I had never disagreed or argued before. We discussed. I didn't know how to handle her raw anger.

And she was pissed. I could feel it radiating from her twenty feet away.

Adaline didn't respond as she watched me pull out pans. The kitchen was eerie. It was the same as the kitchen in our family's vacation home on Lake Michigan. It even had all the same cookware.

"That bad?" I asked.

"She is furious."

"I got that part." I snorted, trying to cover the break in my voice.

"Like me, she fears what we would have done if you'd died. But more so. We asked you not to go. But you went regardless and did not give us a chance to say goodbye."

That hit home like a punch to my gut.

"It is the same with the others. They understand you had to go. However, you did not give them a chance to say things."

I swallowed hard. "I didn't intend to die."

She frowned at the stupidity of my words.

I sighed again, understanding just how wrong I'd been. The stakes were clear. I'd been a coward to leave as I had.

For the first time, I felt Other-Luke shift inside my power. I felt something in the other awareness click into place.

"I'll do pancakes," Noah's voice, rough with sleep, came from behind me. "You have some groveling to do."

5

Sianna flew off in hawk form before I could even open the patio door. I wasn't sure if she was giving me space to talk with Tali or avoiding me.

I'll worry about that later, I decided.

Walking out onto the patio, I moved to wrap Talise into a hug, her back to my front.

She stomped on my foot before walking out of hugging range. "Don't touch me."

"Okay," I groaned. "Sorry for invading your space."

She stared off at the fantastic desert view. There was a pool off the patio at the lake house that was missing here.

"I'm glad he didn't put a pool here." I sat down on one of the patio chairs.

"Me too," Talise acknowledged. "It would have been out of place and wasteful. For as big and empty as the house is, it's surprisingly efficient with solar energy and an independent water supply… in the desert. I'm not sure how Sam managed that."

"The house is off the grid?"

She nodded. "Completely. There's satellite internet, but somehow, I suspect he owns the satellite."

"I wouldn't put it past him."

She blew out a sigh as she came to sit with me. "You almost died."

"I know. It didn't hit home until I saw myself this morning."

"You almost died without me telling you all the things I needed to say. I would have never forgiven you for that."

"Tali, I—"

"You shut up," she snapped. "You had the chance to say things and opted not to. Instead, you opted to run away while our backs were turned."

I nodded in acknowledgment.

"I love you," she said simply. "I always have. You were the *only* reason I kept going for a long time, the only peace I knew in a confusing world of rage and hate. I would give just about anything to see you well and happy… including the fucking shifters. I'd sacrifice them without a backward glance, no fucks given. You knew that, and I suspect it's why you ran. I might be willing to sacrifice a large swath of humanity, but you wouldn't."

Blinking quickly, I shook my head. "You give me too much credit. I ran because it was easier. I didn't think anything bad would happen. I thought it'd be fine, even with all of Sam's dramatics. Part of me still believed bad things only happened to other people."

"Bad things have happened to me, Luke. I don't have the luxury of believing or trusting that bad things won't happen."

I nodded.

"You skated off into danger without a backward wave. I wanted to say thank you for my life. For the balance you brought me and the time you gave me. Thank you for bringing your family to me, for introducing me to Adaline, to Noah.

"Thank you for loving me enough to let me go when it was clear we weren't going to live our happily-ever-after together. And thank you for wanting my happiness enough to watch me build a relationship with Noah. I know he irritates the fuck out of you. He makes me happy. Just the sight of him makes me happy."

"He's so pretty," I choked out. It was Talise's favorite response when asked why she stayed with Noah. We both wiped tears and laughed.

"So pretty. So dumb. But he's my idiot," she agreed, shaking with laughter.

We were silent for a few minutes, letting her words settle.

"I was wrong to go like I did. I'm sorry." The words came from my mouth with quiet sincerity, its own sort of power. "Thank you for helping me. Thank you for being there for Sam's plans. Thank you for sharing your time and life with me. I'm a better person for having known you. My life is better because you're a part of it."

"Don't do that again. I'll never forgive you." Her words weren't a threat. They were a warning.

"I am pointedly aware of what a coward I was. I will avoid such actions in the future."

"You look better," she said after a moment. "Sianna can feed the circle energy to you properly. You need to figure out how to use the circle, Luke."

"I know." I nodded, scratching my head in frustration. "It's like I'm stuck between the two now. I don't transform, so I can't heal with the beast affinities' energy. But there's too much affinity for me to use the circle."

"That's crap," Talise said immediately. "Sianna is all beast affinity and has dumped energy into the circle and pulled energy through Adaline. Whatever it is that you haven't glommed onto yet, get it together. You do this thing where you don't realize something's wrong until you know what to do to make it right."

I sighed again. Of course, she was right. I had a long history of ignoring the obvious until it whacked me upside the head.

"Actually, I don't even believe my own pile of bullshit," I admitted. "I think the beast affinity energy is the same thing as the circle energy, just expressed differently. This has to be something I'm doing, but I have no idea what."

"Figure it out before you get killed, okay?"

"Sounds like a plan," I said, nodding. I tried to smile. It didn't quite work.

By THE TIME we made it back into the house, the rest of my family was awake.

"I've scolded, shamed, and threatened as we discussed," Talise said. "There were man tears and a genuine apology."

Heads nodded in acceptance around the table… except for Beth.

"You're going to beat the shit out of me, aren't you?" I asked her.

"Lucas," Darla scolded.

"There are no little ears! I checked!" I said immediately.

"Still, we don't need to speak like that. It's not necessary."

Her glare dared me to disagree. Deciding I disliked being in the doghouse, I nodded in meek agreement.

"I am absolutely going to deliver an angry kick that disrupts your harem lifestyle and makes you squeal like a little girl. But not until after you're... better than you are." Beth gestured to my body.

"Are we talking physically better? Or, like I need to reach a higher level of understanding and be a better person? Because I can stop growing as a person to avoid that kick."

She glared at me.

"Okay," I said, glancing around the table. "I am very sorry I ducked out like a coward. I truly thought it would be fine and wanted to save us all a lot of drama. I was wrong. I saw my neck this morning and almost puked."

"Puking Peace," Jess muttered.

William's eyebrows shot up. "You think your neck was bad this morning? Fuck you. I will have nightmares about your barely attached head for the rest of my long life. Fuck you for going."

I looked at my mom, waiting for her to scold Will.

Darla placidly drank her coffee, ignoring me.

"I had to go. It had to happen. I'm sorry it went down the way it did, though," I said again, taking my seat.

"Do you feel the circle?" Sam asked, curious.

I thought about it. "In general, no. If I think about it and look for it, maybe?"

He made a harumph of displeasure.

"I will work on figuring that out," I said, hoping to head off more scolding.

Sam was glaring at me.

"What?" I asked.

"Are you going to own up to it?"

"Own up to what?" I asked, confused.

His eyes narrowed.

"I love Sianna? I do. I mean, I thought that was obvious. I don't think she's happy about it, though."

Sam's eyes remained narrowed. "Nothing else? Nothing *Other?*"

I groaned. "How do you know that?"

"I TOLD YOU I TALKED TO OTHER-LUKE! I TOLD YOU SO!" Sam yelled. "I really thought I got that wrong. I was so fucking confused."

"I didn't know, Sam!" I argued back, once again watching my mother sip her coffee, indifferent to everyone else's foul language.

"You never know anything until it's blatantly obvious," Sam muttered. "I shouldn't even be upset about this. Of course, you didn't know."

Swallowing a mouthful of pancakes, Adrian grunted. "I'm missing some of the short-hand on this one."

"There is an Other-Luke. Like I had an Other-Sam. There is an Other-Luke. His power has enough force that it's taken on an awareness of its own."

The family turned as one to stare at me.

I threw my arms up in frustration. "I didn't know. I didn't even suspect it until I started missing patches of time last week. Then, Sianna said she could tell when I wasn't myself."

"Oh." Will shifted uncomfortably.

"Yeah," Adrian muttered.

"What?" I asked.

"That's a thing. I had that when I refused to admit Pip and I belonged together," Will said lazily. "That's nothing to worry about."

Adrian nodded. "Yeah. Same. Rage crushed my hands to little bits when I tried to walk away from Lucy."

Sam's gaze landed on Ethan. "Do you?"

"Do I what?" Ethan asked, tone clipped.

"Do you have an Other-Ethan? Does Joy take time from you?" Sam asked, voice dreamy as he sunk deeper into thought.

Ethan shook his head. "No. I don't think so."

"He's never denied his feelings or true self," Micah explained. "He's never been at odds with the power."

Sam chewed on his lip, not Walking through time but not focused on his surroundings, either.

"What?" I finally demanded after a few moments of silence.

"Jen said something about the cardinal positions growing in power to match yours. I don't know. We'll have to ask her about that. But you stand opposite Will. Adrian stands opposite Ethan. Three of the four of you have Other-selves." Sam took another bite of pancakes while he considered.

"Where is Jen? And Candy, Ellie, and Charlie?" I asked.

"Jen went back to Chicago yesterday afternoon to scope things out. Candy talked Sam into taking her back to her house this morning. Charlie and Ellie are still sleeping," Darla said. "I don't think they let Charlie sleep at all."

"No, I don't think so either," I agreed. "They intended to break his mind enough for him to forget about Ellie."

Sam snorted. "That's ridiculous. There's no separating them in any future that's worth living. Back to the Other-Luke thing. Did he say anything about how to align the pieces?"

I shook my head. "Other-Luke insisted we were parts of the same whole, that there was nothing to reconcile. I just needed to grow up and grow into the power. He was intrigued that you recognized your power as something separate, though. I guess that's not typical for Walkers."

Sam shrugged. "Okay. So, time to grow up, little brother. Time to grow into the power. You accepted the role of Peacekeeper. You went into that arena, knowing what would happen."

"I know," I mumbled, looking at my plate. "And I'm not sorry I did it. Those people need help. If this is the purpose of my life and my power, I'll deal with it. It'll just take some getting used to."

In my mind, I felt another little piece of energy slide into place with my acceptance. I resisted the urge to roll my eyes. Other-me seemed to be spoon-feeding me access to the power.

"Well, what does that mean?" Adrian asked. "You don't shake the ground or anything. So, what does Other-Luke do?"

"I'm pretty sure Other-Luke brings giant waves of relaxed, sexy energy," I admitted.

The table erupted in laughter.

"How does one trade regular Luke for Other-Luke?" Matilda asked. "Because Other-Luke is amazing."

"I mean, you're great, Luke," Lucy continued over the laughter. "But there will be more grandbabies for Darla if Other-Luke sticks around. Raise your hand if you like Other-Luke more than Luke-Luke."

All the hands went up, including mine. And my parents'.

6

After breakfast, I wandered back out into the warm desert air, grabbing Sianna's dress as I walked off the patio and across the hard-packed dry earth.

"Sianna," I called quietly, once I was out of hearing range of the house. "Will you talk with me?"

A moment later, a hawk flew toward my face before it dropped into a coyote in front of me.

I sighed at her. "Really?"

"This is safer, Peacekeeper. I must be wary of my words and thoughts."

"Wow. When did you build the mental link to talk to me with thoughts?"

"You are Peacekeeper. Most with affinities may do this when within range now. If you try to send thoughts to me, I believe it will also work. Legend says commands from the Peacekeeper's mind cannot be disobeyed. My father holds similar power, but not nearly as much."

"Well, now that you mention it, Gary spoke into my mind. I

didn't notice it. But, do you mind if I speak? I don't want to command anything."

The coyote stared at me. I guessed speech was acceptable.

I sighed again, sitting on the ground. When she sat next to me, I had to resist the urge to pet her fur.

"Did you know Darla's family has coyote affinities?" I asked.

There was no response, mental or otherwise.

"Yeah, you're right. This isn't what I want to talk about."

The stare continued.

"This is a super strange conversation to have with a coyote," I complained. It didn't help. I gave it one more good, gusty sigh before accepting this was the best I was going to get.

"I love you," I began. I had to start somewhere, and those words felt like the epicenter of everything yet to come.

"You didn't have to help me last week. You didn't have to help me understand my power. You didn't have to be my ally. You didn't have to walk into danger with me, facing down your entire fucking family. You are so brave and so true to yourself; I am wholly unworthy of you."

I swallowed to help my dry throat, suddenly glad she couldn't interrupt me.

"I would have died on Wednesday without you. My tombstone would read 'Here lies the dumbest fuck to ever live' because I genuinely believed I couldn't have real feelings. I can. It just means that I can also get really hurt. I wasn't brave enough to accept the hurt that can come with real feelings, so I had none. I'm sorry it took me as long as it did to sort out. I'll count my lucky stars that I sorted it in time to survive.

"And when I count those lucky stars and all the blessings that go with them, you will shine brightest of all."

I paused, trying to organize my thoughts.

"I cannot be what you want me to be, Luke." The mental projection was steeped in Sianna's sadness and regret. *"I cannot be part of a family like yours."*

"I know. I was trying to figure out how to say that. But I know family is different for you. I know love and the bindings mean something different for you. I accept it for what it is, Sianna. I would not have you become less than you are. Love that weakens is poorly founded. I know I'm alone in the depth of these feelings. I accept it, but I'll continue to hope for better."

Climbing back to her feet, Coyote-Sianna was Sianna in truth, pulling her dress over her head even as her body took shape.

"They call me Huntress. Do you know what that means?" she asked.

I shook my head. "I inferred that you were an enforcer of sorts."

"Yes, that. But more. Much more."

I waited while she sat next to me, taking my hand without thought. I exhaled in relief as the energy cycled through us. My neck popped as I rotated my head.

"Do not do that!" she scolded.

I lifted my eyebrows.

"Do not crack your neck like that," she said, smiling a bit. "I do not trust your head is firmly attached yet."

"I'm better," I said, gently squeezing her fingers. "A bit tired now, but better. Almost normal."

"The wound is gone. There is a faint line now. No bruising remains. Soon there will be no sign of the injury at all."

I grinned. "Thank goodness my dashing good looks are restored."

Sianna swallowed hard, eyes filling with tears. "I have never failed in my duties so spectacularly. I will never forget that moment or how you looked. It is not lost on me that my father set me up for that failure either."

"Sianna, this was not your—" I started.

"Luke," she said, hand up in a 'stop' gesture. "I will tell you of hunters, and then you will understand. Let me speak, as I let you speak."

I nodded in agreement, understanding then that her words were not about blame or fault. Instead, the words were at the center of her explanation. So, I waited.

She pressed her lips together, thinking as she looked around. "I like it here."

I waited.

She smiled to herself, recognizing my patience. "Does the scruffy beard stubble bother you?" Her fingers scratched through the hair on my cheek.

I smiled at her touch, shaking my head. The beard didn't tweak my senses.

"I like it," she admitted.

I squeezed her fingers again, causing her to sigh.

"We are a patriarchal society, but that does not mean we are lawless. My father cannot be everywhere at once, nor does he care to mete out justice for misdeeds unless there is something to be gained. He would travel across the ocean during the holidays to gain Charlie's allegiance. But, otherwise, he does not care to be involved.

"For the most part, Edgar, Godwin, and John tend to our people. But there are a lot of people, many levels of affinity. The nature of our society makes it easy for atrocities, abuse, and brutality to occur. Particularly in areas where authorities do not monitor and protect as they should, weak affinities, women, and children suffer.

"The hunters serve as our investigators. They are the protectors of those who cannot protect themselves. I was the first woman huntress in the history of our people, and I will protect those who are mine with every ounce of my being.

"Your fox friend—Gary? —was not wrong to fear me. If he had brought danger to one I had sworn to protect, I would have made him repent for his actions and then taken his life. Candace is right to fear me. That one has done wrong to one of mine in the past."

She fell silent, staring off into space.

"How many hunters are there?" I asked to pull her back to the conversation.

She nodded. "When I was young, Nathaniel delegated the responsibility for the hunters to Edgar, Godwin, and John. I was trained to be strong. They allowed me to serve. There were more than thirty hunters throughout the world when I took my oaths. After, Nathaniel reclaimed leadership of hunters. I am now the last. It is no longer a role for me, it is a title. I am the Huntress. The last."

"Just you?" I asked, dumbfounded.

She nodded again. "Some were justly removed for abuses of power—for violating the people they were meant to protect. Some were lost to the madness of age. Some died natural deaths. A few disappeared. The remainder were murdered.

"As the numbers dwindled, my father called me to his side, where I have stayed for most of a decade. I was forbidden to investigate or put myself at risk. I transitioned from being the protector of our weakest to being their voice in my father's circle. He did not always like what I had to say, but he listened.

He respected the work I did for almost one hundred years, but said he would not lose me as the others were lost.

"Edgar and Godwin investigate as they can. John still serves as a protector in areas of the world it is most needed. But my father refused to form a new group of hunters, refused to put the resources behind finding the murderer. The Overlord must grant the power to make new hunters. My father will not do so."

I could sense her thoughts without her saying the words. She thought her brother, Elias, was responsible for the deaths. As her father's favorite, Elias would have the freedom to murder others without repercussions.

"I must stay as I am, Luke. Elias is gone. We may reform our hunters and help our people, particularly with a Peacekeeper to clear the way. My eldest brother would not oppose the idea. He will be glad to be rid of me. I do not believe he would try to claim me, as the Walker says. He cannot stand the sight of me.

"Our people suffer without the protections of hunters. My role as Huntress is about more than influencing my father's fickle mind. It is a promise to the weakest among us that even they are valued. I wear the title alone until we can train more. I will not break my vow to my people. Not even for the love of the Peacekeeper. I am not that selfish."

A few deep breaths later, my lips quirked up. "May I ask questions now?"

"Yes." She smiled. "I am done."

"Do you truly believe I would stop you from fulfilling your role? From protecting others?"

"No," she said immediately, stretching to kiss my cheek. "I know you better. You would not stop me. You would join me. No. You are not the problem. When Edgar accepted me as a huntress, there was an agreement. When I accept a mate with bindings of love, I must surrender my role to the next in line. I cannot change that promise. It was made in full understanding, spoken with power, and agreed to in blood."

I raised my eyebrows.

"It is our truth-swearing ritual. You will see. If anything is more honored than the Peacekeeper, it is the truths we hold. If I try to break that truth, my life is forfeit in the same way Candace's was. I would be mated against my will in a heartbeat."

"Will you teach me all these customs, so I don't make a fool of myself?" I fought to form a smile. I'm not sure it worked. It didn't matter; Sianna didn't look at me.

"I will," she said quietly, squeezing my fingers again. "There can be sex and children between us. That would be celebrated. There cannot be bindings of love."

"Bindings. Plural? Meaning there cannot be shared bindings, correct?" My stomach dropped again. I knew what she was feeling. I knew what was coming.

"No, Luke. You must sever it. You must let me go."

7

"Blah blah blah," I heard Ellie call from the porch as she and Charlie walked out across the open land to join us. "If only someone had told Baby Trellis to avoid sex with an *incredibly* unavailable woman... Oh, right. I did."

"Sex and babies are good," Charlie offered. "I mean, that's most of what family is."

I glowered at him.

"Okay, that's what most families are. It is not what your family is," he allowed.

"How long have you been standing back there?" I asked.

"We followed you out onto the patio," Ellie grinned. "Aww, Baby Trellis is in love."

She patted the top of my head. "Too bad. Let her go."

"I am not the baby," I said on general principle. "Beth is the youngest."

"Pfft. Nope. There's no way I can bait her. She's much more mature than you. You're the baby," Ellie countered. "Seriously, though. I'm sorry, Luke. Neither of you can go back with that binding in place."

I looked at Charlie, who just looked... sad.

"Other people can be hunters without you being a hunter," I said, already feeling pathetic.

She shook her head. "There is energy to it. It is more than a title. The title is given and taken. Shared. If I release the title with no one else able to take it, the energy could be lost to us. My father must allow a new hunter before I can let the title go."

"So, you don't bind to me. I accepted that. I don't even know how I would go about severing the binding, even if I wanted to."

"He-man does. Emma will tell you all about it," Ellie countered.

My eyes stayed on Charlie. He shook his head as he sat down on Sianna's other side, breaking my line of sight. "Even when we were an item, Luke, it was only about sex and babies. No bindings."

Sianna made a harrumph of sound, not quite a laugh. "Bleh."

Charlie leaned forward, pulling a face at her. "Bleh, right back at you. It was like trying to make out with Candy. No thanks!"

Sianna shook with genuine laughter, pushing him over backward.

"We never got to the sexy parts. Too strange for words," Charlie acknowledged. "Just made a good show of 'working toward mating.'"

"This is some of the most fucked up shit," I mumbled.

"Oh, Luke. That's funny. We're barely scratching the surface of the fucked-up culture. I'm hoping Edgar challenges Nate.

That'd resolve half the utter wrongness." Ellie scrunched up her face in distaste.

"And wins," Charlie added. "Edgar would have to challenge and win."

"You saw him change!" Ellie argued.

"I saw him transform with Luke right there. Who knows if he can do it without assistance."

"Let's say Edgar challenges and wins. Then what?" I asked.

"The next capable beast lord becomes Overlord. They have to prove they can transform and keep their mental awareness through the challenge."

"The challenge?" I asked, fishing for information.

Charlie sighed. "Everyone that can transform, keep their human mind, and wants the job squares off in some sort of battle. The last one standing and sane is the strongest among us and named Overlord."

"That is you," Sianna snapped.

"That is *you*, Sianna. Sam is dead right about that. You are the next Overlord." Charlie almost shouted the words. I sensed a long-standing argument playing out.

"I cannot challenge," she bit out.

"There is no precedent for it. A woman has never challenged for Overlord before. But just because it hasn't happened does not mean it can't happen," Charlie argued.

Ellie rolled her eyes, sitting down on my other side. "To this day, I maintain Charlie became a lawyer so he could argue this point in their arena of fucked up battle."

I stared at Ellie.

"I'm not kidding. I think this is why he went to law school," she said again. "He wanted the skills to put forth a logical argument above reproach for why Sianna should lead. He has *never* wanted to rule."

"It is a thankless job," Charlie grated out. "Almost as bad as being a hunter. In times past, our Overlords came from the ranks of our hunters. Nate is the first to break that tradition. The Overlord is meant to lead our people in wellness and plenty. Nate does neither, hiding on his fucking estates, letting the hunters die out, not initiating new ones, not trying to protect affinities. I have a plan."

"I cannot challenge." Sianna's voice was utterly devoid of emotion. "Perhaps Edgar may take the role back."

Charlie snorted, making chicken sounds at her.

She glared at him.

Resigned, Charlie sighed again. "This is going to hurt him. Maybe damage him. You could resurface with that bond intact, challenge for leadership, and stand together as Overlord and Peacekeeper. I couldn't imagine a better future."

"I cannot challenge," she said again. "If we resurface as we are, they would never allow it. You know that is true. They would never allow the Peacekeeper's beloved to stand a battle."

"Meh," Charlie grunted. "I hate that you're right. Not even Edgar would go along with that. You must sever it, Luke. But maybe not forever. I have a plan."

Sianna rolled her eyes at Charlie before talking to me. "There will be sex and children and better life mates for you, man-wife. Gentler. You'll see."

"Man-wife?" Ellie cackled. "Man-wife? That might be better than Baby Trellis!"

SIANNA and I watched in silence as Charlie and Ellie walked back into the house. She still held my hand, resting it in her palm while her fingers wove through mine.

"I don't know how to break it. I need to talk to William." I refused to fall to pieces over this. It was necessary. Important.

It was what Sianna wanted.

We sat in silence for a few more minutes before I started to climb to my feet. "I'll go talk to—"

"Not yet. Please?" Her voice cracked. "We will not go back today. The Walker said four days. Maybe we do not go back until Sunday."

Like a kick to the chest, her raw pain and grief washed through me. I wondered if she'd found a way to hide it while we'd been silent and while Charlie and Ellie were with us.

"Sianna." I sighed, dropping back down next to her. "This is what you want, right?"

She shook her head. "Need. It is what I need. It is not what I want. I will never have this, Luke. I cannot have this without breaking oaths and vows that I hold dear."

As her sobs broke free, I pulled her into my lap, holding her while she fell to pieces.

It didn't help the status of my gold binding to her. I don't know how long we sat like that, but I spent the entire time thinking of ways to avoid severing the binding.

On the more benign end, we could just not go back. Instead, we could screw over the entire population of beast affinities and make a run for it.

On the more extreme end, my family and I could subvert the entire beast affinity population and take over leadership. We'd be fairer and more caring than fucking Nate.

I didn't try to negotiate my way out of this, though. Maybe I should have. Maybe it would have saved us pain if I had begged and pleaded for a different path forward. I doubted it, though. Sianna's commitment to her people was genuine.

Left to their own devices, I suspected Sianna and Hennessy would be fast friends.

By the time the tears stopped, we were lying on the ground in the winter desert, looking at the sky, lost in thought.

"Again?" she asked suddenly.

"I love you," I said quietly, knowing what she wanted to hear without explanation. I felt her head nod from where it was nestled against my chest.

"Can we walk?" She was already climbing to her feet.

"Walking sounds good," I agreed, blowing out a sigh.

Her lips quirked. "We're back to sighs."

I brushed a quick kiss against her mouth. "We're back to resignation. There are options, but not good ones."

"I know. Let's walk."

And so, we spent most of Friday's daylight walking through the desert. She asked about my childhood and my music and told me of the beautiful things she'd seen and the people she'd met.

We didn't touch hard truths or ugly facts, sticking to the gentler parts of life through some unspoken agreement. Sianna spoke more in that single afternoon than she had in the entire time I'd known her.

Charlie and Ellie must have explained what was to come. By the time we returned to the house, forced cheer echoed through the family.

Darla made chicken with dumplings—my favorite—for dinner. As we were sorting through the sets of dominos, Lucy's sister, Linda, touched my shoulder. When I looked at her, she made a gesture to follow her out of the room.

"It's an act of will," she said quietly. "Just like it came into being, you have to will it to break. But, more than that, you have to believe and trust that it is really what you want to happen. If you don't want it broken, the binding will ignore you. So, you have to know it's the right thing to do and then will it to break."

I'd forgotten Linda had forcefully broken her binding to her son, Ree, many times over the years. Of course, she would know how to do it. I nodded.

She chewed on her lip, stalling.

I lifted my eyebrows, unable to muster the patience for this.

"Don't do it," she blurted. "William said he wouldn't tell you, that it would be horrible for you. I disagreed. You're an adult. If you feel it's necessary, that's for you to decide. He shouldn't make that decision for you. But now I regret telling you."

I sighed.

"I know you have to. I know Charlie said that. But don't do it. It will break the part of you that loves and trusts easily. You'll lose that… innocence. The naiveté of people like you, who haven't broken a binding before, is beautiful. It makes me feel better about the world. Like there might be a place in this world for true love and devotion. Don't do it. Find another way. I know there are less elegant solutions. Let's do that instead. War is better than doing this."

"Thanks, Linda," I mumbled as I walked away.

After dominos were done, Sianna and I went to bed and made love once more. Slowly and tenderly, our bodies twisted together, lost in the feeling of each other.

Once she was sound asleep, curled next to my body, I thought about how much I *didn't* want to destroy the binding.

It was the right thing to do for everyone else. It was what Sianna needed to happen. But there was love between us. Even she admitted she didn't want to give up those emotions. There was no sense in destroying the binding. We'd find a way. In the morning, I would tell her I'd decided against it, and we'd just have to figure it out.

The more I thought about it, the more sense it made. I wouldn't do it. I couldn't do it. I didn't want it to happen. At one point, I literally nodded to myself.

Then, I considered what it meant to be bound to someone with love when they didn't desire the binding. What kind of love was that? I would be forcing Sianna to change her priorities and life because I didn't care if my love caused her pain.

I audibly sighed, causing her to stir against me. That wasn't love. No binding at all was better than a binding that intentionally, knowingly caused pain. I didn't want her to suffer because I'd wussed out. I thought of Adrian and Lucy, William and Emma. If this was meant to work out, it'd work out on terms that made sense. Not like this.

One more deep breath in, and another out. I opened my sight, found the gold binding, and destroyed it. I didn't just sever it. I scorched it to the very base of my sense of self, such that it would be unrecognizable. No one would use the severed binding against her. There were no remains.

After it was done, I crawled to the bathroom, curled up on the cool tile, and tried to breathe.

Strange as it sounds, almost being decapitated hadn't been excessively painful. It had happened too quickly; the nerve centers had disconnected before they could really fire.

I'd broken my leg playing soccer when I was eight. That had hurt.

Will had punched me in the head hard enough to crack my skull. That hadn't felt great either.

When Sam had broken the tie in my brain, I'd wanted to die. The pain had been so horrendously bad that during my lucid moments, I'd asked Matthew to kill me.

It still paled in comparison to destroying the binding to Sianna. The pain and grief were so intense, I walled off part of my mind as I processed my new reality. I didn't bother pulling my energy forward. The peace would be a lie. I'd already accepted this; burying the feelings under forced calm wouldn't resolve anything.

Sometime in the middle of the night, I felt my power slide and shift. Like pulling on a new pair of shoes after years in old runners, it felt strange and right. It wasn't quite as comfortable, but the energy felt more seated within me. I recognized the change and then dismissed it as I returned to the twilight haze of rest and healing.

I felt Sianna move around a few times. She didn't come into the bathroom.

By daybreak, I was done coping. I took a shower, shaved, and got dressed for the day ahead without thinking about much of anything.

8

"Oh, holy fuck," Jess breathed, staring at me. Gifted with all-sight, Adaline's sister could see what I had done in full color.

I wasn't expecting her to burst into tears.

"It's fine, Jess," I offered, my voice deep and scratchy.

"Luke," she sobbed, "I can't believe you did it."

As far as I could recall, it was the first time Jess had called me by my name, rather than some variant of "Puking Peace." There was no teasing this morning.

Coming into the family room, Micah took one look at me and visibly flinched. "It's done."

"It's done," I agreed.

"Sam took her back to Chicago earlier. We can go home today," Micah said, trying to avoid looking at me.

William followed a waddling Emma into the room. Jess's sobbing and Micah's not looking at me must have given it away. "Linda told you."

"She did."

"I told her not to. I refused to do it."

My lips quirked at that. "Hypocrite."

"What you call hypocrisy, I call experience," Will countered. "C'mon. Let's spar." He headed toward the patio door.

"Let's not," I countered, chugging a glass of water. Walking around in the desert for a lot of the previous day hadn't helped my hydration levels.

"Luke, trust me on this. Let's spar."

"Will, I really don't feel like getting beaten up." My voice was monotone. "Addy can't help me heal as much now, and Sianna's gone."

"Charlie's here," he argued. "You need to get mad, Luke. You need to get raging angry, or it all just turns numb. From the way Jess is sobbing, I'm guessing it's ugly, akin to what I did—"

"It's so much worse!" Jess wailed, panting for breath. "You cut it. He *destroyed* it. There's nothing now. No sign it was ever there to begin with. Just gone. All that's left is this weird sense of duty and survival. It's like his power swallowed everything else. There's *nothing* else other than calm acceptance and… I don't know what the fuck to call it. Bemusement."

"That's not true," I argued, frowning.

I felt Will's power shift. "Luke, Mom is dying. Every day she gets a little bit older."

I tilted my head. "Are you trying to hit me with the fear? I don't think that works anymore."

"That's interesting," Will said, shrugging. "Come on. Let's do this."

"You're not going to let this go?" I asked.

"Nope. Time to fight, little brother. Let's go!" He clapped his hands in my face.

I put my water glass down with an eye roll and followed him. "I'm not sure who's shorts these are but try not to ruin them."

"They're yours. Sam and Addy went and bought us a lot of Costco clothes on Thursday. I can ruin them."

Out on the hard-packed earth, we turned to face each other. "Go," Will said. "Take the first strike."

"You're the one that wanted to do this," I said. "I don't particularly want to hit you."

Just like that, I saw his fist coming toward my face. I stepped out of the way.

Will paused, surprised. "Very nice. Usually, you just stand there like an idiot."

"You went slow with that. I saw it coming."

He hesitated. "I didn't slow it, Luke."

Before either of us could process it, Micah took a swing at my head. I hadn't heard him come outside, but I felt his presence within arm's reach and blocked the strike with my forearm.

"The energy is centered," Micah said. "He's using it now for heightened senses."

Will snorted. "It is on, little brother."

Somewhere in my mind, I realized we were sparring with increased speed, both dodging strikes for all we were worth. I got in a good center body hit that stole Will's breath, but he also got in a kidney kick that made me hobble in pain.

We didn't stop, though. For damn near an hour, we fought. Micah occasionally mixed things up or called a break.

"Enough," Emma yelled from the patio. "If he isn't pissed off by now, it's not going to happen, William. It's time for breakfast."

We stepped apart, both breathing hard.

"Good. Good job," Will panted, slapping me on the shoulder. "Now, if you could just learn to keep your head attached, we'd be all set."

"Why was this easier?" I asked Micah. "I don't understand."

Micah lifted his eyebrows in surprise. "You don't feel the difference in your energy? If Jess is up to it, ask her to show you. You rarely understand until you see it."

Stepping back onto the patio, I took a bow for the applauding audience. My entire family, plus Charlie and Ellie, had watched our little show.

"He didn't even piss himself this time," Matilda cheered.

"That was amazing," my dad praised. "That's how Will spars with Matthew. No more kid gloves for you."

I nodded, ignoring Tali and Adaline whispering together at the other end of the patio as they both wiped at tears.

It was done. They could cry if needed.

"Breakfast?" I asked, suddenly starving.

"Casserole is coming out of the oven in ten minutes. Go get cleaned up," my mom suggested, voice flat. She wasn't happy with me. At all.

It was done. She could be mad if needed.

Ten minutes later I was back in the living room after another quick shower and some fresh clothes. "We're going home today?"

Sam nodded, eyes fixed on me.

I lifted my eyebrows.

"There were other ways," he said. "You could have asked."

Everyone in the room went still.

"I thought of three thousand alternatives. They all left me at the same place—forcing my love upon someone who doesn't want it."

"Good. It's good you realize that. This is an okay place to be," he said with a nod.

"Was I supposed to be somewhere else?" I asked, wondering why Sam hadn't offered his oracle talents last night. "Where did you take her this morning?"

"I took her back to your house." He pressed his lips together, debating what else to share. "I guess it doesn't matter now. It mattered if I told you yesterday, but not now. In some futures, you refused to break it or couldn't break it. In others, you broke it but hated her. In the worst futures, you break it and turn cold."

"Cold?" I lifted my eyebrows.

"Indifferent," Adaline offered. "I'm not sure we've avoided that, Sam."

Sam shrugged. "I think this is an okay place to be. He's not avoiding us or trying to escape reality. I think we're okay."

William walked up behind me, smacking me upside the head as he passed by.

"What?" I asked, confused.

"That was an 'I love you' smack. No indifference for you. Been there. Done that. We can avoid it, Addy. Don't worry about it."

"Where to from here?" I asked Sam, hoping for some tips. It seemed best to ignore Will.

"Home. I thought we already said that?" Sam asked.

"We did. But I meant, where do I go from here?"

Sam's head tipped to the side. "You'll have to decide that, Lord Peace."

I sighed, sitting down at the table. "Thanks for cooking,

Mom."

Darla waved away my thanks.

Just as I reached for my silverware, Matthew stabbed me through the hand with his fork.

"Are you kidding me with this?" I asked flatly. "Now it's four tiny stab wounds instead of one larger one."

He twisted the fork a bit before yanking it out. "Heal it."

But the wounds were already closing without any effort on my part.

"Lord Peace," Sam said again as Matthew got up to get a clean fork. "Great. We've got that going for us."

"Is he purposely ignoring me or actually doing his time shit?" Will asked Adaline after breakfast. "Usually, I can tell when he's doing the time thing."

He'd been trying to talk to Sam for nearly five minutes. It was hard to ignore William for five minutes.

Addy scrunched up her face. "It's more of a space thing. He's looking through the houses without his body. Give him a minute."

"Come again?" my dad asked, nonplussed.

"He wants to make sure there are no surprises at home," Addy said as if that was the confusing part.

"Okay, but when did he start doing the looking without the eyeballs?" Hank asked.

Addy shrugged. "He's been working on the space stuff."

Hank looked around the table, hoping someone else knew about this. His eyes landed on Ethan.

"Mmm, he said something about trying to look a few weeks

ago," Ethan offered, also shrugging. "What difference does it make?"

"I'm having a hard time keeping up with my children," Hank snapped, uncharacteristically upset. "He Walks through time and is now Looking without his body? Do I have that right?"

Adaline's mom, Ava, pulled a face. "I don't know if this has a name. I didn't know he could do this. Is this something he does or something you do, Addy? I know you can Look through the eyes of other living things."

Addy nodded. "I look through eyes. He's looking without eyes. He'll show me how when he knows for sure."

Ava and Hank shared a sympathetic look that almost made me laugh out loud.

"That wasn't what I was asking. Is what he's doing part of the power of the Walker, or is it your power as the Mistress, just used differently?" Ava clarified.

Adaline shrugged. "We can ask—"

"There will be no asking," Micah cut in. "My Walker could not do this. You will not tell anyone else you can do this. You need to start protecting information about your power."

Adaline frowned at Micah, causing him to shift uncomfortably.

"I'm serious," Micah said after a minute. "We need to stop sharing information so freely, even within our Harbor circle. I'm willing to bet Nathaniel found out Luke was standing circles as Lord Peace because the Harbor members update internet message boards every week. I searched for 'Lucas Trellis Peace.' I got back fifteen different message boards talking about him standing circles as the Peace pillar."

Charlie gasped even as Ellie nodded.

"I read those for a while," she admitted. "I thought they

were funny. But it didn't dawn on me that Nate would do a basic internet search."

"My name is on the internet tied to being empowered?" Sam asked, joining the conversation.

"Your name is on the internet as the Time Walker," Micah corrected, "as is Adaline's as Mistress Life."

"That's a problem," Sam and Hank muttered at the same time.

"Was there anything going on at the houses?" Will asked.

"You're not worried about this?" Sam retorted.

"No, I'm not," Will replied. "I knew about it as it was happening. Gregg told us he was spreading the word. Hennessy's been burying most of the message boards into the search results wasteland of pages ten to a million that no one ever looks at. Someone would have to search for 'Sam Trellis Time Walker' to get any meaningful hits, and those people already know what you are."

"Meh, they'd probably have to have his full name. I've buried the Sam Trellis Walker hits pretty good now," Hennessy countered. "What were you trying to ask him, Reap?"

"Yeah!" Will said, remembering his original question. "Why did burning the binding fix his circle shit?"

Darla cleared her throat.

"Sorry, Mom. Lost track of it," Will admitted.

Somehow, Will *never* ended up doing dishes. Not once.

"I don't know," Sam said, answering Will's question. "Why ask me?"

Will threw up his arms. "Because you know everything?"

"I do not," Sam disagreed.

"What day are my babies going to be born, Sam?" Emma asked.

"February second at three-thirteen in the morning," Sam said immediately. "But of course, I would look for that!"

Will's mouth dropped open in shock. "How long have you known that?"

Sam shrugged. "Since the day I took the name. It was the first thing I intentionally looked for."

"Aww," Emma cheered. "You would have won godfather on that even if you hadn't worked the system."

Sam smiled smugly at Adrian. "Told you. It was always going to be me."

"Why wouldn't you tell me that, Sam?" Will demanded, enraged. "You know I've been stressed about it!"

"I thought you wanted to be surprised," Sam said, all innocence. "Why didn't you ask?"

Will's mouth hung open, catching flies.

I couldn't help it. I laughed at that, but I had the good sense to cover it with a cough. There were quite a few coughs and sneezes around the table at the same time.

"What's going on at the houses?" Will asked again, tone flat as he glared around the table.

Sam shook his head. "Three people are waiting for us. Gary, Candy, and someone I'm going to kill."

He said it so casually, so easily, I would have believed I'd misheard if Jake hadn't choked on his drink.

"Uh, what?" Matthew asked.

"Gary, Candy, and a dead man," Sam said again, eyes on Darla. "Mom, Dennis is in your house, sitting in the big room. Do you want to see him before I rip him limb from limb and toss him Outside?"

The color drained from Darla's face as her teeth ground together. "Why is he in my house?"

"I don't know. I don't care. He's not staying," Sam said, only then showing signs of his rage in the echo of his voice.

"How do you know him, Sam?" my mother asked, voice chilly.

"I couldn't always control where time took me, Mom. You know that."

"Why wouldn't you have talked to me about it before this second?" Her words were more clipped, but her voice wasn't raised. Instead, she radiated shame and remorse more than anger.

"Why would I ask you about this?" Sam asked, his words also clipped. "I wish I didn't know him. I will kill them all on sight. I am the Walker. It is my right to judge how energy is used in this world. They used it poorly."

"Who are we talking about?" Lucy whispered to Adrian, who shrugged in response.

"Dennis is my second eldest brother," Darla said, eyes still on Sam.

I rocked back in my chair. *Oh, shit.*

"He's there because of me, Sam," I said. "I'm sure Nate thought he'd be a welcome presence like Candy and Gary. He's a relative. Mom and I figured out on Thursday that her family has some very minor beast affinity. She produces the smallest of small pings on my radar."

"Do you want to see him?" Sam asked, ignoring me.

Apparently, he already knew that. *Thanks for the heads up, Sam.*

"No," Darla said. "And I also don't want—"

Too late. Sam was already gone.

"ADALINE! GO! NO KILLING!" Darla roared.

She was too slow. Adaline followed Sam before Darla could even start speaking.

"Oh shit!" Darla yelled. "How do we get back without them? I don't even know where we are!"

"So, we have some time," Will said, leaning back away from the table, eyes on Mom. "Let's talk about Dennis and why Sam would be willing to kill him."

"I told you! He's my second brother, and he's an asshole. He beat the shit out of me in high school when... I objected to him negotiating certain aspects of my life with his best friend. Now, someone tell them—"

Will started laughing. It wasn't a happy sound. "I can feel your fear from the memory, Mom. Forty years removed the residual fear is still there. I know you're leaving out the details of what happened. It's embedded in your fear. God speed, Midas."

"ETHAN!" Darla yelled. "YOU TELL HIM—"

"Nope," Ethan cut her off and even popped the 'p' for emphasis.

"Luke!" she tried.

"I mean, I can. But if he's still there when we get home, I'm not going to be happy."

Micah leaned across the table to take Darla's hand. "It will be fine. You raised good humans. He won't make a mess in the big room."

"Micah!" Darla yelled over our cynical laughter. She was both horrified and trying not to laugh herself.

"You have been the most dangerous person in the room from the day I met this family," Micah said, shaking his head. "You should not be surprised they would protect you."

"Okay, we can go," Sam said cheerily as he reappeared by the couch. "I'll come back later and do the dishes."

"Sam," Darla breathed, bracing herself. "What did you do?"

9

"He's not dead. Addy said no," Sam said with a shrug. "I hurt him a lot, then she healed him some, then I stuck him Outside."

"What is Outside?" Charlie asked. "We've talked about this before, but it's never made sense."

"Outside," Sam said like it was obvious. "It's Outside."

"Outside of what?" Charlie tried again.

"Oh. Sorry. It's outside of time and space. Or outside *our* time and space. Like, another dimension or alternate reality, however you want to think of it. I have a house there."

Of course, he did. Sam had houses everywhere.

"Grey. It's all grey. A great, big grey nothing," Matilda added with a shudder. "It's a 'bring your own colors' kind of place."

She had followed Sam Outside last November.

Sam grinned at her. "My house is lovely. We can go one day. But now that you mention it, everything in the house is grey."

Matty pulled an I-told-you-so face.

"Dennis is in your Outside house?" Darla tried to clarify.

Sam scoffed. "Oh, no. Fuck that guy. No, he's floating."

"Samuel," she barked.

"I already told you I'd do the dishes," he offered.

Jake turned to me. "Talk to me about what you can do to shifters."

"Beast affinities," I corrected automatically.

"Fine," he bit out. "Can you hurt him more than Sam? Should we make Sam go get him?"

"Boys, we will not do this!" Darla scolded. "Sam will go get him, apologize, and send him on his way. I haven't seen him in over forty years. This is ridiculous."

Matthew smacked my arm. "Answer the question."

"Are you coming home? What's happening?" Adaline asked, reappearing next to Sam. "You told her we'd do the dishes, right?"

"I have to do the dishes. I swore," Sam said, unrepentant.

Adaline rolled her eyes, unimpressed. "Are we going?"

"We're trying to decide if Luke can hurt him more than I can," Sam replied.

Addy looked at me, awaiting an answer.

"ADALINE!" Darla yelled.

"It's worth a shot." I nodded.

"Someone to practice on," Charlie agreed. "I was going to volunteer, but this is better in case you Edgar him."

"Edgar?" my dad asked, trying to keep up with our nonsense.

"He's an elder that got...." Charlie's voice trailed off as he shivered in revulsion.

"Stuck," I finished. "He looked like a bigfoot. But I fixed it. I wouldn't Edgar you, Charlie."

"We shouldn't use 'Edgar' as a verb." Charlie looked around guiltily. "By far, he is the most approachable elder and an amazingly kind person. But he'd still chew me up and spit me out."

"You think?" I asked, surprised.

"Yes, Luke. Yes. The elders are scary. Well, okay, Edgar, John, and Godwin are terrifying. Nate is insane. Nate Junior is marginally better. The two psychos are gone. Daniel is fine. He doesn't belong where he's at, though, and he knows it." Charlie looked at Sam. "Are we going?"

Sam nodded. "Everyone up. Grab a hand."

"Seriously?" Jake asked, glaring at him.

"Do you want to get lost between time and space?" Sam asked. "No thanks. Mom would be pissed. We'll hold hands."

"I'm already pissed, Samuel," Mom bit out.

"Well, that's because you're silly," Sam said easily, clearly not considering his words before he spoke. "Ready? One, two, three."

We were back home before Darla got a chance to respond.

Micah looked around. "See? No blood."

"Go get your uncle," Darla growled, glaring at Sam. "Or I'm going to be truly angry."

"Alright, I'm going," Sam said, affronted. "Keep your hair on."

He was gone before she could respond.

As one, my entire family worked hard to avoid eye contact.

"He's feeling saucy today," I muttered.

Beth snorted in response, unable to completely lock down the sound.

"He's very happy about this," Adaline admitted. "I believe he's been looking for them for a long time, Darla."

My mother didn't reply. Instead, she threw herself down in her favorite chair, arms and legs crossed, waiting.

IT TOOK Sam a full five minutes to reappear.

"Sorry," he yelled over the man's screaming. "I couldn't find him."

"Well, he's broken," Matthew yelled back to Sam. "His mind is shot."

As one, my family turned to look at me.

"It's very loud, what with the screaming and all," Adrian yelled, noticing my hesitation.

"Fine," I muttered, not liking that I was about to help him, only to hurt him again.

Taking his limp wrist in my hand, I got the irregular measure of his pulse and caught the pattern of his breathing. Then, remembering Sianna's words of caution, I pushed the net of peace around the man, excluding myself. He fell silent as soon as the net settled.

"Wow," Matthew muttered. "He's quiet but still broken."

"I know," I muttered, sending a wave of centering peace into the man. His heart stuttered, losing its rhythm before finding a more consistent pattern in the net of my energy. Then I tossed his arm away and withdrew all my energy. He'd be fine.

"Wow," Matthew said again. "That's new. It avoids shock?"

I nodded. "I figured it out when I was working with the older kids. Their systems were so used to the horror, removing it was a different kind of pain. That's the first time I've done it without being in the net, though."

"Doesn't look like a net," Jess muttered. "No holes in it."

I shrugged. I hadn't tried looking at it, but I could feel it.

"You'll show me how?" Adaline asked, interested. "I've not done that."

That threw me for a minute. "Sure."

"Peacekeeper," the man croaked, trying to roll himself upright.

"Uncle Weasel," I responded, voice cold.

"Coyote?" Darla asked. "They said coyote?"

I snorted. "He's a weasel."

"Dar?" the man asked, trying to look around.

"Why are you in my house, Dennis? You are not welcome here." I doubted my mother's voice had ever been colder.

"I can't see nothin'," he muttered. "I don't know what happened. First, I was here, waiting. Then I was somewhere else."

Adaline sighed, glaring at Sam. "He had glasses. Did they fall on the floor?"

"They're over here," Emma called from the other end of the room. "I'm not bending for them, though."

Will picked up the glasses then tossed them across the room to Adrian, who caught them without looking.

I fought not to roll my eyes. At times, Will and Adrian seemed like extensions of the same person… not unlike Matthew and me.

After wiping off the glasses, Adrian handed them to our would-be uncle. Dennis sat up then, looking at the horde of angry family members encircling him. His eyes finally landed on my mother.

"My God, Dar. You look exactly the same, maybe just a little more… soft."

My father—my even-tempered, gentleman of a father—outright growled in anger.

"It's a good thing! In a good way!" Dennis yelled, almost cowering. "She was all hard edges, suspicious and angry when we were young."

"Why are you in my house, Dennis?" my mom asked again, resigned. "You're not welcome here."

"I know," he mumbled, "I know. Tried to explain that. But I didn't have no choice."

"Sure, you did," Will countered, now hovering over Dennis. "Probably should have told them to fuck off, man. It's not healthy for you here."

Charlie grunted, shifting uncomfortably. "No."

Will turned to Charlie, eyebrows raised.

"If he was told to stay here and wait, he didn't have a choice. With his level of affinity, and as a weasel? No. If they told him to stay, he'd stay even if it meant death."

Dennis gasped in pain as he tried to crawl to Charlie. "The Prodigy. The young one. Merciful one, please. Let me stand."

Charlie sighed, bending down to meet Dennis's eyes.

"Be still," Charlie murmured. "Be calm. Who holds you here?"

"J-John," Dennis whimpered.

Charlie nodded, unsurprised. "Where are Candy and Gary?"

"Gary's in Adrian's house, eating leftovers and drinking beer. Candy's in Luke's house, taking the world's longest shower," Sam answered.

Charlie's eyes shot to Sam, narrowed in anger.

"I don't know," Sam said, hands raised. "I intentionally didn't look. I don't want to know. Truth be told, I still have words waiting for her."

"Come here, Luke," Charlie ordered. "Release him from John's command. Your uncle's not here as a spy. I'm guessing they offered him up as a sacrifice."

"I don't understand," I admitted, moving to Charlie even as Dennis whimpered. "I don't see anything...." My words trailed off as I touched Dennis's head. "That's disgusting."

Charlie nodded in agreement. "The elders are terrifying. Don't discount them because they don't transform."

"Can the rest of us understand?" Jake asked, annoyed.

"There's a mental compulsion driven like a nail through his mind," Adaline offered softly. "He could not leave, even if he wanted to, even in his terror and pain. Though he is delighted to see his sister again. There is genuine love."

My gaze flicked to my mom. Her eyes didn't soften in the slightest.

"I'm not sure how to do this, Addy. Do you want to do it? I completely missed it when I helped him a minute ago," I admitted.

She shook her head. "I tried earlier. When Sam and I were here. Before Sam sent him Outside."

Well, that's not promising, I thought. *How am I going to do this if Adaline can't?*

I took a deep breath before sitting on the floor with my uncle. Would-be uncle. *This is too strange for words.*

"Dennis," I said, sending peace through his mind.

As his eyes focused on me, I could feel the natural parts of his mind shift away from the unnatural ties and compulsions.

"What the hell?" Jess muttered. "There's more than one compulsion. Some behavioral ties as well. For what it's worth, Puking Peace, I couldn't see this before, either. Not until you cleared the way."

"There's a whole chain of them," I agreed, untwisting the mental landscape. "Going back years and years."

"You should hold him in the net," Adaline directed. "Like you did before."

I hesitated. "No. I don't know what all of these are, Adaline. I don't want to get stuck in one of the ties."

My family hovered silently while I worked my way through the mind. "Some of these suppressed emotions. How is that possible?"

Darla actually snorted. "It's a hierarchy thing, Charlie? Anyone with more juice than him could mess with his head?"

Charlie waggled his hand in a so-so gesture. "Yes, but it's also a specific talent. Not everyone could do it. And even fewer people can *undo* it. The elders have broken minds before with poorly spoken commands. Godwin and Nate have talent at unwinding, but Luke is undoubtedly the best person on the planet for this work. No offense, Adaline."

"None taken," Addy murmured. "I told you. I tried and could not do this."

"Anyway, if my father or grandfather had the ability, they would have removed everything they considered soft. Affection and empathy were heavily frowned upon amongst the menfolk in my family."

I paused in what I was doing to stare at my mother.

"What?" she demanded.

I looked around the room, first to my father, then at each of my brothers in turn. Then, I looked back at her.

Darla nodded, a regal, proud lift to her chin. "I raised my boys better."

"You raised a family of empaths… and whatever Sam is," I countered. "Maybe a little bit of an overcorrection?"

She grinned. "You are each your own person. I had no part in all the *extra* crap."

I grimaced, flinching at the wrongness of the words.

Before I could speak, Sam's words came into my brain. *"Ignore it. We'll talk about it later. Interesting that you can hear the wrongness now. Things people believe to be true but that are wholly false—it sounds wrong. Dad does it too."*

I nodded, going back to the task of cleaning out my uncle's mind.

10

An hour later, I looked around, only then realizing I was mostly alone in the big room.

"Hi," I whispered, forcing a small smile.

It didn't help. Candy's eyes still filled with tears.

"Hi," she mouthed, unable to speak as she choked back a sob.

I sighed, moving my uncle's head from my lap. He'd fallen asleep after I'd cleared about a third of the crap from his mind. I wondered who he would be when he woke up. Stuffing a couch throw pillow under his head, I left him on the floor.

He might have been manipulated, but the guy had hurt my mother. I wouldn't go out of my way to ensure his comfort. But a throw pillow seemed reasonable.

I pulled on Candy's hand, tugging her up from the couch. She nodded, following me out of the room. "Where is everyone?" I asked.

"Went to their homes, I guess. Hank and Darla went to your

house. She didn't want to be here with him. And they didn't want me there with them."

I raised my eyebrows, surprised. "They said that?"

"Well, no. They were fine in the desert house. But I wouldn't want to see me," she muttered, head hanging.

"Hey," I said with forced cheer. "Guess what Micah told me this morning?"

She didn't respond and didn't look up, just pulled her hand away from me.

"It turns out that if you do an internet search for 'Luke Trellis Peace,' you get all sorts of hits about me standing in Harbor's circle as Lord Peace."

Her eyes shot up to mine. "Are you serious?"

"You were there for dramatic flair, not fact-finding," I said, nodding.

She chewed on her lip, thinking.

"Okay?" I asked after a moment.

"Is my brain knotted?" she blurted.

"What?" I asked, caught off-guard.

"Charlie said your uncle had a lifetime of orders tied up in his brain. Is my head like that?"

I blinked, confused.

"Would you check? Please?"

"Candy, I think I would have..." my words trailed off as I doubted my earlier perceptions. "Okay."

I touched her head gently, letting a small pulse of peace free to see if anything jumped. Instead, she snuggled into my chest, relaxing into the feeling.

"There's nothing," I murmured, kissing the top of her head as I hugged her. "You're fine. A lot of fear, grief, and remorse, though."

She shivered, holding on tighter.

"Candy," I breathed, smoothing her hair. "I'm fine."

"I should have let them kill me. It'd have been better than seeing you bleeding out like that. Adaline is amazing."

I shook my head, disagreeing. "Mostly, it was Charlie and Edgar." I hesitated, swallowing my own knot of grief. "And Sianna."

I don't think Candy realized her fingers dug into my back.

"I would have died without her," I said, nothing but the truth in my words.

We were quiet for a minute, standing together but lost in separate thoughts.

"You are Peacekeeper now."

I nodded. There was no denying it.

"You're better too. I can feel it. Calmer."

I nodded again. "Centered."

Her head tipped back so she could look me in the eyes. I felt the emotion flash through her right before she stretched up, trying to pull my mouth down to hers.

"No," I said. The word came out more firmly than I'd intended, even as I unwound her arms from around my neck. "Friends, Candy. Nothing more."

Her gaze dropped to my chest, cheeks flushed with embarrassment. "She can't be with you, Luke. So, if that's what you're thinking, it won't happen. Not in the way you want, at least."

I blew out a sigh. "I know. But that doesn't mean this is a good idea. We tried this already, Candy. We're great friends. That's it."

"Luke—"

"No. No, thank you."

"You hate me now," she mumbled.

And, with the words, I noticed it—just a little touch of manipulation. She intended to bring me back to her, even if it involved pity. She'd keep working this angle every chance she got.

Her eyes flicked up to mine, full of tears again.

I took a step back, crossing my arms over my chest as I glared at her.

The tears disappeared, replaced by confusion.

"So, an interesting byproduct of being more centered, or maybe of being Peacekeeper," I started, wrinkling my nose at her. "That tiny bit of manipulation you're working at is oh-so-apparent to me. It stinks. It's disgusting."

Her eyes went wide as she shook her head in denial.

"I defended you when Sianna called you selfish. I defended you when you 'testified' against me. I do not hate you. I'd like us to remain friends. Please don't make me regret it."

"I wasn't—"

"You were," I cut her off. "Maybe you didn't do it intentionally, but that makes it just a little worse."

She hesitated, considering.

"This," I said, gesturing between us, "is not happening. It ended when I was just Luke. The 'Peacekeeper' thing does not change it. Friends, or not friends, I'll leave it up to you, but check the bullshit at the door, Candy."

"And now you should leave," Sianna said flatly from a few feet down the hallway.

Candy jumped in surprise. I didn't. I'd felt Sianna even as she'd landed in my backyard, a quarter of a mile away.

With a nod, Candy was out the front door, probably on her way to Jake and Matilda's house, where I'm sure Charlie and Ellie waited.

I didn't turn to watch as Candy left, and I didn't turn to look at Sianna. With another sigh, I leaned against the wall behind me.

"Turns out you might have been onto something with the 'selfish' side of Candy's personality."

Sianna gave a small huff of laughter. "I am always right. You should accept this now. It will make things easier."

I nodded, sliding down the wall to sit on the floor.

I could feel her hesitation.

"I'm not in pain," I assured her. "I'm fine."

At my words, her grief and loss rolled through my brain.

"I am not," she whispered, taking my hand. She kissed my knuckles as she helped herself to my peaceful energy.

I yanked her down into my lap, folding my arms and legs around her, wrapping us both in a little cocoon of my energy.

"I have information," she mumbled.

I nodded, head leaning on her shoulder as she wrapped her body around mine.

"Later," she agreed.

"WHAT THE FUCK are you two doing?" Will said right before he smacked me in the back of the head.

I blearily looked around, confused.

"I thought you were breaking that binding for the good of animals everywhere or some shit?" Will asked.

I'd fallen dead asleep with Sianna in the hallway outside of my parents' big room.

"Yeah, that's a thing," I said groggily. "Just sleeping. Sianna?"

She didn't move as I shook her. For a horrible second, I wondered if she was still breathing.

"You are less likely to reforge that binding if you just avoid each other. It's exhausting and extremely painful to forge and cut that kind of thing over and over. I imagine it's much worse with whatever you did to it," Will counseled. "The fatigue is normal."

"How did you do this repeatedly?" I breathed, realization dawning.

Will had done this over and over, hundreds of times, trying to let Emma be free of him. I'd understood that logically before but had a new respect for it now.

He sighed, bending to pull Sianna out of my lap. Then, cradling her carefully, he walked down the hall toward a guest bedroom. "Find some food for us."

A few minutes later, Will walked into the kitchen as I sliced chicken breasts for sandwiches. He picked up a hunk of chicken and shoved it in his mouth.

"Whatever," he said, even as he chewed. "Your fancy gourmet shit is lost on me, little brother."

He picked up the unsliced avocado half I'd left on the counter, flung the seed out, and scooped the whole thing into his mouth, tossing away the skin. "Same effect," he gurgled around the food.

I laughed. My mother would have been horrified.

"Good," Will said, smiling. "You're still in there. I do actually want a sandwich, so keep slicing."

"Jackass." I shook with laughter.

"I am a jackass," he agreed. "And I fucked up my life. I will never get back the years I spent trying to set Pip free. It was agony. For both of us. I'll live with that knowledge forever."

I froze, eyes on him.

"It's the truth, Luke. I will forever know that I hurt the only person I've ever loved with my whole heart. There are so many things in this life I love, but there has only ever been one queen of my heart."

"Sappy jackass," I corrected, then dodged the expected smack as I neatly folded together the French bread sandwich and sliced it in half.

Then I watched as William took both halves.

"You're going to eat the whole thing? Really?"

"I told you I wanted a sandwich. Sandwiches always taste better when someone else makes them!" He grinned.

"It's an eighteen-inch loaf. You don't need an eighteen-inch sandwich."

"Says you," he grumbled around an overstuffed mouth.

"Bread was kind of stale anyway," I muttered, going back to the fridge to look for something else."

"Keep telling yourself that if it helps," Will gloated. "Back to this thing, though. If you're not going to allow it to exist, stop seeing her. Stop falling asleep in the hallway with her. It'll damage you, Luke. Forging and breaking something like that over and over destroys part of your ability to care about others."

"I won't accept the binding again," I called, head stuck in the fridge.

William kicked me in the ass.

"Then *stop snuggling* in the fucking hallway!" he bitched. "I'm serious."

"Fine," I pulled my head out of the fridge. "I'll eat at home. Mom's leftovers are dated. I'll stop with the hugging. But she was upset."

Will snorted.

"She was!"

"I don't doubt it," he said. "But Pip's tears got me every time. One good hug, and then there was naked frolicking. It seemed like a great idea, over and over again, right up until I got on that plane to come back to Chicago."

"Why did you do that?" I asked.

He snorted again.

"No, seriously. After a few *years* of torture, why didn't you spill your guts and move to California to be with her? That part has never made sense to me. You wanted to give her time and space to be free, blah blah blah. But surely it sunk in at some point that you were a fucking moron."

Will boosted himself up to sit on the counter.

"Mom is going to lose her mind if she finds you sitting on the counter."

"Oh, shut up, Pollyanna. It's fine. I'm the favorite. I'm never in trouble."

I rolled my eyes, sitting on the counter across from him. "Spill it," I prodded.

He shrugged. "There was some fear that if I said I wanted to stay, she'd tell me to go. Then where would I be?"

"FEAR OF REJECTION?" I howled with laughter, almost falling off the counter. "Since when are you afraid of *anything*?"

"Are you shitting me?" Will laughed. "I'm afraid of everything. Literally everything. You walk around with your peace energy hanging out, influencing you all the time. You think you're the only one like that? Fear's a constant in my life, just like rage is a constant for Adrian. It just doesn't stop me."

He paused, considering. "It doesn't stop me often. Maybe it kept me away from Pip longer than it needed to. But I truly did want her to find happiness somewhere else."

"Huh," I muttered, considering. "It's really always there?"

"Always."

"Huh."

"What are you going to do about Sianna?"

"I don't know," I admitted. "I don't think I can just outright avoid her."

"What are you going to do about Candy?"

My eyebrows shot up.

"Oh, please." Will laughed. "I can spot an opportunist from a thousand yards, and you're an easy mark."

"I put a hard stop to that," I said, the words angrier than expected.

"Good," Will grunted.

"LUCAS, WHY IS YOUR ASS ON MY COUNTERTOP!" Darla yelled, turning into the kitchen.

My mouth dropped open, hands gesturing between William and me.

"GET DOWN RIGHT NOW, LUKE!" she roared.

I shook with laughter even as I wandered out of the kitchen, followed by William.

"I hate you," I muttered, still laughing.

"Oh, Poor, Puking, Pathetic Peace, woe is you," Will whispered back, also laughing.

"What happened to my avocados?" Darla yelled after us.

11

Two hours later, we sat around the dining room table trying to avoid eye contact.

"This is super fucking awkward," Jake muttered, comfortable in his swearing.

The kids were absent, preferring to spend Saturday afternoon with Jess's husband, making anatomically correct snowmen and women.

"Still at the table," Hank muttered back, "but your assessment is not wrong."

"It's like a kiddy table, but worse," Matilda added, looking out of the corner of her eye without turning her head.

We were all trying not to stare.

Dennis sat in the doorway, not quite in the dining room, awkward in his wheeled desk chair with a TV tray in front of him.

"I don't care," Darla snapped. "He's not eating at my table."

Matthew slapped my shoulder.

I shot him a look.

He looked from me to Dennis and then back to me, the message clear. *Find out why he's here.*

I sighed. "How are you feeling, Dennis?"

"Uh. Good. I'm good, Peacekeeper. Th-th-th." He paused, taking a deep breath. "Thank you. I don't know what you did, but I feel… different."

"Why did you come here?" I asked. "Were you in the arena on Wednesday?"

"N-n-n-no, sir," he stuttered again, almost hyperventilating.

I frowned, looking at Matthew. He shook his head. We both looked at Jess, who shrugged.

"You cleaned all the crap out, Puking Peace. He's not used to this kind of mental space," she offered.

I shook my head, already climbing to my feet. "He's terrified."

I touched his right hand gently. He flinched.

"She'll kill me," he breathed. "If she knows what I did when we were kids, she'll kill me."

The lightbulb went on over my head. He feared Sianna as Huntress, defender of the weak.

"You knew it was wrong," I said, voice cold. "Why did you do it?"

"I don't know. I've thought on it for years and years. Since I met my wife, had my girls, moved away from Dad. The thought makes me sick. I thank the dear Lord every night that my sister was strong and fierce," he mumbled, not meeting my eyes.

"Truth," Micah muttered, eyes on Darla. "He regrets and longs for forgiveness."

"I don't care," she said, looking away from Micah. "I really don't."

"Dar—" Dennis started, his words cut short when I yanked away the peace I'd offered.

"Do you know where you sit?" I asked, eyes locked on his. "Do you know what surrounds you?"

He didn't even blink. "I sit in judgment before the Peacekeeper, before the Huntress, awaiting death."

"You sit in my mother's dining room, idiot," I scolded. "And neither Sianna nor I are the scariest threats here."

I wasn't expecting him to start crying, but actual sobs broke free. "My nephew. My nephew is Peacekeeper! Praise Jesus! The Lord is just and kind."

I looked over my shoulder, glowering at Darla.

She grinned at me. "Did I fail to mention my family was *extremely* religious?"

"You did not mention that," I answered, "but, oddly, I'm not surprised. Maybe I should thank Dennis for all my Sunday mornings of sleeping in."

Darla's smile fell as her eyes narrowed, even as she shook her head. "All Sunday church meant was a good whipping for not sitting still while praising God. I preferred my children to talk with God in their own ways. I think you're doing just fine, maybe better off for the Sunday sleep-in."

I nodded, thinking back over my childhood. My mother had never backed away from conversations of faith or the afterlife, never denied the presence of a higher power. But, consistent with all things, we were encouraged to think for ourselves, question, and reason our way through life's challenges.

Meeting Mom's eyes again, I bowed my head a bit, thankful for my family and upbringing. I had no idea how Darla had survived with her spirit intact, but damn if I didn't respect her even more for it.

Turning back, my would-be uncle was mopping his face with his paper towel. Darla hadn't even given him a proper napkin. I bit back my smile. She had more than earned this little bit of mischief if it made her happy.

"Do you know what it means to be empowered?" I asked.

Eyes back on me, Dennis nodded. "I know about those pansy empowered assholes."

Oh, great, I thought, *from praising God in one breath to belittling others in the next.*

I could hear Darla snort behind me.

"Okay," I said, drawing out the word. "Let's do some introductions. How's that? We'll go around the table. I'd tell you not to worry about remembering names, but I doubt you'll forget anyone."

"At the head of the table, you know Mom, obviously. Next to her is my dad, Hank. You know the Huntress. Ava and Jess are in-laws."

They waved, both grinning. They knew what was coming.

"I am William, eldest son and Lord Fear." With Will's power-infused words, Dennis was back to sobbing.

"I am Emma, Lady Love." The tears slowed as he fell under Emma's spell.

Adrian let it sit for maybe a moment longer than was nice. "I am Adrian, Lord Rage." Interestingly, instead of feeding Dennis anger, Adrian seemed to draw it away.

I shot him a confused look.

"Rage is a common reaction to fear. I'd rather he not have that defense," Adrian said with his nice-guy smile. I almost laughed.

"I am Lucinda," Lucy said, the air in the room whipping around Dennis. He would have fallen out of his chair if I hadn't propped him up. "Take a guess at what I can do, asshole." Thunder cracked outside for good measure.

"I have to admit. We're getting better at this." I nodded as the group chuckled.

Jake and Matilda shared a look.

"I am Matilda, Lady Light," she said, shining brightly enough that I shielded my eyes from her.

Dennis squeaked at that one. He'd heard of her, apparently.

"And I am Jacob, the Anchor, which is a fucking stupid name. More like a wild card." Even as he rambled, he pulled the light from Matilda, turning it to fire, then extinguishing it in the palm of his hand.

"I am Ethan, Lord Joy, and I am disinclined to share my energy with you."

Micah sighed, eyes on Adaline. "I am Micah the Desolate, Lord Hate and Redemption, for redemption can only come to those who ask for it. And you've long since known redemption, Dennis. I have nothing to offer you."

Adaline's eyes shone as she smiled. I wasn't following it, but there was some form of acknowledgment and maybe an apology in Micah's words.

The table fell silent as shame rolled around the room. We weren't being nice. This was not how we behaved.

"It's fine!" Darla chirped. "I'm enjoying it. I know it's a little petty. It's fine. Let's finish and then we can move on. This is great healing fun for me."

As one, we turned to Sam, who pulled out his little smile. "Hello, I am Samuel, the Walker. We've met." The words echoed with a slight touch of his power. "You will repent, beg forgiveness, and never again offend one of mine. Or I'll leave you where I put you."

Dennis was back to hyperventilating, so I gave him a shot of peace.

"I am Adaline, Mistress Life. You will abide by his words and respect those who belong to us, or I will let Sam do as he chooses."

Noah grinned. "I'm Noah, Lord Passion, and those lusty thoughts for my oh-so-pregnant sister-in-law will get you killed."

Dennis flinched back in shock, decidedly not looking at Emma. He turned to me. "She's an actress, right? I think she's an actress? The most beautiful woman in the world?"

I nodded, smiling as another wave of proper fear rolled through Dennis, courtesy of William. "But I wouldn't go there if I were you."

Dennis nodded in agreement. "I wasn't. I'm sorry. Sorry, I'm sorry. So so—"

His words were cut off as a fount of water exploded out of his nose and mouth. The orb of water flew to Talise's outstretched palm. She tossed it like a ball before smirking at Dennis and dispelling the water into mist.

"Go ahead," Tali said to Matthew. "He doesn't need my name."

Matthew smiled his kind, genuine smile. "Hi, Dennis. My name is Matthew. If you fuck with my little brother or make my mom cry, I'll snap your brain like a rubber band. I am Captain Fucking Chaos, and you belong to me as much as Luke."

"That was pretty good," I complimented. "I felt that wave of energy."

Matthew nodded in acceptance and agreement, still smiling.

Miranda wrinkled her nose.

"What?" Matthew asked, frowning at her.

"Can we go outside for mine? Darla will get mad if I earthquake her house."

"That's true," my mother said immediately. "Let's skip your show and tell. That's Miranda, Lady Earth."

"I bet I could call the minerals from his bones," Miranda muttered. "That'd probably be bad, though."

Matthew nodded, kissing her hand.

"I am Bethany, Lady Hope." Beth sighed dramatically, sending her energy flying wild throughout the room. "Do you know what it is to live without hope, Dennis?"

His eyes stayed glued on Beth, more entranced than he'd been with raw love.

Beth smiled sweetly, yanking all her power away. "Do not believe, even for a second, that Luke is the most dangerous person in this room."

Before the words were done, Sianna was gone from the table, from the room, from the house. Just gone.

I frowned, concerned until I caught William's glare.

"My name is Jessup Garland, Dennis. Friends call me Hennessy. That's *not* you. And you already know what I control."

That caught me by surprise. I looked at Dennis, cowering over his little TV tray.

"Horrible things happen when a man of faith breaks loyalties with all he holds dear," Hennessy said, voice neutral. "We understand each other."

My mouth dropped open in shock. I had not seen that one coming.

"I am Charlie, Prodigy Lord, and I will fucking eat you if you hurt these people, you weasel."

Prodigy Lord? What? I tilted my head at Charlie. He waved off my question. We'd talk about it later.

"I am Candace, a beast master among cats."

"And maybe the only person less welcome here than you," Candy thought, the words coming to my brain clearly. I didn't think she'd meant to share them.

And then, not to be outdone, Ellie took a deep breath, sucking all the wild energy from the room and dimming the light overhead. "I am Eleanor Facet, next queen of the siphons. I don't even need to be within reach to break you and your entire bloodline."

Queen of the siphons? My eyebrows shot up at her.

She grinned at me, winking. "True story, Luke!"

"Abomination," Dennis breathed at Ellie.

She smiled back at him, not bothering to respond directly.

"What did I *just* tell you?" Sam roared, shaking the house around us.

Dennis flinched back, tipping over his chair and landing in a heap on the floor.

"Okay, that was fun," Darla said, clapping her hands. "Luke, go get a chair out of the garage. Get Sianna while you're out there. Charlie and Ellie scoot to make room. Dennis, get up. You look like a moron."

"SIANNA?" I called out the back door. She wasn't far. I could feel her wandering along the back fence in the winter darkness.

She came to the door in wolf form.

"You'll scare the dogs," I said, frowning.

Snaking around my legs, she padded her way into the house. The dogs didn't even move.

"I guess I'll just go get the chair then?"

There was no answer.

"You know, Sam moves shit with his mind! Why can't he get the extra chair?" I yelled back to the dining room.

Again, no answer.

"So much for that all mighty Peacekeeper thing," I muttered, lugging the chair into the house. "'No, no, Luke. You almost died a few days ago. I'll go get the chair,' SAID NO ONE," I kept bitching, irrationally angry over nothing. I got extra chairs all the time.

I tossed the chair into the empty space, only then realizing Dennis was sitting in my spot.

I glared at my mother.

"What? It was taking you forever. Sit down and shut up. You whine a lot," she said. "Besides, you're holding up dinner."

"What's for dinner?"

"Pot roast," Sam said smugly. Pot roast was his favorite. Darla was saying 'thanks' in her own little way.

"William sat on the counter first, Mom," I snitched.

"What?" Darla asked, eyes going between Will and me. "What are you talking about?"

"Earlier. You yelled at me for sitting on the counter. I only did it because William did it first," I continued, tone unmistakably juvenile.

"I raised you better than to do things because everyone else is doing them, Luke," Darla scolded. "I mean, really. You're a grown man. Time to think for yourself. Did you know I didn't want you on the counter?"

"Yeah, but—"

"No buts," she said. "You knew better. Grow up."

I rolled my eyes at William, who wasn't even trying to hide his laughter.

"Has anyone else ever noticed that Will is *never* in trouble? He swears at the table and gets away with it. He sat on the counter today, egging me on. He started it, but I'm the one that got yelled at."

Darla looked around innocently. "Of course, William's not in trouble. He's bringing me grandbabies to love."

"BOO!" the table yelled in unison.

My dad was laughing hard enough to cry. "I wondered how long it would be before someone noticed!"

"What a crock of shit!" Jake yelled. "Matty! Babies?"

"Nope, not yet," Matty said, shaking her head. "Maybe after you learn to put your socks in the hamper and stop shoving them into the couch."

"Well, I'll stop doing that now. It was only funny because it made Luke nuts."

I glared at him. "I don't think I can walk into your house without my eye twitching. Even now."

"Everything has a place of peace," Jake mocked, laughing at me.

"This is normal," Micah said, nodding at Dennis. "It's fine."

I could feel Dennis wigging out again, but was happy to let him sort out his own emotions. Of more interest to me was Wolf-Sianna, who sat behind Charlie and Ellie, avoiding my eyes while her emotions ran wild.

"Can I help?" I asked, trying to project the thought.

There was no response. I wondered if I had done it correctly right up until I heard Charlie's voice in my head. *"Leave her be, Luke. She didn't mean it, but what Beth did was absolutely horrible for*

Sianna. She is not prone to hope. To be doused with it unexpectedly, languish in its relief, and then have it ripped away is a special kind of torture."

I swallowed hard, eyes going to Beth at the other end of the table. She was watching me.

When our eyes met, she raised her glass, toasting me.

She knew exactly what she'd done. And she wasn't sorry.

Note to self: Never, ever fuck with Beth.

Her lips twitched up like she'd guessed my thoughts.

I blinked, unable to look away.

"My brother," Beth mouthed, dragging her finger across her throat, then shaking her head in disapproval.

My mouth dropped open in shock, even as I shook my head.

"I caused that. That's my fault, my stupidity," I said to Beth over the family chatter. "That wasn't her fault."

Conversation stopped as everyone wondered what was happening.

"We talked about this," Beth said coolly. "She stood in front of us and swore no harm would come to you. She was wrong, so she can fuck *all the way* off."

Stillness accompanied the silence at the table.

"Beth, she saved me. I would have—"

"She saved herself," Beth interrupted. "And you in the process. If she'd failed, Sam would have gone batshit, and we both know it. You lived, so she lives. But we're not friends, and she doesn't get to keep my energy. Not now."

Beth took a swallow of her wine. "Maybe if that binding had stayed. Maybe if that binding went both ways. But now, after she's forced your love away? Nope."

"And that's why she's not Baby Trellis," Ellie stage whispered. "She's way meaner than the rest of you boys put together."

"It was intentional?" Charlie gasped in shock, his angry eyes on Beth.

"Whatever do you mean, Charlie?" Beth asked, turning her mocking gaze his way. "I'm done with this conversation. Back to the other asshole in the room. Why are you here, Dennis?"

12

ennis looked around the table, eyes wide with confusion.

"This is normal," I assured him. "An off day for it, but normal. Why are you here? How did you end up here? Were you in the arena on Wednesday?"

I let loose a little peace to keep him calm this time. Now that we'd scared the crap out of him, the guy was likely to have a heart attack if left to hyperventilate on his own.

"No Peacekeeper, I was not in Chicago until this morning. My girls and I live in Iowa," he said quietly, eyes focused on me.

"When did you move, Den?" Darla asked, surprised. "I didn't think you'd ever leave southern Illinois."

"Not long after you, Dar. Two years. I met Winny when her car broke down outside the house, and I loved her immediately. Dad hated her. So, when her car was fixed, I got in it and drove away with her. Never went back."

My mom's lips twitched up into a bit of a smile. "I'm glad for you."

He nodded in thanks, eyes drifting around the table. "Me too."

I wondered what he meant. Was he glad for himself? Or glad for Darla's escape? Without warning, Dennis's thoughts came to me.

"—fine. Just fine. Wonderful, beautiful family. So much family. So much love. Baby sister's done just fine for herself."

The tenderness in the thought brought me up short. I felt terrible for scaring the hell out of this man.

"Winny and me had two girls. Renee and Sarah are long since grown with kids of their own. My Winny passed last fall after a long battle with breast cancer."

"I'm sorry," Darla said, blinking fast. That cut just a little too close to home after Darla's battle with breast cancer in the summer. Our eyes met. I knew she was also ashamed of our little show and tell.

"So, I'm on the farm by myself most the time, just me and the dogs. I sold off most of the land to the neighbor so the girls would have getting started money anyway. Ain't much to do these days. In the spring and summer, it's alrigh'. Winter, though, there ain't much going on. I ain't thought of that animal nonsense in a lotta years. It never gained me nothing but trouble raisin' chickens.

"Then, last night, late, a man come to the door. He said I had to come with him to Chicago to see my sister and pay my penance. I couldn't say no, and I wouldn't have, even if I could. So, we got out here to this great big house surrounded by all these other great big houses this morning, and I thought for sure he had it wrong.

"He walked in like he owned the place. I thought he knew you. I followed him in. When I realized you weren't here, I told him I'd wait outside. Somewhere else. He told me to sit and not move 'less nature called."

He sighed, wiping his eyes before he continued. "Asked if I knew the Lord, and I said 'yes, sir.' Told me to pray for my immortal soul, for I'd surely meet my maker soon enough."

Charlie sighed again. "They must have traced your family lines, Luke. They hunted him down and plucked the long-past memories of your mom from his head and brought him here for you to... work with. Peacekeepers have a heavy hand for justice. And John is older than dirt. Maybe older than Micah. I'm not sure."

Micah grunted in disapproval. "I will kick your beast lord ass, prodigy or not."

Charlie grinned down the table at him. "It was too easy to pass up, man. Who's older?"

"Me," Micah allowed. "By a long stretch."

Charlie nodded, smiling before he turned back to Dennis. "You knew me on sight, Dennis. You referred to me as only an affinity would. You knew the Huntress as well. How did you know us if you've been removed from affinities?"

Dennis's eyes went vacant. "Did I? I did. I dunno. I feel the Peacekeeper. They told me 'bout the Peacekeeper. They told me about the prodigy and his wife, the abomination—their word! Their word!" he corrected immediately.

"Okay," Charlie said soothingly. "Don't worry about it. It's fine. All fine."

"Help him sleep, Luke. He needs rest," Charlie said in my mind. *"Just let him rest where he is. Don't move him. The circle's energy might help him if Jake opens it to him."*

"Dennis," I said softly. His eyes darted to me immediately. "Sit back in your chair. Yes, like that."

And then he was out.

Charlie smiled. "Well done."

"I've had a lot of practice with that trick." I smiled back.

"Still annoying," William muttered.

"What did you pull out of his head earlier? Do you know?" Charlie asked.

I shook my head. "The newer stuff was like spikes through the mind. The older stuff was more like twist ties and zip ties that his mind grew around throughout his life."

Charlie shrugged. "I'm guessing they put some thoughts in there for him to ponder. And you should *not* feel bad about that little power display. If the elders get ahold of him again, they should know what they face. I don't think they have any idea what awaits them here."

"They have to have some idea now," I disagreed. "Sianna knew what we were the night she arrived."

"Sianna pays attention, and you were all here at the time," Charlie replied. "They know Sam and Addy are here. There's no hiding it with the type of wards that stand here. They probably know Matilda is here. I'm not as confident about the rest of you."

"I am familiar with Godwin and John. I've known Edgar for a very long time, since before he was Overlord. Nathaniel and I have met and are not on good terms," Micah added. "They know I'm here. They can probably guess what this place is, Charlie."

An unfamiliar smirk played across Charlie's face. "Well, if they go digging through his mind again, they'll know for sure.

You all need to practice that shit. It was good. Enough to scare someone without abilities. You need to be scarier. Don't bother with words. Take each other's energy and throw it like it's a game. Tali was absolutely perfect. The nonchalant 'I can rip the water right out of your body' display was terrifying, even for me."

Wolf-Sianna behind Charlie grunted. It sounded like agreement.

"Why would they dig around in his head again?" Darla asked, affronted. "They need to leave him be. He was a monster of a teenager who grew into a decent human being."

Charlie hesitated. "I don't think they're going to leave him alone, Darla. I don't think anyone in your direct bloodline is safe from intrusion. So, if there are people that don't know what you are yet, it's time to have that heart-to-heart."

Hank sighed. "I'll call my sister. My parents are gone." He turned to Darla.

"I have no idea," she admitted.

"Your mom has been dead more than twenty years," Hennessy replied. "Your Dad's still alive, living in the same house. He has dementia now. Both of your other brothers are in jail. One of them robbed a convenience store, the other killed his wife."

Darla blinked at him, at a loss for words.

Hennessy lifted his eyebrows. "It's what I do, Darla. Ain't nobody coming for this family."

Sam's voice went dark and echo-heavy again as he glared at Hennessy. "I've asked you. Multiple times."

"And I've told you there's nothing worth finding. I wasn't wrong. Look me in the eye and tell me you don't feel bad about tossing that repentant, gentle man Outside."

Sam shifted uncomfortably in his chair even as Micah outright laughed at him.

"A Walker with a conscience." Micah grinned. "Thank you for his humanity, Darla."

"You're welcome," Mom said smugly.

"Open the circle to him, Jake," I prodded.

Jake scowled at me. "Why?"

"Charlie thinks it might help his mind heal."

Jake's scowl remained.

I lifted my eyebrows.

"He hurt Mom!" Jake finally objected.

"It's true. He did," Mom said. "He hurt me so much, I vowed to run away and find a better life for myself. Ta-da!"

"Really?" Jake asked.

"Really," Darla agreed. "I got a touch of vengeance with show-and-tell. I don't wish harm to him."

"How about Grandpa?" Sam asked, angry eyes still on Hennessy.

"That man can rot in the cesspool of his own mind, Samuel. You don't need to do anything more to him," Darla replied. "And don't call him 'grandpa.' It turns my stomach."

"What's next?" I asked Charlie. "What do I do from here?"

"What do you mean?" Charlie asked.

"There's a ring of strong affinities about a mile out from our wall, but they seem more like defense than an attack force."

Charlie nodded in agreement.

"What am I supposed to do from here? Are we at odds?" I asked. "I don't know how things shook out."

"Sorry little brother," Will murmured, "but trying to take your head off puts us at odds with at least some of the beast affinities."

"I agree," I said immediately. "I just don't know what to do from here."

"Go home, get some sleep," Charlie suggested. "I want my bed and my clothes. We're going home tonight. Someone's lending me a car."

I opened my mouth to disagree.

"They won't touch me, Luke. Not now. Not after you've cleared me," Charlie said before I could form words. "Candy and I are free and clear. Sianna says the ring of affinities outside the compound will stay as long as you wish. They are here to offer her backup in keeping you safe.

"She talked to both Nathaniel and Edgar earlier. Nate has recognized you as Peacekeeper, despite your association with empowered circles. He couldn't deny you after a thousand people stormed the arena floor, chanting for his head. He came very close to death by an angry mob on Wednesday. They have seen you, felt your power. They heard about the kids you helped. They don't give a flying fuck about you hanging out with empowered people.

"You're Peacekeeper. You don't answer to anyone. Let the elders come crawling to you. They know you were due to return today. They left you gifts." Charlie paused to gesture at my uncle. "Sianna says Edgar will visit tomorrow."

"So, just go home?" I asked, somewhat confused by the anti-climactic resolution.

"Go home," Charlie confirmed. "Rest while you can. This is the calm in the eye of the storm, Luke. Nate doesn't want a Peacekeeper in his way. He's unqualified to hold his position. Any beast lord within reach or any beast affinity that's talked with him for more than ten minutes knows it. You're a threat to him. But he can't come at you straight on. He won't come here and risk facing Sianna. She'll wipe the floor with him, and every beast affinity on the planet knows it."

Wolf-Sianna grunted again. She seemed to be smiling.

Charlie rolled his eyes at her. "Sianna's hoping he comes here. She'll welcome that battle now."

Leaning forward to glare down the table at Beth, Charlie continued. "Despite what some people think, it was Nate who set you up to lose your head. He broke faith with Sianna and brought shame to her with your injury. She will make him answer for it if she gets the chance."

"I still vote for a Nate-Edgar cage match," Ellie argued. "Sianna would just kill him. Edgar would make it hurt."

Darla's eyes were narrowed in thought. "Should I expect Edgar for dinner tomorrow? Who's going to be here?"

"Are we doing Sunday dinner?" I asked. "We did a weird Saturday dinner. We've been together most of the week."

Darla made a face. "I've had a bit of a day. And now I have company that I haven't seen in forty years. Can we skip Sunday dinner this week?"

There was an uncomfortable moment where we all looked around, lost. I was suddenly sorry I'd suggested it.

"Sunday football, queso, and taco bar in my basement!" Will offered, eliciting a sigh of relief from around the table.

13

"Good evening, Peacekeeper." The soft, feminine voice greeted me as I opened my front door.

I squealed like a little girl before almost falling off my front porch step in surprise.

"What the fuck?" I yelled. Wolf-Sianna was at my side. So, who was in my house?

"Hello?" the voice said, startled. "Peacekeeper?"

"Who are you, and why are you in my *dark* house! Turn on the fucking lights!"

In my defense, I was surprised and not thinking clearly. My smart lights were smart enough to turn on, though.

She was about five and a half feet tall with platinum blonde hair and big baby blue eyes. "Peacekeeper?" she asked again, blinking in the sudden light.

My mouth hung open. "What the fuck?" I asked the wolf by my side.

The woman standing in my living room could have been a stand-in for Marilyn Monroe, complete with all the curves.

Wolf-Sianna stared back, somehow exasperated.

"You have nothing to say about this?" I asked her.

Silence.

I turned to the new woman. "Who are you, and why are you in my house?"

The big blue eyes were swimming with tears. She dropped to her knees where she stood, head bowed. "Apologies, Peacekeeper. The Huntress said you would not want me to await you outside."

I glared at the wolf again. No response.

"Who are you? Why are you here?"

I was already scolding myself for standing there like a fucking moron. If Will found out I'd walked into my house, found an intruder, and then stood around asking questions, he'd skin me alive.

Rightfully so, given the last few days.

Sianna disappeared from my side, headed back toward my parents' house.

"My name is Jane, Peacekeeper. Janie. It is my great honor to offer you assistance, but I'll leave if you wish."

I could feel Sianna returning and Charlie running down the block.

"She is harmless, Peacekeeper. Young. Of Godwin's line, actually. If she works at it, she may become a beast lord. Right now, she is just a rabbit," Sianna said. "The elders insisted you have a companion and assistant. I thought she would be most fitting as she is a calm person, also inclined toward music. I thought you would sense her, that you knew she was here."

"I wasn't paying attention to the house," I admitted, glaring at Sianna.

That ticked her off. "You must use all your senses now. All of them! Charlie told me they are centered properly and that you can access the circle. You have many powers now. You must use them to keep yourself safe!"

"I thought that was why you're here?" I rebutted, furious that we were having this conversation in front of this new woman.

Sianna's expression froze. "And I did my job so flawlessly, you damn near lost your head. Stop this. She will help you cycle energy and is a worthy companion."

In true Sianna fashion, she was gone again, sure to get the last word just as Charlie was heading up my walkway.

"What happened?" he called.

"There's a woman in my house!" I yelled.

"Just one?"

"SHUT UP, CHARLIE! THERE WILL BE NO HAREM!" I roared even as Charlie laughed.

"Charlie!" The woman ran past me and down the front steps in a flash.

"Janie!" Charlie cheered back, swinging the woman around as he hugged her. "What are you doing in Chicago? I thought you were in California these days."

"Uncle sent for me," she said, as if that made sense.

I guess it did. Charlie nodded.

"Luke, this is Janie. She's my baby cousin and extremely harmless."

I threw my arms out in exasperation, unable to find words.

"They're going to send people and gifts to you. Get used to it."

"Fucking creepy!" I yelled, storming into my house. I wasn't rude enough to slam the door behind me, though.

"Don't mind him," I heard Charlie say as they followed behind. "He doesn't understand yet."

"What the hell is all this stuff?" I shouted.

My living room was filled with plants and flowers. My dining room table was overflowing with fruit baskets, muffins, and loaves of bread. There was no clear surface to be found anywhere in my kitchen for all the crock pots and coolers.

"Gifts," Charlie said. "This isn't stuff the elders sent. This is probably stuff from the families of the kids you helped, Luke. I know it never really sank in, but I'm going to repeat it. You are a god to us."

I blinked at him, lost for words.

"These are offerings to the god that saved our children and was wronged by our leader," he clarified, speaking slowly to be sure his words hit home.

"Tell them not to do this," I suggested. There was so much food, so many gifts. "What am I going to do with all this?"

"There are people standing guard over you and your family right now, Luke. More than a hundred people, rotating around the clock at all times. They'll stay to ensure your safety. Maybe they'd like some dinner?"

That knocked the steam out of me. Strangers were standing watch to protect me, facing the real possibility that their unhinged leader would snap and try to come for me. I could feel them. I could feel their focus and sense their pride in and devotion to keeping me safe.

I stared at Charlie as I processed this new reality.

"It's going to be okay, man. It really is. But this is part of it," Charlie soothed. "You can send Janie away, and you can send the people standing guard in the middle of the fucking cornfields—in January—away. But it'd be right up there with taking a shit in the middle of your mother's Sunday dinner table."

"I will go if you don't want me here. I understand," Janie offered, eyes focused on the floor.

"You will not," Charlie said with a glare for me. "He doesn't understand that he needs help managing this yet. He won't kick you out. He was raised better than that."

Charlie was laying it on a little thick. I glared back at him.

He grinned at me.

I smacked myself in the forehead, realizing something.

"What?" Charlie asked.

"There's an insulated shed in my backyard. Big enough to be an extra room. Sam insisted it have electricity set up. There are enough amps to put another fridge out there. And there's a gate on my back fence. I'm the only one with a gate on the back fence to get to the walking path between the fence and the wall."

"Time Walker." Charlie smiled again. "Are you thinking of all the weird nuances about your house now? I know Matty's house has some interesting features."

"Yep," I admitted. "I don't have a basement. Mine is the only house without a basement."

"Hmm."

"Hello!" Ellie yelled from the front door.

"Ellie!" Janie bounced as she cheered. I tried not to look.

Charlie noticed me not looking and laughed, eyebrows raised.

I shook my head.

He shrugged. The gesture said *Why not?*

I went back to glaring.

"I APOLOGIZE," I said as I closed the door behind Charlie and Ellie. "You're welcome to stay in a guest room. I didn't mean to dishonor you or befoul your ancestors or anything like that."

Janie's lips twitched up. "Overwhelmed?"

"Yes, very much so," I admitted, blowing out a sigh.

"You can't do this wrong," she assured me. "You can't screw it up. We want nothing but your contentment, in whatever form it takes."

I nodded, decidedly not watching, as she took a deep breath and exhaled slowly.

"Uncle said there was a Peacekeeper. The Huntress told me too. I didn't expect this… relief. This freedom," she murmured before gracing me with a true smile.

I smiled back. I couldn't help it. She had that kind of smile. "Going bunny is rough?"

I will not think about Playboy bunnies. I will not think about Playboy bunnies. I will not…Holy shit, I'm ashamed of my brain. I gave myself a mental head slap of mortification.

"Oh!" she laughed, her giggle like a tinkle of bells in the room. "No, not really. But when I push for more… it's difficult. I know I can do it, though; everyone says so. I can feel it, like there's space to do more. I just don't know the other animals well enough yet, I guess."

My brow furrowed in confusion.

"You look confused." She smiled again. I smiled right along with her like a fucking moron. "The Huntress said you didn't know much about affinities."

"I don't," I acknowledged. My chest tightened at the mention of Sianna.

Janie nodded. "The animals that don't come by instinct come by knowledge and practice. Hard work. Uncle thinks it may be easier with you, and I think I agree. My mind moves easier with you here."

"Huh. That's interesting. All the shapes that Sianna takes? She had to study each of the animals?"

"Yes, but the Huntress is gifted. She was born with two forms and had eight others before her twentieth year." She picked up the lid of one of the crockpots. "Did you eat? This is pulled pork from Edgar's great-granddaughter, and it's the best thing you'll ever eat."

"I ate with my family but don't let me stop you."

"Oh! No. This is your food. I would not take it from you."

"Janie, there's no way I'm eating all this food. I'm offering it. Help yourself."

Her lips turned up as she bowed her head in thanks.

"Please don't do that!" I blurted. "This is incredibly strange for me."

Her face fell. "I'm sorry to upset you, Peacekeeper. What did I do?"

"My name is Luke. Can we go with that? And, like the bowing and kneeling? Can we skip that part? I don't know what to do with that, and my mother will lose her damn mind if she sees it."

Janie blinked at me, obviously confused.

"I swear I'm a pretty normal guy, Janie. I like music and cooking and food and hanging out with family and friends. I have no idea what to do with obeisance."

"But you functioned as empowered before taking the role of Peacekeeper. Your circle—"

"Most of my circle calls me Puking Peace," I interjected. "My circle—my family—we're a little different, I guess."

Her lips turned down in an expression of confusion. "Okay. I'm sorry."

"You don't need to apologize. I'm sorry. I'm sorry I'm making this weird."

Even as I spoke, I could feel my emotions twisting uncomfortably. I was upset and out of sorts. My energy was not automatically soothing the emotions, though. For a hot minute, I wondered if something was wrong with me again. But thinking about the energy called it forward, settling me.

Fingers touching my face and tugging my head down snapped me back to the present just as Janie's mouth closed over mine.

"Yikes!" My voice cracked on the word as I tried to break free. "And let's not do this. Sorry! Sorry! My fault."

I didn't expect a bunny to be quite *so* strong, but she must have worked out regularly. I couldn't break her grip. So, I did a dip and dive routine that involved some not-so-manly whimpering as I tried to escape without touching her womanly bits.

"Okay. Okay. I forgot about that!" I squeaked. "Sorry. I'll keep my energy to myself. Got it! It hits you worse than it hits Candy. Okay."

She was still panting, pulling at my clothes.

"JANE!" I yelled. "Janie! Stop it!"

She didn't seem to follow. For lack of a better option, I ripped the energy away. Rather than leaving it at my normal, neutral level, I sucked it away from her.

She yelped, tripped over her own feet, and landed in a heap in front of me. "Oh no," she wailed, holding her head as she sobbed.

"SHIT!" I yelled, recognizing I'd caused her physical pain.

I tried to come up with a solution that wouldn't involve hurting her or me and came up utterly blank.

"Sianna!" I called. "Please help! I don't know what to do with this!"

She was through the back door and into the kitchen before I'd even finished speaking.

"Fool," she scolded as she pulled Janie into a sitting position. "Why are you taking the peace away. Stop that. It hurts. Go back to normal. Don't pull it away unless you're punishing someone."

"I screwed up, and then there was too much and—"

"Take her to bed and make babies. What is wrong with you? You are the only man on the planet who would have a problem with this!" Sianna yelled.

It hit then. For the first time in my life, I knew what true rage was. It was not run-of-the-mill anger. No. I tasted rage. My natural energy recognized the threat to my wellbeing and swallowed the emotion. I was lightheaded and numb in the wake of the two warring emotions.

"Peacekeeper!" Sianna snapped. "What is wrong with you?"

When I met her eyes, she slid back away from me, pulling Janie behind her on the kitchen floor.

I watched the women move. I recognized their fear. I just didn't care.

"Luke?" Sianna asked, voice softer. "Luke, come back to us. Can you hear me?"

"I'm going to go spar with William." The words were flat, monotone.

14

I pounded on William's door, knowing better than to just walk in.

When he yanked the door open, I fell into the house. I guessed I had been leaning into the pounding.

"You're going to break my fucking...." His words trailed off. He shook his head a bit. "Let's do this."

I lost some time between walking in his front door and going splat on his basement wall.

"You think your walls are reinforced?" I asked, back to myself. "Seems like I should have broken the drywall."

"Basement. Giant concrete hole in the ground. Drywall's just for show," Will panted, dropping to the mat. "What the fuck happened? Did you crack your skull on the wall?"

I touched the back of my head. It wasn't bleeding, but it hurt. "Meh."

I grabbed two clean water jugs and headed to the cooler in the corner. "Matthew?" I asked.

Will grunted, not turning to look. "He hates the plastic bottles."

I dropped a full jug next to William and plopped down onto the mats to chug my own water. "So thirsty. Always so thirsty."

"Ask Tali?" Will suggested.

I nodded. *I should ask Tali what that's about.* As I thought it, Will's words drifted by me unnoticed.

"—happened?" Will asked.

"One more time. I wasn't listening," I admitted.

He turned his head, blinking at me. "Your eyes aren't glowing now. You look more like you. Not quite right, but better. What happened? You were fine earlier."

"There was a woman in my house when I got home."

Will was already shaking with laughter. "Harem?"

"No harem." I groaned. "My house is packed with shit. Gifts. Plants, flowers, food… don't cook for football Sunday. And this woman. I was confused, to put it mildly. Charlie whacked me upside the head with some perspective, figuratively at least. After he left, I was talking to the woman—Janie—and was decidedly uncomfortable."

"Why?"

"Okay, think of Marilyn Monroe."

"Yeah?"

"Now make her eyes bigger and bluer. Longer, natural platinum blonde hair. That's Janie."

"So? Since when do you have a problem talking to women? How are you not already BFFs? You're mostly a woman anyway, man-wife."

"Ah, shit," I muttered.

Will shook with laughter. "Yeah. Ellie told Adrian and me. That shit's sticking. Priceless."

"Anyway, I was out of sorts and wondering where the fuck my peace energy was when I needed it. The energy responded, and... things just got out of hand."

"I'm missing some of the shorthand," Will admitted.

"Not as much with Sianna, but with Candy, the peace energy generally led to energetic, happy sexy time."

"Ah. The peaceful energy led to energetic, happy sexy time for everyone else with Sianna. We all liked that outcome." Will grinned at the ceiling, listening to Emma move around in the kitchen.

We sat in silence for a moment while I waited for Will to get it.

His laughter finally broke free in giant huffs. "The Marilyn Monroe knockout made a pass?"

"I freaked out a bit when she tried to pull my belt off," I admitted.

"You are the only single, straight man on the planet that would have a problem with this particular situation. You know that, right, Pollyanna?"

I couldn't help it. I laughed. "Do I have to be Pollyanna and man-wife in the same conversation?"

"I don't know. Do you?"

The exercise mat shook under us as we both laughed.

Will sat up to look at me. "So, what's the problem? What happened?"

My good humor fell by the wayside.

"Oh, are we sparring again?" Will asked, eyebrows raised. "Your face is looking angular."

I froze, looking for a mirror.

"There's no mirror down here, and it's already fading. Again, what happened?"

"Sianna came to help and told me to go to bed and make babies, that I was the only man in existence with my issues."

Will pulled a face but didn't laugh this time.

"I don't change gears that fast," I admitted. "And I didn't welcome the harsh reminder that she'd rather I be *with anyone other* than her. She might have a soft spot for me, but she doesn't have real feelings and doesn't understand that I did. I took it poorly."

Will pressed his lips together, considering how to respond.

I cut him off. "I know there needs to be distance. I know she's not into any kind of relationship. Scorching that binding is the worst thing I've ever done or survived. I'm not super eager to do it again. But it was still a hard smack across the face. I got mad. Truly angry. I know what Adrian means when he says 'rage' now. My peace swallowed it. Everything went numb. I came here."

Will nodded. "Okay. Good."

"That's it?"

"You come to me when it goes numb, Luke. Me or Micah. You come to me before you risk hurting anyone else. You can't do irreparable harm to me. That's not true of everyone else. You come here when the feeling goes away. It's going to happen again. It'll sneak up on you."

I nodded. "I knew you'd kick my ass out of it."

"And I did."

"They were afraid. Terrified. I didn't care. There was nothing—no sympathy or remorse, no desire to calm the situation. There was nothing."

"Yep," William said. "If you stay like that too long, it's hard to remember why you should feel things. It's hard to stay engaged with life. I won't let you do that, Luke. Last night you did something vulgar to your psyche. It'll be a while before you're okay again. You don't take that out on anyone but me."

"Thank you," I said lowly. "I wouldn't expect you to be the brother to save my ass, but here we are."

"You can stay in a spare room if you want."

I chewed on my lip, considering.

"What?" Will demanded.

"How are you so fucking good at this? 'Relationship counselor' is not a talent I would expect from you."

He threw his head back, laughing again. "This isn't my first rodeo. You're doing fine, Luke. You'll figure your shit out so long as you keep your head attached. Adrian was much worse. That night I beat the shit out of him in the backyard is still among my worst nightmares. He's just so fucking stubborn.

"Jake was just plain old stupid. I really worried that I'd have to kill the shrew and hide the body if she made Carrots cry again. I hate Bella for the shit she said to Matilda. I hate her on a level only Micah would understand. And I hated Jake for his own apathy and stupidity.

"But Jake knew he was dumb, and he knew how to fix it. So, once he and Matty got together, he held on for dear life. In the end, all his stupidity cost me was a pair of shoes."

He hesitated. "Sam was so much worse. Maybe worse than Adrian. I really thought he was going to die because I couldn't figure out what he needed. He asked, over and over again. 'Tell me what you love.' I didn't get it. I thought he was going to die.

"Ethan and Micah, Matthew and Miranda, Noah and Tali... they did fine on their own. Though, I had a few pointed conversations with Noah. He was more like Jake. Just lost, not dangerous. Matthew didn't need my help. I'd wager he'd known where he went wrong long before Miranda turned up in the big room.

I think he's probably more intelligent than all of us combined, including Sam.

"Beth and Hennessy were annoying. *Staying out* of that was horrible. I knew he loved her like I love Pip from the day he saw her. I knew it. He kept backing away. In true Beth fashion, she just kept at him, teasing, hinting, and baiting until he was finally caught."

"I think Beth might be slightly evil," I admitted.

"She's not evil. She's vindictive. Get it right. She's very protective of us. And you almost got beheaded. I'm with her on this one, Luke. You and Sianna are not a thing. It's better if she's not comfortable at Sunday dinner."

I sighed, reminding myself this was what Sianna wanted.

I SLEPT in a spare room at Will's on Saturday night. I couldn't face Janie or Sianna after that shit show. I'd sleep and eat in the morning and then be in a happier frame of mind by the time I went home.

"Fucking Sam," I muttered under my breath, more out of habit than anything else. I kept picturing him laughing at the idea of me living with a harem of women. I was hiding at my scary brother's house to avoid the women in my own home.

"I'll fix it tomorrow," I said to myself. I projected that thought into the world. I would manifest it forward and call it into existence. "I'll fix it tomorrow."

"You keep telling yourself that!" Emma called from the next room.

"Is there a camera in here?" I yelled back.

"No," Will yelled. "You're just loud, you fucking moron. Go to sleep. This isn't Sam's fault."

I could hear Emma laughing.

"I've lived alone for a while," I called back. "Sorry. I didn't realize I was being that loud."

I could hear the bed squeaking in the next room, followed by a sigh.

"Are you kidding me?" I yelled.

"Oh, shut up! Pip is super pregnant. There are a lot of pillows and adjusting involved in going to bed. Stop making her laugh. She'll have to pee, and we'll have to start all over again!"

"Why are these walls so thin?"

"I think Sam planned for us to have kids in all these rooms!" Emma yelled. "They're thin so we can hear the kids."

"These fucking houses!" I swore. "Just remember, the kids can hear you too. Don't scar them for life!"

It was quiet for a moment, then I could hear shuffling feet. Emma was up and moving.

The door to my room slammed open. "That's it," Will growled. "Go to your own fucking house and deal with your harem. Pip had to get up to pee. You're an asshole."

"I'm sorry," I said with sincerity. "But, when she's not pregnant, we could have fun sleepovers here. It's like being in adjoining tents."

"It's not that bad!"

We both listened to Emma pee, then we sighed in sympathy when she tried and failed to stand up from the toilet.

Will glared. "Go to sleep." He slammed my door on his way out. "I'm coming, babe!"

I was still chuckling to myself as I drifted off to sleep, not quite realizing I was out.

When I woke up, I wasn't alone in the room. Sianna stood at the window, looking out over my family's cluster of houses.

"Sianna," I breathed. "What are you doing? We'll wake them."

She jumped with surprise, turning to meet my eyes. "Why are you here?"

"Keep your voice low," I said, pointing to the shared wall.

She shook her head, not understanding. I climbed out of bed to stand closer to her, but the minute my foot touched the floor, we were in the field behind the houses.

"Oh. We're dreaming?" I asked. I pulled my foot from the ground and was back in the bedroom. "What do you see?"

"We are in the field," she murmured. "You should not be here."

"I'm in the bedroom at Will's house. You're standing by the window, and you should not be here," I retorted.

She frowned. "It is a dreamscape, Peacekeeper. Go back to your rest and leave me to mine. Do not come to me like this again."

"I don't think I did this, Huntress. Sorry to disturb you." Adjusting the blankets where I lay, I tried to will myself back to normal sleep.

After a few minutes, it still wasn't working. I turned on my side, so I didn't have to see her in my peripheral vision.

"Just wake up," she snapped.

I sat up to face her again. "I've been trying. Not working."

"Wait. I will shift to a rabbit, so you run away in fear," she mocked.

"Why would you do that?" I yelled, suddenly furious again. "Why would you bring her to my house and not tell me? Why spring that on me?"

Sianna crossed her arms over her chest, turning away from me. She wasn't going to answer me.

I collapsed, back to lying flat on the bed, blowing out a gust of a frustrated sigh.

"You look ridiculous," she snapped. "You are lying in the field."

"Shut up," I growled, done with the whole thing.

There was silence for a few moments.

"She is a good companion for you!" Sianna shouted. "Gentle and kind. Musical. Curvy in the way you like. Capable of bringing strong children."

My frustration was rapidly turning to anger. "I don't shift gears that fast, Sianna. Not twenty-four hours ago, I literally destroyed my love for you. I need a little bit of time. And I know this offends everything you hold dear, but I don't give a flying fuck about making babies. It's not on my list of priorities. So, don't bring any more women into my house."

She swallowed hard, tears dripping down her face.

"Fuck my life," I muttered, lost. "Why are you crying? Go back to yelling at me! I will live for a very long time. I'm sure I'll get around to making babies. I'm pretty sure at least one of Emma's twins has an affinity. There will be babies. Just not right this second."

"I did not think you would do it. I did not think you would sever the binding," she said miserably. "I did not think it would happen. I fell asleep trusting you would leave it, then tell me it would stay."

I blinked. "You didn't want it. You gave me a lot of reasons why it had to go. You gave me a whole list of things that were important to you. You told me this is what you needed."

She nodded. "I did. It is."

"But?" I asked.

She shook her head. "I did not think you would agree. It is your right to take what you desire."

I stared at her. "You have to be fucking kidding me."

She opened her mouth to say something.

"No. No!" I shouted. "This has to be a fucking joke. You are an intelligent, grown, kick-ass woman. There's no fucking way we're playing these games. You told me what you wanted. I did it, and it damn near destroyed my sense of self. Jess sobbed her eyes out when she saw me this morning for all the pain I'd caused myself. Don't come wandering into my dreams sobbing now. No. Get out."

"I heard him today. I heard your brother tell you that we should keep distance, or it will hurt you," she said quietly, walking toward me.

I stared at her, waiting for whatever was to come.

She touched her forehead to mine, then brushed her lips against mine. "I will stay away. I will keep you safe and be here if you need me, but I will not come to you again. The young one will tend to you, and your love will heal. I am sorry, Luke."

I started awake, the weak sunlight of a winter's dawn coming through the windows.

15

By early Sunday afternoon, Janie and I had sorted through the food and gifts and made a lap of the people around my house.

"So surreal," I muttered.

"You'll get used to it in time," Janie murmured, weaving her arm with mine as we walked through the uneven field.

"Hope not."

"Why?" she asked, surprised. "This is like every person's dream. There's a whole bunch of people that want to pander to your every wish, myself included." She did a pretend curtsy in her jeans, picking up the hem of her long winter coat.

"But can I pander somewhere warmer? Do we have to stay here?" she asked, teasing.

I smiled. "You were in California, right? What were you doing?"

"Studying pandas!" She grinned, knowing the answer would make me laugh.

"No. Really? You're a bunny who wants to be a panda?"

"You got it," she cheered. Her face fell a bit. "I'm not there yet. I think it'd go better if I could touch one and really sense its energy, but it's a bear, number one. And, number two, I think the zoo would frown upon it. So, I'm studying Chinese for traveling. I want to go see them in the wild."

"I had no idea there was so much work involved with transformation," I admitted. "I thought you just imagined it, and it happened."

"Well," she hedged. "That's true for our natural animals. I can go rabbit in less time than it takes to get out of these boots. But any other animal takes work."

I pulled open the gate to my yard for her.

"What is Charlie's natural animal?" I asked.

"All of them," she said wistfully. "No. Really, I think he is naturally a wolf and maybe some type of cougar. He had two families of animals from the start, so they knew he would be special. But, really, he's a prodigy. Any animal he's touched or studied, even in passing, is his. He can take well over a hundred unique forms, not counting any kind of hybrid he might do."

"Wow." I grinned. "Charlie the Prodigy, indeed. I wonder if Matty knows he can do that."

"The Huntress has nearly as many forms, though she's worked harder and longer for them. She's a better fighter than Charlie ever thought of being too. Uncle said Charlie fought to protect Candace, though."

She looked at me, awaiting confirmation.

I nodded, pulling open the back door.

"You claimed Candace?" Janie asked, tone more serious.

"I did. I will not see her mated against her will."

"You are not lovers?"

"We are no longer lovers," I corrected. "We dated for a while."

Her lips pressed together, showing a frown of disapproval.

"Not a Candace fan?" I asked. "You're a Charlie fan. An Ellie fan, too. You didn't even call her a vampire."

"Of course, I didn't! She is not a vampire." The affronted scowl was kind of adorable. "Charlie and Ellie love each other very much. If he was anyone else, the elders would leave them in peace. They might even applaud him for making alliances."

"Well, he's done that in spades," I agreed.

"Yes, he brought you to us!" Janie grinned again.

"By way of Lady Light." I nodded. "Ellie and Matty are best friends. I met Charlie and Candy as we planned Matty's wedding."

Janie's eyebrows shot up. "Lady Light? She has shown herself?"

"She lives across the street, Janie. I thought you knew that. She's married to my second dumbest brother."

"She's here?" Janie squeaked. "Here in the cornfields?"

"Directly across the street. She's a tiny little redhead who hates the cold."

"I'm not good at sensing that kind of thing yet. Who else is here?"

"All of my family," I said, suddenly cautious. I didn't think I was being pumped for information, but I didn't know this woman at all. "Where is your family?"

"Oh! Uncle Godwin travels, but makes his home in Spain usually. My parents lived in Florida until the neighbors realized they weren't aging. Then they moved to California to be closer to me. My brother attends to John's needs—"

"To his great honor," I interjected with an eye roll. I was sensing a pattern.

"He is not quite as honored as me. John is not fun. You are. Do you play all the instruments here? The Huntress said you were musical."

"I am." I nodded. "I do."

"Godwin's father was also musical. Maybe Edgar's too. You should ask about that. Maybe it's part of the peace?"

"Maybe," I agreed. "I feel better with music. I haven't played since Wednesday. That's a very long time for me to go without music. The world brings it to me when I don't play, though."

I paused, wondering why I'd said that last part out loud. It was the truth. I heard music in everything from the gust of the wind to the undertones of voices muttering in the dark. There was music in the sound of breath and the beat of a heart. But I didn't usually admit to that little touch of strangeness.

Janie took it in stride, not even raising an eyebrow as she flipped on the coffee maker. "I love this coffee maker. I love great coffee."

"Anything worth doing," I agreed, pulling down a pair of mugs.

"Your house is very neat. The only thing that needed cleaning was your living room."

"You cleaned my living room?" I asked, confused.

"No, not me. Nathaniel and his sons were ordered to do it."

"There's nothing to clean—"

"There was blood and vomit everywhere."

My mouth dropped open. "Oh. I forgot about that. Nate was in my house? Nate cleaned up Sam's puke?"

She nodded, causing the hair on my arms to stand up. She frowned, noticing my uneasy feelings. "What's wrong?"

"That man wants me dead, and he was wandering around my house? Who would even make him do that? He's the fucking Overlord! Who orders him to do anything?"

"John," she said easily. "John ordered it, and Uncle saw it done. Nathaniel could not have harmed your home or anything in it, Luke. John's words cannot be disobeyed."

I blinked, confused again.

She grinned. "I like that you just blink when you're lost. It makes watching your expression fun. John and Uncle are old. John was Overlord for a long time. When he no longer felt safe in the role, Uncle took the responsibility. But John kept some ability to talk to others, no matter the distance. Uncle can do it as well, but John mastered it. Mental commands cannot be disobeyed."

We were quiet while she got creamer and a spoon for her coffee.

"I think you have that power, too," she continued. "Right now, you could tell me to take off my sweater and let you motorboat my boobs."

"Oh, my God!" I yelled over her tinkling laughter. "I thought we agreed you wouldn't make those jokes!"

"Not that you'd need to command it. I mean, I'm happy to oblige."

"Janie!" I could feel my face flame in embarrassment.

"You're so red! I love this! A Peacekeeper who blushes. It's so sweet."

"Shush!" I scolded. "I don't know what to do with that kind of flirting! Stop it!"

"If I keep going, will you spank me?"

"Gah!" I ran out of the room, both laughing and horrified.

I closely examined every inch of my living room. It was spotless. I thought one of the end chairs might have been replaced, but I wasn't sure. If so, it was the exact same chair.

"He did a good job," Janie murmured, coming into the room with her coffee. "I inspected it yesterday. There is no sign of what I'm sure was a bloody mess. Are you going to play the piano?"

"I was thinking saxophone."

"Don't worry. That's not sexy at all," she teased with an eye roll. "Hang on. Let me get cozy. I wish I wasn't wearing pants. Then, I could try to work some *Fatal Attraction* show-and-tell."

I glared at her, not picking up the instrument.

"Let's hear it. Work the mouthpiece and show me the fingerings."

"We can't be friends."

Janie's nose crinkled. "You'll get used to it."

JANIE'S HAND waved in front of my face.

"Luke!" she yelled.

I stopped playing. "Huh?"

"Holy shit. You've been playing for almost two hours. You have to stop now."

"Why? I do this all the time."

"My uncle and John are coming. They'll be here within half an hour. Uncle said John has tried to talk to you several times, but it doesn't seem like you hear him."

My eyes narrowed. "I'm not sure I want him in my head."

Her lips pursed in confusion. "No. He can't affect you. You can affect him, though. I think. Anyway, they'll be here soon.

Edgar was going to come but got caught up with something else."

"Okay." I looked around my living room. There was nothing to straighten up. "Is there something I should be doing to prepare for them?"

"Oh. No. I guess I just didn't want them to surprise you. The Huntress said to smack you to get your attention. I didn't think that was appropriate. But she said she would let the others know. Who are the others?"

"I imagine the security guards if they're back, and the rest of my family. So, you'll probably get to meet everyone." I smiled to assure her it was a good thing. "Why are you nervous? What aren't you telling me?"

"I'm not nervous!" she objected.

I lifted my eyebrows, not bothering to call bullshit. I could feel her lack of peace radiating off her. "Can I help?"

"I would like to stay!" she blurted. "I know I screwed up last night, and it was a little rough going at first, but I would like to stay."

"Okay?" I stretched the word into a question.

"They're going to suggest someone else. I know it. There's no romance between us, and they will offer others. I would like to stay, though!"

My mouth dropped open. "Holy shit. Would they just keep sending random women until I took someone to bed?"

"Probably. And, fine if you'd like other company for love-making. But I would still like to stay. I think I could work well with you, and I know you'll help me transform. I just know it. I can feel it."

I sighed, frustrated beyond belief. I spent a moment searching for the right words. When they came, they were flat.

"I don't want you to go. If someone must be here with me, I'd rather it be someone Sianna and Charlie trust. I trust them and am more willing to trust you by extension. I'm not taking *anyone* to bed anytime soon. I will not have a rotating door of women in my life."

"Oh."

"Okay?" I asked again, still feeling her unease.

"You don't like me." She sounded deflated.

"I like you just fine. We've had a lovely day together. Thank you for helping me not look like an idiot earlier."

She waved the words away. "That's not what I meant. You're not attracted to me. You'd rather I look another way?"

"What?"

"I think I can do that. I know Charlie and the Huntress can. I've never tried. Never felt the need to do it before. I don't hide from anyone. But I can work on it."

"Janie, that's seriously fucked up. That's so fucked up, it gives me a headache. Please don't be this person."

"What person?"

"The person so entirely focused on trying to become what she thinks I want that she forgets who she is. You just be you. I'll be me. And it'll be fine. You're absolutely gorgeous the way you are. But it still doesn't mean I'm jumping in the sack and making shifter babies with you."

She flinched.

"Sorry. Beast affinity babies," I corrected myself.

"Okay," she muttered. "But you're okay with me staying?"

"Yep. Absolutely. If someone must be here, I'm glad it's you."

My sentence was punctuated with a car door slamming in front of my house. Janie jumped. "Oh shit! They're here. No!

No!" she slapped my arms and hands as I moved toward the front door. "I'll get the door! You sit!"

"Peacekeeper, Peacekeeper, Peacekeeper," she chanted under her breath as she moved into the entryway.

I guessed calling me Luke in front of the elders would be frowned upon.

"Am I like Beetlejuice now?" I asked, catching her completely by surprise.

And that's why Janie was giggling like a little girl when she opened my front door to the *three* visiting beast affinity elders.

16

"Child," Godwin greeted her, voice stern. "Are you well?"

Janie sucked in air, trying to gather herself. "Un-Uncle! I apologize. I am well."

She was still working to stifle the nervous giggles. I could tell.

I walked up behind her and poked her in the side, causing another little rupture of laughter.

Of course, she's ticklish, I thought, laughing to myself.

"Go that way." I pointed. "Coffee?"

"Coffee!" she agreed, all but running toward the kitchen.

"Gentleman, you're welcome to come inside. I believe you know your way around." My tone was polite, but only just.

John entered first, bowing his head to me and walking toward the living room. His face was expressionless, but I could feel the humor radiating from him.

Godwin entered next, bowing his head and offering a handshake. "Greetings, Peacekeeper. We are honored to be in your presence. Thank you for allowing us into your home. By my life, no harm to you or yours."

His words rang with sincerity. He was overjoyed to have a Peacekeeper once again. I could feel his joy and hope, even without touching his hand. Then, accepting the handshake, his intentions came through, loud and clear. He and John intended to see me honored above all others, a boon to their people, even if they had to tear apart their society to see it done.

My head tilted as I processed the truth he'd shared with me. It was an intentional act. He'd shared it with me on purpose. There was an offer of friendship and help embedded in the gesture. I wasn't sure how to respond, so I nodded before Godwin followed his brother into the living room.

"Will Micah be joining us? I hoped to see him," he called back to me.

"I imagine so," I said, eyeing the last person on my stoop. "Daniel, right? Sianna's brother?"

"Peacekeeper," Daniel said in a soft voice, eyes meeting mine. "I am glad you're well. I had hoped to know you but will understand if I am not welcome in your home."

I shook my head, waving him in. "I'm just surprised to see you. I felt you cross the wards. You are no threat."

He also offered a hand to shake as he came inside. I took it, more out of habit than anything else. With the touch, I got a deluge of shame, worry, love for Candace, and... something more. "You're empowered?"

He nodded. "Primarily fire and a bit of life energy. I am welcome as an elder because I can offer a small amount of healing."

"Candy is well. She went home with Charlie last night. She wasn't injured."

His eyes flicked down in shame and embarrassment. "Thank you."

I offered my hand again. He looked at me in surprise for a moment, not getting it until I lifted my eyebrows in a dare.

He exhaled hard, rolling back on his heels and rotating his neck as my peaceful energy washed through him. "I was concerned for her. When no one had seen or heard from her. I thought maybe you… were displeased with her after my father's games."

I shook my head, gesturing to the living room. "I understood what happened. I wouldn't see her dead over something readily available on the internet."

I followed Daniel into the room just in time to watch Janie deliver tea to John and coffee to Godwin.

"Daniel," she said, stretching to kiss his cheek. "You're okay? Better?"

"I'm well, Janie," he assured her, quickly offering a one-armed hug.

"He has glass-bottled Coke," she said, smiling.

Daniel smiled back with a nod, making his solemn face livelier.

She looked at me, her expression asking what I wanted to drink.

"Beetlejuice," I said, perfectly serious.

"You are a pain in the ass, Luke!" she scolded before she caught herself.

I shook with laughter as all three elders stared at her in shock.

"Coke's good." I grinned.

She stomped out of the room, annoyed.

"Sorry, she's fun to tease," I muttered, sitting down in the end chair across from Daniel. The two brothers sat together on the couch. I appreciated the seating arrangement. "To what do I owe this visit?"

Daniel and John both looked to Godwin, who smiled as he sipped his coffee.

"First, I hope you found your home satisfactorily restored upon your return?" he asked. "It was a horrible mess, an unspoken testament to the level of your injury. Edgar assured us you were healing, but it was difficult to believe given the state of things here."

"Thank you for cleaning up the mess. You also left a visitor in my parents' house. It was quite a surprise. He caught hell from my middle brother before reconciling with my mother. I don't have a fire and brimstone turn to me. Please leave my family and friends in peace." My tone was polite but firm, my eyes focused on John. *No more mind spikes.*

"Hmm," John said, looking to Godwin.

"My brother wonders if you were able to untangle the mess of your uncle's mind beyond his compulsions to sit and stay," Godwin translated. "Forgive him. He rarely speaks aloud. Leadership comes with the ability to command. The power grows as we age. John's energy has concentrated in communication, both mental and verbal. He is most comfortable when a misspoken word will not destroy a life. I end up speaking for both of us since his words don't influence me. Though, with you among us, perhaps he will join us in conversation again."

"I removed John's compulsions with no effort. They were akin to giant metal spikes. The older compulsions and ties took more effort. My uncle's sense of self grew around them throughout his life. But it's done."

There was a gasp from John and a staying hand from Godwin. They seemed to be having a little mental sidebar.

I looked at Daniel.

"There are a host of people like your uncle. Hundreds, maybe thousands. Like the children in the church," he said in his calm, placid tones.

"Wow, Edgar did spill the beans," I noted as Janie handed us each an open Coke bottle and headed back to the kitchen.

Daniel nodded. "Most of the people in the arena knew of the children long before your arrival. My father knew of them. He didn't care. Ten or twelve lives don't matter much to him, regardless of what they might suggest. So, there was no question of what you were, even before your power rolled through the arena that night."

I glanced at the brothers, still locked in mind-meld mode.

I looked back at Daniel.

He rolled his eyes, sparking a laugh from me.

"Peacekeeper," he started.

"Please. Luke. I prefer Luke. If I'm to call you Daniel, you may call me Luke."

"Luke," he said, sounding guilty. "I owe you the humblest of apologies. I follow Greggory of Harbor's online chronicles of the Walker and Mistress. I am sure I told my family of a Lord Peace at some point, though I was not involved in the capture of Charlie or Candace. My father knew what you were the minute he saw you. He knew you stood circles from the first moment; I am confident of it. He did not expect you to be able to accept the beasts' offering of energy as you did. You have not answered the offering yet, but we have no doubt you are capable."

I wondered what "answering the beasts' offering" entailed but put it to the side as the guilt from Daniel tried to swallow my ability to focus. He was painfully genuine, and, if I wasn't mistaken, kind. It upset him to know his knowledge had brought anyone injury, let alone me. "Did you slice off my head?"

He froze, staring at me. "No, but I took great delight in burning my brothers' bodies to ashes for the offense. I would thank my fierce little sister for her deft blade if she were here."

"Then, we're fine. No apology is necessary. It's on the internet. I didn't consider it dangerous knowledge to be shared. Peace is the worst superpower—I honestly didn't believe anyone would care."

He swallowed back a laugh before hesitating. "Candace is dear to me. She does not—"

"She's dear to me too." I cut off his understatement. He'd go to hell and back for her. The love absolutely radiated from him. "We're great *friends*."

His mouth dropped open in surprise. "You claimed her. My father said you claimed her?"

"I did," I agreed. "I would not see a friend in those circumstances."

He exhaled hard, chugging his Coke.

"Ah, good." Godwin smiled. "Good news all around."

"Is it?" I asked, surprised by his cheer.

"The best we could hope for, I should think. You are whole and well, willing to speak with us, able to undo ties and bindings that do not belong." He nodded to Daniel. "And love shall persist long enough for the lady to recognize its worth."

Daniel smirked at Godwin. "Unlikely. But I would not want her harmed."

Godwin took a turn at rolling his eyes.

"I can't handle the eye rolls." I laughed.

Godwin grinned at my laughter. "Smirking and eye-rolls have been around longer than us. And we must adjust to the age as well as we can. Back to the topic—"

The words were cut off by my front door opening.

"Lord Micah," Godwin said happily as he rose to his feet.

His expression fell as Micah was followed by Ethan, then Noah and Talise, Beth and Hennessy, Adrian and Lucy, William and Emma, Sam and Adaline, Matthew and Miranda, and finally Jake and Matilda.

I didn't know what to make of the order of entrance, but there was a formality to it. My living room was suddenly standing room only.

"Oh," Sam said, the slight sound escaping him as his eyes landed on John. "You."

"Me," John said aloud, eyes wide with surprise and glued to Sam. He completely missed Godwin's flinch of shock. "How?"

"I don't know," Sam said, laughing. "But, hello."

"You found the girl," John croaked, lips turning up in a semblance of a smile. He was out of practice, though. It didn't look natural.

Sam nodded, also smiling. "I wondered if I would find you eventually. I'm unsure if I found you or you found me, though."

Silence fell while everyone in the room waited for more of the odd exchange.

"Uh, Sam?" I asked, breaking the awkward pause.

"Dreams," Sam said as if that clarified everything.

I sighed, unsure what to do.

"We are no threat to the Peacekeeper. None at all! I swear it. I swear it on my own life," Godwin was suddenly terrified and using his outside voice, eyes fixed on Matthew.

Matthew's expression was closed in anger. When the words

came, they were loaded with the power he usually hid from the world. "The Walker may kill you. He is merciful and fair—the quickest means to the desired end. I am not so kind. If I come knocking, I'll take your sanity and leave just enough memory for you to regret the loss."

Godwin's mouth opened and closed without words. "I will not see him harmed again," he finally sputtered. "My life before his. We are allies. I swear it."

Matthew nodded, acknowledging the words.

I stared at Matthew, shocked. The hair on my arms was standing on end in warning, as much from his controlled use of energy as from his words. *What the fuck, Matthew?*

He turned to me then, eyes devoid of emotion. *"I will drag them all down into madness if you die by their hands."* The words were crystal clear in my head. He must have been practicing the mental speech stuff with Adaline.

I had not talked to Matthew since Wednesday, since my injury. I couldn't remember him sitting with me on Thursday while I was in and out of consciousness. I'd spent Friday with Sianna. We'd come home on Saturday. I realized I'd spent more time with William than with Matthew over the last few days. It was an odd shift.

Note to self: Go talk with Matthew after this! Holy shit. He is not okay.

"This circle is not yet full, but there is a quorum," Micah said, pulling me from my internal blathering. "Know what you face should another mishap befall him."

"Lady Light," Daniel breathed, literally falling out of his chair to his knees to bow to tiny Matilda.

"I'm going to be honest," Matty said. "I don't get the reverence. It's fire, light, power. But we all have power. So, what's with the bowing and scraping?"

Micah sighed, glaring at her. "They're young."

"They are young and glorious! Look at them. I have never seen such an uncorrupted circle." Godwin's terror had turned into something like fan-boy excitement. "Lady Light, no truth may be hidden from you. Throughout all of time, your predecessors have stood on the side of right."

"That's crap! People lie to me all the time. Jake lied about farting last night," Matilda objected. Her face scrunched up. "Maybe I don't know how to do that yet?"

Micah sighed again.

"It comes with your power, Lady. You will find that those who stand in your light cannot hide from you. You'll see. These are amazing times! A Peacekeeper that unites Affinities and the Circle. A clean circle with all the elements and a real Time Walker. Your arm, Mistress? Is that a mark of accordance?"

Adaline looked to Micah, who nodded.

"Show him the accordance. Maybe he knows something I don't." Micah seemed to be suggesting a possibility, but there were instructions embedded in the words. There were other marks not to be shown.

Addy took off her coat. Then, she pulled up the sleeve of her sweater, exposing the swirling, moving tattoo. Lightning bolts and vines circled from her left ring finger, all the way around her palm and up her arm. Next, she lifted the hem of her long skirt, showing the tattoos going down her leg. "It runs the entire length of my body."

"You found the girl," John breathed again, nodding at Sam. "That is well done."

Sam took off his coat.

"What are you wearing?" I asked. "Who let him buy that?"

"Jeans go with everything," Sam objected.

"It's true. They do. You match. I'm so proud," I said, trying not to laugh. "But since when do you wear shirts with designs. 'Hell kittens?' Really?"

"You'd love this shirt if Jake was wearing it," Sam rebutted, holding out his arm to show the vines and lightning marking his hand and arm as well.

I attempted to hide my surprise. The accordance marks had changed since I'd last paid attention. Addy used to have lightning, and Sam used to have flowering vines. I didn't know what it meant that the marks had changed.

Sam looked at me as if I'd spoken out loud. "They change and move constantly. Sometimes it's clouds with the lightning. Sometimes the vines have thorns."

"Did I ask?" Had I spoken aloud without meaning to?

"No, but I could feel your stare. Don't stare. It's rude. Admit it. You like the shirt."

Micah sighed again. We were disappointing him. "Mistress?" he barked in warning as Adaline moved toward John.

"I'm fine, Micah," she murmured. "He's Sam's friend. I'm just going to see."

"You have a friend?" I asked Sam, surprised. Sam didn't have friends outside our family.

"I do." Sam smiled, seeming proud of himself.

"There's nothing, Sam. No injury. Just too much energy, like when you came to me. You are welcome in our circle," she said to John, walking away. "You as well," she said, squeezing Daniel's shoulder. "Monday nights. Luke will tell you. It may help you. We can go."

She and Sam were already leading the way out the door

when Godwin yelled after Emma. "Lady Love, your children, one of them. He is... like us. But more. We will help."

Emma nodded, smiling her thanks. "Sianna told me."

"Thank you," Godwin called to no one in particular. "Thank you for showing yourselves. Thank you for making us welcome. You are welcome among us as well. Not yet. No. Not yet, but we will make it so."

"A true circle of power!" Godwin exclaimed after everyone cleared out. "Not in all my years! I suspect not in all of Micah's years! All of them, and it is not yet full! It's a legend come to life."

"How exactly do you know Sam?" I asked John.

He turned to Godwin.

"No!" Godwin scolded. "There is no one here you could harm. Daniel's mind is well guarded, the young one is out of the room, and the Peacekeeper is right here, should something go wrong. Speak!"

John glared at his brother. "Arf arf," he said, making the pretend dog-bark noises with a perfectly straight face.

I didn't know what to do or say. Then, Daniel lost it, breaking down in rolling laughter that seemed out of character for him.

"More than two hundred years he's not spoken, and now he's making jokes," Godwin said, expression flat as he looked at me. "Brothers are annoying."

"Amen to that," I agreed, chuckling.

"They are family?" Godwin asked, distracted.

"Seven brothers and a sister," I said, eyes back to John. "How do you know Sam? He does not interact with people outside our family often. He doesn't like other people."

John shifted uncomfortably before putting his mug down on the coffee table. He cleared his throat, looking around.

"Janie!" I yelled. "Could you go straighten the garage? Load up the drinks in the fridge and stuff?"

"The garage is clean. It's as cold in the garage—" she called back, confused.

"I know. Just for a minute," I said, smiling an apology as she walked into the living room. She shrugged, heading out to the garage.

"She is gentle. I do not want to harm her," John croaked, nodding. "Sam has visited my dreams in the past. Once as a young man. Again, maybe five years ago. Then shortly before the holidays last month. We've had conversations on what it means to have power, care for others, and lead. When he came into my dream before the holidays, we saw each other but could not find a way through the dreamscape. I had not put together that he was the Walker until now. I don't understand."

"Have you met many Walkers like that?" I asked, dumbfounded. This was not part of Sam's list of recurring dreams. I wondered what else he'd dreamt about without mentioning.

"No, none," John said flatly. "I would not be glad to meet a Walker in that way."

"But Sam?"

John gave me a put-upon look. "You will not convince me that one is normal."

I laughed, surprising my guests. "Sam is not normal. That is a true statement."

"I think maybe you are all different," Godwin murmured. "Call her back."

I blinked, confused for a moment. "Oh. Janie!"

She didn't respond.

"Try the other way," Godwin suggested.

"Um," I hesitated. "I don't think I do it correctly."

"I don't think you do either," Godwin admitted. "We each tried to talk to you earlier. It didn't work."

I frowned. "Charlie has spoken to me like that. Sianna as well."

"Janie, we're done. You can come back." I projected.

Daniel shook his head. "You're projecting it everywhere. That part is not right yet. The bindings must be present for it to work."

"What bindings?" I asked, surprised. "I'm not doing the harem thing. I know progeny are a hot topic…"

I stopped as they laughed at me.

"Noted. No harem," Godwin said, grinning. "The young one is helpful? You welcome her company?"

I nodded. "She has indicated she would like to stay. So please leave her be."

Godwin frowned. "Of course. It is not our desire to disturb or upset you."

He turned to Daniel, waiting for something.

Eventually, Daniel sighed. "Sianna said she'll visit soon. She won't be joining us today."

Godwin's frown deepened. "She is well?"

Daniel lifted his eyebrows. "She's Sianna. Have you ever known her to be anything but well?"

"Perhaps she will speak with Edgar," he muttered, turning back to me. "He will visit tomorrow if that is acceptable to you. He has started to coordinate bringing the lost children here. Chicago is his home. He wishes to serve as your primary contact. We will all remain here for a time.

"Nathaniel and those of his line unfamiliar to you are

forbidden from direct and indirect contact. We must judge the state of things before allowing him within reach," Godwin finished.

I looked at Daniel, surprised.

He shook his head. "He is unfit. That's not a secret, and I don't contest it. He loathes me."

"I will talk to Charlie," John whispered.

I lifted my eyebrows. "You will not force him to do anything." I meant the words to come out a question, but it didn't work out that way.

John smiled. "I will not. Even if I could, I would not. Charlie's mind is different."

"He does not want to lead. Why not Edgar or one of you?" My eyes landed on Daniel again.

"I cannot withstand a challenge from my brothers, Peacekeeper. They will kill me if given a chance. And leadership must pass forward, not backward."

"Sianna?" I asked.

All three men sat back, away from me.

"That is a different struggle. She will not challenge her father, and her brothers will refuse to face her," Godwin muttered. "There are... complications there."

"Because she's a woman?" I asked to get a reaction.

"That is an issue," Godwin allowed. "Some affinities will not allow a woman to lead. Though, I wonder if your presence will shift those minds. But gender is not the only issue. No. Charlie is the next Overlord."

I looked at John, raising my eyebrows. "Sam says Sianna is Overlord in the best futures."

"That does not surprise me," he whispered. "I will help her assume the role if she wants it, and I believe she knows that. It is to our detriment that we did not allow a female Overlord in the past. Sianna needs to have that conversation with Edgar if that is our path forward."

I frowned at the implication, certain that Edgar would never hold Sianna back.

Godwin shrugged. "Edgar will visit tomorrow. Perhaps she will speak to him."

17

"How does this work?" I asked Janie.

"It's a stove. You turn the knob. The fire appears."

"No, I mean, how does your working here work?" I turned the fire down to warm the milk.

"My what?"

"Your work here. You're working for me, essentially. Helping me. Taking food out to… everyone. Who also kinda work here. How does that work?"

I could tell she was trying not to laugh at me again.

"Why is this funny?" I demanded. "I'm serious. Don't you have a job and home and bills and stuff? Surely the people standing guard have obligations."

"Well, I'll sublet my apartment in California. My family will help with my bills. The people that stand guard do it in their off-hours."

"Ugh. No. We need to figure out something else." I caught

myself waving my hands in an "it's gross" gesture and stopped. I wondered if Janie noticed.

"What are we going to figure out?" She laughed. "You think we're going to start a collection pool to pay everyone wages? No. It is our honor to—"

"No! Nope! That's not what I'm suggesting. I'll talk to Sam. Or maybe my dad. I don't know. We'll figure it out."

"Figure what out?" she asked again. "You don't have a job either."

I blinked.

"I can't tell if that's an 'I'm confused' blink or something else, but I'm really hoping you do the 'ewww' hand thing again."

"I have money. I'll pay people. I just don't know how to do it. I'll talk to my dad."

She laughed again. "You're going to pay us from your piggy bank?"

Does she not get this? I wondered. *She must know, right?*

"Uh, no. I have money. Real money. A lot of it. Think about this house. Think about this weird little subdivision, Janie. I don't know how much money—it fluctuates. But I make enough to pay people for their time."

Her jaw went slack as her eyes narrowed. "Trellis. Trellis Industries?" Her head shifted like she was looking through the walls. "Sam Trellis."

"Yes. Correct." I nodded. "So, we need to figure that out."

"Does Uncle know?" she asked tentatively.

I frowned. "I don't know. I think so. Why?"

"Some people with affinities have trouble with steady work but would be good guards," she said, fidgeting uncomfortably. "The elders try to find a purpose for all of us."

"Okay," I said, nodding again. "I'll talk to Edgar about it tomorrow. Sianna knows. They must know."

Janie shook her head. "She would not tell if you did not give her permission."

My anger flared again as I poured the warm milk over the shaved chocolate. "I'm not going to stay up. I'm not feeling great. Stir. This is all yours. Have a hot chocolate party."

"No pirates?" She pulled a pout.

"We'll do *Pirates of the Caribbean* tomorrow night. I'm beat suddenly."

She touched my hand. "Your energy seems… angry. Did I do something?"

"No, not at all," I said, giving her a quick hug. "Thanks for everything today. Help yourself to anything. I'm going to bed. I'm not great company. Sorry."

I high-tailed it out of there, afraid of taking a rotten mood out on Janie.

"SIANNA," I called out the window again. I knew she was out there. I could feel her.

I'd been calling for her for almost ten minutes. She wasn't coming.

I wondered if she could feel my anger somehow and was avoiding me.

I washed my face and brushed my teeth, exhausted in truth. It had been a long day and a longer week. *A week ago, Sianna and I were making snow angels, laughing like children.*

The wind was knocked out of me at the thought. I was

suddenly sitting on the edge of my tub, thinking of everything I had gained and lost in seven days' time.

I almost died.

I found love and lost it.

I gained a new purpose.

The world went black.

When I came to, I was lying in the fields behind the house, my head resting in Sianna's lap as she ran her hands through my hair.

"Rest, Luke. You must rest. No more dream walking," she murmured, noticing my open eyes. "She is right. I would not share your secrets. The knowledge that belongs to you is not anyone else's business. Do not be angry because I refuse to play spy."

I sighed, relaxing my body.

"Rest," she breathed again. "Stay here with me and rest."

"Edgar will be here tomorrow," I mumbled.

"I heard. I do not know what he has to do with anything," she said, answering the question before I could ask. "We will find out tomorrow."

"You will see him?"

"Rest now. Stay with me and rest," she soothed, not answering my question.

I did as I was told, too exhausted to argue.

I HEARD JANIE YELL SOMETHING, then someone was shaking me.

"Huh?"

"LUKE! WAKE UP!" she roared.

I dragged my eyes open. "'s wrong?"

"You banged your head? What the hell?"

She was starting to panic. I felt the panic. Panic wasn't fun, so I let my peace free.

"Oh," she breathed. "Um. Okay. Are you awake? Please be awake. Are you awake and doing this on purpose? That'd be nice, but I don't think that's what you're doing. Um. Bed? Maybe bed?"

"Hm?" I muttered, attempting to roll over.

But I wasn't in bed. Instead, I was lying the wrong way in my bathtub, legs hanging over the side. I blinked the sleep from my eyes. "Huh?" I asked again.

"Oh, holy fuck."

There were panting noises. And a hand. It was a nice hand in a nice place doing nice things. I looked around, again thinking something wasn't right. *Why am I lying in the bathtub?*

"S'anna?" I mumbled, confused.

"Okay, that's fine. Fine with me."

There were lips now too. Kissing my abdomen and drifting downward. But the voice was wrong.

I bolted upright, almost falling again. "Whoa! Oh." I grabbed my head, swallowing bile. I must have cracked my head on the bathtub, but it wasn't bleeding. The wound had healed itself, leaving the headache.

"Sorry, Janie. Sorry," I mumbled, only then realizing she was on her knees in front of me.

"Bed? Maybe bed?" she suggested, still breathing hard, eyes fully dilated in the bright bathroom lights.

"Janie, I'm sorry. I'm going to pull the energy away slowly. I'm sorry."

I watched as her expression cleared.

"You have money?" she asked.

I nodded, confused again.

"You will buy me the very best vibrator on the fucking planet if you keep doing this to me."

I laughed. She was so serious, so annoyed. And I'd fucked up royally, *again*. It was either laughter or tears, so I went with laughter.

"Keep laughing, Luke. Whatever. There will either be a *lot* of great sex very soon—like now—or an epic array of vibrators to keep me company on nights like this. What the fuck happened? I saw your foot hanging out of the bathtub on the way to my room."

"I don't know," I admitted. "I tried talking to Sianna. She ignored me. I washed my face and brushed my teeth. Then I was thinking, sitting on the edge of the bathtub. I must have fallen asleep."

"And now that you're awake, you want to have a lot of great sex?"

"I admire your persistence and willingness to ask for what you want," I said with a small smile.

"I'm going to work on the body shifting thing so I can look like the Huntress."

"That's wrong. And I'm fairly certain I'd know it was you."

"I wouldn't try to dupe you! But, if she's what lights your fire, I could get into that role-playing."

I sighed. "I'm sorry. I didn't mean to douse you with the energy again. I wasn't with it."

"You and Sianna? Really?" There was a softness in her eyes that looked an awful lot like pity.

"Not anymore," I muttered, headed for the linen closet. "It lasted about three days before she kicked my ass to the curb."

"I've never heard of her taking a lover," Janie said, eyes on me. "Want to talk about it? It's still raw, huh? You got pissed earlier. I didn't put together that it was the mention of her."

"There's not much to talk about," I admitted. "She wasn't a fan of the idea of a relationship. We had a little bit of miscommunication. It's over."

"Sit," Janie murmured. "Give me the washcloth. Let me see."

I sat on the edge of the tub again while she gently sorted through my hair.

"She is an amazing person," Janie continued. "A fierce protector and strong advocate. But I don't think she does relationships, Luke."

"I can confirm she does not do relationships," I said, tone flat.

"You are Peacekeeper. You just need to make the desire known," Janie offered with hesitation.

"No. I wouldn't do that. What kind of relationship would that be?"

She sighed then, sadness radiating from her. "You're not bleeding anymore."

I turned, weaving my fingers through hers. "Thanks for checking. I figured it was closed. What's wrong? Are you suddenly sad there's not a gushing head wound to deal with?"

She shook her head, eyes damp.

I waited, watching her try to find words.

"You're not supposed to be like this," she said at last. "If I met you in a coffee shop or at a concert, I'd absolutely crush on you. You're kind and sweet and a little silly. You run away when you think you might do something that would hurt me. Guys like you are hard to come by. I'm bitter that you're Peacekeeper."

I exhaled my frustration. "I went through this with Candy and Sianna too. This is who I am, Janie. I'm not going to change. It's irritating that you are all waiting for me to turn into an asshole."

"Maybe the Peacekeeper always starts out like you are now? I don't know. But, in my experience, people in power demand what they want and take for granted that it will be done. My uncle is a good person, but he's still terrifying to me. I don't believe he'd hurt me, but I know he has other priorities than my happiness."

I frowned. "Janie, you are responsible for your own happiness. Each person on this planet is empowered to control their own happiness."

"No. No, Luke. You have that wrong. I am at the beck and call of higher-ranking family members. I was perfectly willing to come to Chicago for this, but I would still be forced to come here even if I wasn't. I can't disobey a command."

I thought about John's mind spikes and realized I had spoken from a place of privilege. I nodded then, accepting her truth even though I hated it. "I need to think about that. I hadn't considered the mental compulsion or the forced patriarchy."

"Don't get me wrong," Janie said with a sad smile. "I believe my family wants me to be happy. I just don't know that they'd consider my definition of 'happiness' when making decisions about my life. And I know you would never mean to override someone else's desires, but it will come with time. People in power exert power. It's hard to see you like this, see who you are now, and know it's going to change."

I didn't argue her point. I still didn't agree with her, but time would prove one of us wrong. I stood up from the tub to wrap her in a hug.

"I'd like you too," I admitted. "If I had met you under other circumstances, at another time, I would have asked for your phone number and called you immediately."

There was a huff of laughter against my chest. "Time. Just some time for things to settle. Then, lots of sex. While I'm waiting, the world's best vibrator."

I laughed again, flushing.

"You think I'm kidding. I'm not. I'll subscribe to the 'pics or it didn't happen' motto too."

"Gah!" I yelled, still laughing. "No."

"Yup." She giggled. "This is going to be fun."

18

Janie was not kidding.

By the time I'd woken up on Monday morning, there was a whole text thread with product links, a wish list, and pictures that I tried (and failed) to avoid looking at.

I covered my head with my pillow as I rolled onto my stomach, contemplating my life choices.

"Good morning," she called cheerily from my doorway.

I groaned, already embarrassed. I'd struggle to look her in the eyes again.

"You know what's fun?" she asked.

I pulled the pillow tighter over my head, knowing what was coming.

"Sex!" she cheered, climbing onto the bed next to me and yanking at my protective pillow. "Orgasms! Did you watch the video?"

There's a video?

"No, I did not watch the video," I grumbled. "I can't even look at you right now."

She climbed over the top of me and pulled the covers down on the other side of the bed. A minute later, she was snuggled against my side, chattering away.

"So, I was thinking. If you intend to pay people who work for you, it doesn't just need to be the wealthy, connected families that come here. And you're Peacekeeper. I know you don't get this yet, but there's a lot of coordination and work to being Peacekeeper. Serious work. Work that must be done. And there are five bedrooms in this house. Five!"

"I'm not super awake," I mumbled. "What is it that you want?"

"I want my besties here with me," she blurted. "Really, I think—"

"'s fine," I said, dozing back off as I listened to the music of her heart and the sound of her breathing.

"Really?" she chirped.

"If Sianna and Charlie say they're okay to be here, it's fine with me," I mumbled, tossing an arm over her midriff. "Now, shhh. Lemme listen."

And I was out again, somehow still exhausted.

"WHY ARE YOU STILL IN BED?" Sianna barked. "The young one is worrying herself sick. Get up!"

"Huh?" I sat bolt upright in bed, just in time for my head to explode. "Ugh." I crumpled back down, pulling the covers straight.

"What is wrong with you?" she asked, coming over to dig my hand free of the bedding. "Are you sick?"

"Dunno," I mumbled. "Head hurts. Tired."

"Peacekeeper," Sianna said, her tone no-nonsense. "It is well past time to be awake. It is near noon. Edgar will be here within the hour." She paused. "The energy is not cycling. Janie!"

I flinched at the loud noise and flinched again at the touch of cold hands.

"No, I don't feel it," Janie offered. "You don't either?"

"No." Sianna was not happy about this turn of events.

"'s wrong?" I slurred. I could feel two unhappy stares on me. "What'd I do?"

"Luke, you're scaring me," Janie whispered. "Do you think you have a concussion?"

"He does not have a concussion," Sianna said, tone flat.

"He passed out last night and banged his head in the tub. There was blood in the tub and in his hair, but no wound."

"He is fine. Just dumb. Go downstairs," Sianna said softly. "Maybe outside."

"But," Janie started.

"Walk to the house at the end of the cul-de-sac and meet his mother. Her name is Darla, and she will love you. Go now. Go on."

I drifted back to sleep in the trailing silence.

"Luke," Sianna said, her voice laced with undertones and energy. "Luke, wake up. It's time to be awake now. No more dream walking. Can you hear me, Lucas?"

"I'm awake. Kinda," I muttered. "What are you doing with your voice?"

"Open your eyes, Luke. You must wake now."

I dragged my eyes open, looking at her. A sheen of sweat had broken out on her forehead. She seemed to glow in the natural light of my bedroom.

"What are you doing?" I asked, confused, even as my power twisted and pulled at my control, wanting to be free.

"Pull the power forward, Luke. Let the energy go. It is fine."

I stared at her, sure there was a reason I didn't want to do what she suggested. But my head hurt so much, I couldn't focus, couldn't remember.

I came up blank, finally letting the energy go just to release the pressure in my head, if nothing else.

I resisted the urge to moan in relief. *So much better.*

"I will tell her not to tease you," Sianna murmured, running her hand across my cheek and through my beard stubble. "Let the energy out."

As she said the words, I could feel the energy slamming out of me and through Sianna. Her eyes closed as I touched her face. We both sighed as our lips met, though I'm not sure if I kissed her or she kissed me.

Oh yeah. This is why I wasn't supposed to let the energy go, I realized, slowly pulling it back.

"I will tell her she cannot tease you like that," Sianna whispered again. "But it was funny."

"I hate this," I mumbled.

"She is a rabbit, Luke. Lots of… energy. Do you know what happened?"

I shook my head, lying flat as I stared at the ceiling.

The kissing was over.

I couldn't look at Sianna without regret, loss, and anger. So, I'd look at the ceiling.

"You dream walked to me last night. Remember?"

I grunted in the affirmative.

"You must have banged your head. I did not realize it until she woke you. She was alarmed. You let your energy free."

"I remember that part. We can zoom right past the vibrator discussion."

Sianna dove for my phone on my nightstand, already laughing. "She sent pictures. Your energy is tied up in sex right now. You will not sleep with her, and you would not want to hurt her. I understand. You cannot force the energy back, though. You will hurt yourself trying to do that now. Bringing her… friends is a good idea."

My eyes narrowed in suspicion, catching on to something I'd missed when talking to Janie. "Why did you pause like that before saying 'friends?' She has special friends, doesn't she? Janie's bringing her girlfriends here?"

Sianna laughed again as naughty sounds came out of my phone. She'd found the video. "There will be better camera angles."

"Shit." I groaned. "Tell her no? Please tell her no."

"I already told her it was fine."

"Sianna," I whined. "No. No harem!"

"Stop it. The young one needs attention, and you are unwilling to oblige. Leave them to it or join them if you wish. It is fine. You do not realize it, but you will need the help."

"Why did you pick her to come here?" I asked. "Be honest."

Sianna hesitated, a small smile playing across her face. "She is sweet and simple, does not engage in politics, and wants to be a panda more than anything, simply so she can tumble out of trees and eat bamboo."

I laughed. Only knowing her a day, Janie's logic for wanting to be a panda still didn't surprise me.

"She would not bring intrigue to your life, and I thought you would like her. You liked the curvy one best. I thought she would soothe some of the hurt, Luke. I do not want you to hurt."

"And you?" I asked. "I should not hurt, but you can?"

"We should not discuss this." She sighed, resigned. "I should not even be here."

"I'm still mad at you." It was the truth.

"I am trying to do what is right for my people and for you. I know it is not right for me. But I gave up hope long ago. I will be fine, Luke."

Again, I thought of what Beth had done to Sianna. Again, my stomach turned in revulsion. I had never considered using my energy like that.

"Edgar is coming?" I asked, changing the subject.

"Soon. You should get up."

"Yeah, okay. I'm awake. Energy's better. Thank you."

She nodded, not looking at me. I realized we'd had this entire conversation without looking at each other.

She paused before walking out the bedroom door. "It is good. I heard you talking last night—what you intend to do for the people that work here. It is good. It would be a hardship for many. An honor, but a hardship."

"It never occurred to me to ask. Where does your money come from? I guess I assumed some structure within the society provided for those that worked within it."

"We each pay the Overlord a portion of our income. But Edgar supports my travel and duties."

"Sianna?"

She paused again.

"*You* were my favorite. The curvy facade was nice. Fun to look at. But it paled in comparison."

"Edgar will be here in fifteen minutes." And then she was gone.

19

The house was empty by the time I made it downstairs. Janie must have been visiting with Darla for the afternoon—a thought that gave me chills. Sianna had gone back to her perch.

So, I answered the door when the bell rang.

"Peacekeeper," Edgar said, surprised. "Where are the others?"

"Out and about, I guess. Please come in, Edgar."

"Thank you, Pe—"

"Luke," I cut him off. "Please. Luke. People who save my life get to use my name."

Edgar's lips twitched up as he walked into the house. "Fair enough, Luke."

"You look much better," I noted.

When I'd first met Edgar, he'd been trapped in a bad tie, stuck in a form something like a bigfoot. The next time I saw him, he appeared to be a man in his late fifties or early sixties, but tired and wan. This afternoon, Edgar appeared to be a hale young forty, ready to run a marathon if needed.

"Likewise." He smiled at me. "Much better with your head firmly attached. But yes, I am feeling better. The energy is returning to me and balancing. I haven't transformed since Wednesday and will give it more time before I try. But I feel I will be safe doing so."

I nodded, wondering what that meant. "Coffee? Tea? Something else?"

"Water?" he asked.

A minute later, we were seated in the living room chairs, facing each other. My piano was directly behind me, calling for my attention. I didn't know what to make of it. My music didn't typically distract me from conversation. I shook my head in confusion, wondering if Edgar's tentative unease was somehow calling to my musical side.

"Daniel mentioned he was invited to your circle. I believe he is curious," Edgar started the small talk. He was still. His emotions were calm. But there was a part of him buried deep that was not at peace.

"He is welcome," I nodded. "So is John. I believe Adaline would like to try to balance his energy."

"It's interesting that your family should be so empowered and so willing to share their power," Edgar murmured. "It is nearly unique in history."

I shrugged, not sure what to say. "While we're talking about family, I should let you know I intend to hire and pay the people standing guard. The people that work for me will be compensated for their time."

Edgar's face went blank. "That's not how this works, Luke. You would offend them."

"I have the means to do it. Surely you know who my family is. I'll talk to my dad and brother and figure out the best way to do it. But I won't have any of them suffer a hardship on my account."

"Something like a business? A business would pay them, not you directly?" Edgar asked.

"Probably," I agreed.

He nodded. "I believe that would be welcome. They will not take from you directly. But an organization that is set up for your benefit would be acceptable."

I stared at him, unable to process that logic.

"In truth, the care of those in service to the Peacekeeper should be the responsibility of the Overlord. He is paid a small portion of each of our people's paychecks for the caretaking of the greater community. I know Nathaniel will not pay them, though. I try to assist those most in need, but I do not have your brother's resources."

"We're in agreement, then."

He nodded again. "I'm glad for it. Thank you for your generosity. I came to beg a different favor. This is an unexpected boon."

"How can I help?" I asked.

"We've been organizing the children that need assistance. I was hoping we could plan for some of your time this week."

"Of course. Mistress Life is also willing to lend her aid. Adaline and I will work with the children that need help. Let us know when and where."

"Wednesday? At your estate?"

My eyebrows shot up. "The arena?"

Edgar nodded. "That is your property. My brother has vacated the premises, as well as your estates in Rome and

Madrid. I believe he has retreated to his own home in London. John has taken some steps to ensure Nathaniel remembers his role, but it is a stopgap. We will address it. Until then, you are welcome in your home without fear of his influence."

"I am home, Edgar. My family is here."

He pressed his lips together. "I thought you might say that. Some families will need—"

"They're welcome to stay at the estate," I said. "We can talk to Sam about converting the house if needed."

Edgar shook his head. "There is already plenty of room in the house and outbuildings. There are also other families willing to play host."

"How does the Peacekeeper have an estate here? If my facts are right, there hasn't been a Peacekeeper in nearly a thousand years. This land was nothing but forest, grass, and native tribes at that point."

His lips twitched again. "It's true. There are affinities among the natives that my father could connect with, even across continents. A lot of land has been claimed in the Peacekeeper's name without a Peacekeeper present, including this land.

"You have many holdings throughout the world. The comfort and care of a Peacekeeper are vital to us, even when we are without one. The older affinities, in particular, invest heavily into your holdings. My father, Jude, was not a wealthy man. His entire life was devoted to caring for affinities. In turn, we cared for him. It was much the same with his predecessor, Francis.

"Functionally, I purchased the land here before Illinois was made a state, back when I was still Overlord. I carried my father's wards to it and have improved the dwellings throughout the years. Sianna was raised there."

"Then it's your home, not mine." I wondered what was involved with 'carrying wards.' I'd have to ask Micah or Jen.

"No, Luke. I claimed the land and entrusted it to the Peacekeeper. It is your legal property. Thank you for letting me live there while we awaited your return to us."

"I have the means to buy my own property, Edgar. Take that land and fill it with people that need a safe haven. I have the means to go to the families too. They don't need to come here."

"Let them come, Luke. Let them come and see you. If you go to them, you invade their homes and upset what balance they have. If they come here, their home is still their domain. They will come to you."

I nodded. "If you feel that's best, I won't argue."

"Thank you."

Edgar's eyes had been fixed on a spot over my right shoulder throughout the conversation. I turned then, trying to guess what he had been staring at. Nothing. There was nothing that would draw the eye.

"Where is Sianna?" he asked, tone subdued.

"She's outside doing… what she does. I can call for her," I offered.

His smile was sad. "I like that you suggest calling to her, as if she'd miss me coming within a mile of this place, miss the car pulling up, miss my entry into the house, and miss our conversation. No. She knows I'm here. She doesn't want to speak to me. I would still like to know what happened."

I lifted my eyebrows in a question.

"I saw that binding of love. I felt it. What happened to make you destroy it? I would not think you capable of it."

I stared for a minute, considering how to answer. It turned out I didn't need to find words.

"She asked it of you. She asked to be free of genuine love so she may continue as Huntress?"

I continued to stare, my frustration and anger slowly coming to a simmer.

"I have wronged her and you. I am sorry for your pain, Peacekeeper." His words were subdued.

"I'm sorry for hers," I said, tone sharp.

Edgar gave a slow nod of agreement. "She has not known much of kindness and love. I meant for her to be free of the requirements of a hunter when she found her place in this world. I meant her to set that responsibility at my feet, to blame me when she stepped away from the role. Never, in my wildest dreams, did I expect her to be the last hunter."

"You know, in the world of the empowered, hunters are something completely different. It throws me every single time we use the word," I said. I didn't want to talk about Sianna without her in the room.

"You need to study your histories more, Peacekeeper. That's not entirely true. Your hunters started like ours. First, they were the law enforcement for the Circle of the Mistress and Walker, ensuring balance among your kind. Then, as the Walker drifted from the center, dragging the Mistress with him, your hunters became a force in their own right. Like so many, the power they claimed made them laws unto themselves.

"Our hunters started down that path. My brother is many things. A leader is not one of them. As his oversight and care faded, our hunters became the sole arbitrators of right. Unfortunately, their actions did not always coincide with our practices. Many of the hunters fell victim to the people they had wronged, and I can't bring myself to cry for their loss. As for the others, well… I believe our Huntress took care of the perpetrator. If I am not mistaken, she's waited a very long time for the chance to face Elias. He tormented her as a young woman."

We sat in silence as I considered his words. I'd have to ask Micah or Jen about the origin of our hunters too. I should have been taking notes.

Eventually, Edgar spoke again. "Your brother stands in the dead center of that circle, doesn't he?"

"He and Adaline stand center, yes."

"But the actual center. He stands in the very center, correct?"

I furrowed my brow in confusion. "I think you misunderstand the center of the circle," I replied. "They stand in the actual center, yes. But they move around. We walk through it. Sometimes others join them."

"I know what the center of the circle is, Luke," Edgar said, tone flat. "Over time, as the Walker and Mistress drift in purpose, the circle does not balance with them at the center. They'll move. The circle will rotate to adjust. Or the circle will only close at certain times of the day. Maybe the Mistress can't or won't stand with him. As the pair gets shadowed with selfishness and wrongful death, the balance of the circle shifts. Godwin babbled nonstop about your family shining bright with four elements and a pure Walker and Mistress. They stand the center? The actual center?"

"They do," I acknowledged. "Would you like to meet them? I'm not sure Sam is home, but I know Adaline is."

"No, not today. Not now. I'll leave you to your day and look forward to seeing you on Wednesday. I don't believe John or Daniel will join your circle tonight, but they are curious. They would like to experience it if they are truly welcome. The

Mistress made that offer without discussing it with your brother. They will await Samuel's invitation."

I laughed at that. "They are welcome. They do not need to await an invitation from the man. Sam worships the ground Addy walks upon. He would never make her guests unwelcome. It is more her circle than his."

Edgar made a sound somewhere between surprise and approval before standing to go. He seemed to hesitate, unsure what to do with himself.

"You don't need to rush away, Edgar. You're welcome to stay."

"No. I had hoped to talk to Sianna. To both of you, together."

"You know as well as I do that she can hear you," I reminded him.

He sighed, frustrated and sad. "I do. But I would not have this conversation without holding her hand. I would rather never have this conversation, but the binding between you is gone. John tried to convince me I had imagined it. He could detect no sign of it and was convinced I wished it into being. I know better. And I owe her a conversation. Next time."

I followed as he moved to the door. As he turned to say goodbye, I offered my hand in peace and wasn't surprised when he took it. I was reasonably sure Edgar would pull off the side of the road somewhere for a good cry on his way home.

His sense of self screamed in my mind for his lack of peace and his pain.

"Can I help? Is there anything at all I can do?" I asked, lost.

He swallowed, considering his words. "Do not fault her for my failings. I was wrong to make her take that oath. It is my fault you are now in this predicament."

"You take too much blame upon yourself," I said, surprised by my own words. "She's an adult. She opted for this solution when others were available. We're in this predicament because I didn't understand that I was supposed to put my wants before her needs."

His eyes narrowed. "You are not at fault for being a good person, Lucas."

"Neither are you," I said, smiling a bit.

He smiled with me, then left without another word.

20

Janie strolled in an hour later, carrying a food container from my mother.

"I really hate you," she said, grinning. "That's just unfair."

"What's unfair?"

"I've met your mother and your father. No one is allowed to have *two* parents that awesome. Your dad calls me 'sweetheart.'"

I smiled, secretly wondering if Hank and Darla had mentally married me off to Janie in the last few hours. "What do you have?"

"Your mom and I made fudge. I've always wanted to make fudge, and I have never actually made it before."

"There's fudge in that container?" I asked with narrowed eyes.

"I'm told peanut butter chocolate fudge is a particular

favorite, and I should only give you a piece when you've been especially good." Janie's grin turned devilish.

"I'm the Peacekeeper. I demand fudge." It was worth a try.

She snorted, rolling her eyes. "Too late. You already ruined that for yourself. How are you feeling?"

"I would feel better with fudge."

"I would hate to upset your sensitive tummy," she cooed, lips pursed to hide a grin.

I sighed.

"Poor Persnickety Puking Peace," she said, breaking down into giggles. "You let them call you that?"

"I don't think you truly understand my family dynamics," I started.

"You puke a lot?"

"He vomits surprisingly often," Sianna said, coming into the room from the kitchen. "Are there other kinds of fudge? Just chocolate peanut butter? No straight chocolate?"

"Huntress," Janie said with respect, bowing her head a bit as she handed Sianna the container.

My mouth dropped open. "Don't eat all the fudge!" I yelled at them. "My mom only makes it once a year, and it's incredible. May I please have a piece of fudge?"

Sianna's eyes rolled up in her head as she chewed a piece of chocolate. "This is better than the hot chocolate," she said, still rolling the candy around in her mouth.

"I know! I want a piece, too!" I demanded.

"Not me," Janie said, patting her midsection. "I ate roughly my own body weight in fudge while we were packing it up. I'm good."

"That's my container? That's my single container of Mom's

fudge for the year? She only makes one container for each of us!" I yelled, starting to panic.

They were going to eat all my fudge. I normally rationed that fudge so it lasted a month. Sianna was already on her third piece.

I reached, trying to take the container from her.

"No," Sianna said. "No fudge. You have not done your exercise in a week."

"But my head got—"

"No, no fudge," she said again, walking away with the container.

I glared at Janie. "Why did you give her the fudge?"

"Because she is Huntress," Janie said easily. "You're upset about this. I can feel it rolling off you. You're really upset about the fudge?" She was starting to laugh.

"Yes! I look forward to it all damn year. I had no idea this was fudge day! Mom doesn't tell us when she's making it because we nag."

"She told me that."

"She only makes it once a year!"

"She told me that too."

"I can't believe this!"

"You know what else she told me?" Janie asked, sounding superior.

"What?" I snapped.

"The recipe."

I froze. "You're looking especially lovely today, Janie."

"If I make you fudge, can we have sex?"

I tried to think of a reason why I should say no. I came up with nothing. My mouth moved without words coming out.

She cackled, enjoying herself. "I won't do that to you. I'll make you fudge, you big baby. But you'll watch the video."

BY THE TIME Sam showed up, I was at my piano, working through my fudge frustration. Janie had borrowed Matthew's car and gone to the grocery store.

When she'd complained about me not having a car, I'd started to wonder if I needed one. Everyone else had cars. Someone was always home. Maybe I could just borrow a car forever. Then I thought of driving Noah's car with the rubbers in the glovebox. Twenty minutes later, a replacement for my previous car was ordered from the dealership. No more borrowing cars.

"Edgar was here?" Sam asked, appearing directly behind me.

"Sam!" I shouted. I suspected he enjoyed startling the crap out of me. "Would you please fucking walk across the street and knock on the door?"

"It's cold out," he said. "Edgar was here?"

I turned to look at him, taking in the edgy fidgeting and rapid breathing. He'd been playing in time again, in no mood to bicker or joke.

"Yes, he was here," I acknowledged, tone soothing. "Do you need help? Are you calm?"

"Did he tell you? He didn't tell you. He didn't talk to her. I told him. I told him on Wednesday that I would look. He knew what I meant."

I moderated my breathing to a slow, steady rhythm and started to pull Sam into the web of my calm without using my peace.

"Don't do that!" he snapped. "I'm not unbalanced, just

upset."

"Your heart is racing," I countered. "I can feel it. You are decidedly not at peace. I'm not pushing the energy at you, just trying to help you center yourself."

He blinked. "Edgar talked about the center? That's why you used that word. He told you the center moves. I don't know if he's right, but I know Micah's circle only closed at sunrise and sunset because his Walker couldn't close it at other times of the day. So, I don't know what it means that Addy and I can close a circle at any time and stand anywhere."

I stared. Sam's ability to Walk through time was amazing in every way, but his ability to process and understand all the different possible futures, meanings, and cues was nothing short of mind-boggling. He retained so much detail from each possible future, he could usually identify where we were without asking even basic questions.

He flopped down on my couch, exhaling hard. "I don't want to tell this story."

"I probably don't want you to tell this story either," I admitted. If the story was bad enough to make Sam this edgy, it wasn't going to be a happy tale. As luck would have it, Sam was also the world's worst storyteller.

"Sianna," Sam said, voice laced with power. "You must come inside. You must know this. Nothing will move forward until you and Edgar recognize each other for what you are."

We waited in silence for more than ten seconds.

"Don't make me name you," Sam yelled. "I don't want to do that."

She appeared almost immediately. "Edgar cannot be my father. When we met, you called me the last of the Overlord's sane begotten. That means Nathaniel."

Sam glared. "Edgar has been your father in every way that matters. Don't devalue his worth over a trick of biology."

"We're calling fatherhood 'a trick of biology' now? Do you want to tell Hank, or should I?" I asked, almost laughing.

"He speaks the truth in my case," Sianna corrected me. "Edgar was my keeper and caretaker from as early as I can remember."

"From the day your mother died," Sam corrected her. "Nathaniel had no interest in you until you showed significant gifts."

Sianna drifted down to sit on the piano bench next to me, eyes locked on Sam even as she took my hand. "You know of my mother?"

Sam's eyes shot to me. "I'm terrible at storytelling. Edgar should have talked about this. You should have made her come inside."

"It hurts him to see me. I feel his pain when I am nearby. I would rather not do that," Sianna whispered. "But you know of my mother? You can tell me of her?"

"Which 'him' do you mean?" Sam asked coolly, eyes back on her. "Edgar or Luke? It's true for both, but I didn't think you recognized Edgar's heartache."

Sianna frowned. "Edgar is in pain because I have no match. He has longed for me to have a partner more than anyone else."

Sam nodded. "He wishes you to know love. But that's not the source of his pain."

Sianna and I both watched as Sam chewed his bottom lip.

"Samuel!" I barked, reacting to Sianna's tension. "Go back to the part about her mom."

"I don't want to tell this story! Can we call him? Sianna, will you call him? I'll go get him if he will Walk with me. Tell him I said you must know. It must happen. Now. Before Luke helps the children."

"He won't talk to me about her. I've asked," she said, voice low. "Godwin told me she was a great beauty and admired by many. My father killed her when she challenged his authority."

Sam's brow furrowed. "That's all you know?"

She nodded.

"Please call. Please ask him." Sam begged. "I won't tell it right."

"Sam, we have the Harbor circle tonight. We don't have to do this right now. We have to leave in about an hour. Let's talk about this later." I was working hard to *not* push peace at him. He was freaking out.

"I'm not going," he said, not even looking at me. "Neither are you. Adaline will do the circle tonight with the others. We'll have another circle Wednesday night after you visit the children. John and Daniel will join that circle, and we'll see if it stands more evenly with you. Otherwise, I think you have to join Addy and me in the center."

I frowned.

"Stop it," Sam scolded, still not looking at me. "No circle with your power like this. You'll scare them. It will freak the rest of Harbor out. No."

I continued to frown, knowing he was right. I loved the circle, though.

"Don't pout," Sam barked, still not looking at me. "Bigger things are going on than you missing the circle for two weeks in a row. Get it together. Call him, Sianna."

"I do not need a phone to do that, Walker," she murmured.

Sam's face scrunched up. "I forgot about that. I'm not good at it."

"You are young. Have patience." Sianna sighed. "He is upset. Distraught. He is not sending words, just feelings. He rarely does this."

"Will he Walk with me if I go to him?"

"Yes, he awaits you now."

Sam was gone in an instant, leaving Sianna and me sitting together on the piano bench.

"What comes to us, Peacekeeper?" she asked, subdued and lost in her thoughts. "I have asked about my mother my entire life. She is not spoken of. Some behave as if she was a shameful woman. I was punished for even asking the question as a child. Why would the Walker involve himself? Why would he hesitate to tell me what needs to be said?"

I squeezed her fingers, leaning forward so she'd look at me. "Sam is truly terrible at explaining what he sees. *Terrible*. For all his power and his dedication, he is a gentle person. He would not want to tell you things that might hurt."

"He told me I was going to chop off your head!" she yelled, suddenly angry. "That hurt me! Even when I barely knew you, I knew I would do no such thing. It hurt that he would say that!"

Sam reappeared with Edgar before I could respond. Their eyes darted between us, taking in Sianna's anger.

"Do you want us to come back later?" Sam asked, confused. "I had to use Sianna's bindings to get Edgar. So, we won't go back to the estate, just across the street. I hate using the bindings like that. It doesn't always hold and then bad things happen."

Sianna literally growled at him. It was not the growl of a human throat but a feline growl of warning that said something like, *"Stop being obnoxious, or I'll eat your face off."*

Sam's lips twitched. "Just checking. Edgar, I'll pour you a whiskey. Jake has better whiskey."

He was gone again and back in a flash with a bottle and three glasses.

"No fourth glass?" I asked, somehow knowing there would be no whiskey for me.

"You don't need whiskey. You need to pay attention. Everyone else needs whiskey," Sam said, once again not looking at me. My stomach rolled as it sank to my feet.

"I-I had hoped to talk about this earlier," Edgar muttered, sitting on the edge of the couch. "When you wouldn't come in, dear one, I figured it was for the best to leave it be. I didn't foresee the Walker insisting upon this."

"Foresight is my thing, not your thing," Sam said, his slight smile showing for Edgar. "Please. I cannot imagine your pain. I don't know that I would have survived as you have. But we are stalled. She must know before the challenge. She won't do what she needs to do if she doesn't know. And things are moving faster than you realize. Nathaniel is preparing as we speak."

"She won't challenge my brother." Edgar's eyes shot to Sianna. "Never. Not under any circumstance. You will promise me. Swear it to me."

Sam shook his head. "Don't do that to her. I don't think she will challenge him. I believe it'll happen otherwise." He paused, staring until Edgar nodded. "But should that fail, she may choose to challenge, and it may be the only way forward for your people."

Edgar was silent as he processed Sam's words, finally giving a nod. "Fine. But please, dear one. I don't want to see you challenge him. It's not your place."

"Start with Jude. Or maybe Francis," Sam said quietly.

Edgar glared. "Do you want to do this?"

"I really don't," Sam admitted, shamefaced. "I mostly want to go home and eat self-pity fudge, but that makes me a coward."

"You know what would make this conversation easier?" I suggested, seizing the opportunity.

"You're not getting my fudge. This is no time to bicker about fudge. This is important."

I could feel the dread rolling off Sam. "Your level of fear and cowardice is scaring me."

Sam met my eyes, blinking quickly. "Maybe worse than Micah's story. Maybe."

The air left my lungs in a giant whoosh of dread as if someone was standing on my chest.

Edgar's ears perked up. "I don't know Micah's story and have always wondered."

"You'll have to ask him. It's horrible and not our story to tell," I said, wishing I had whiskey too.

Edgar nodded in understanding before downing his drink in a swift motion and refilling the glass from the bottle on the coffee table before him. Sam sat in one of the straight back chairs, turning to face Sianna and me where we sat on the piano bench. I couldn't decide if he wanted to watch us or wanted to avoid looking at Edgar.

"You play piano, Peacekeeper?" he asked.

"Several instruments," Sam answered for me. "Music is a part of him."

Edgar nodded again. "It was that way with my father as well. The Peacekeeper before him was not as musical, but he loved music and nature. Your brother is right. We will start with Francis."

21

"The world used to be wilder," Edgar started, his expression removed as he assumed the role of storyteller. "Sianna mentioned your idea about the loss of wild things, Luke. There might be truth to it, but there is no changing it. We cannot go back, only forward.

"Even when things were untamed, beast affinities had trouble with mental balance. There are stories about where we came from and how we came about. They are not worth discussing right now. Suffice to say, there have been affinities for at least as long as there have been people empowered with control over human energy and emotion. During our strongest times, we were blessed with a Peacekeeper, someone to help us maintain the mental and emotional balance needed to be both human and beast.

"You have a long legacy, Luke. There are journals and letters in your libraries. You should explore them over time. Each Peacekeeper has added something to the legacy. However, I doubt you care for the land or wealth of your title. The Peacekeeper holdings don't come close to what the Walker over there holds. Primarily, your estates have been used as safe houses and Overlord dwellings. I'm glad you're willing to let that continue.

"We'll put that aside for now too. Our tale starts with Francis, a man of peace who lived in the twelfth century. He was born to a wealthy family in Italy and grew into a heart of service. He had four children with a lovely woman named Agnes. You know John and Godwin. They also had two daughters, Cecily and Estrid."

Next to me, I heard Sianna gasp and saw her eyes go wide with shock.

Edgar ignored her. "Once John had grown to adulthood, the previous Overlord made way for him. When a person of stronger affinity and character arises, we stand a challenge and transfer the burden of leadership to one more worthy. It is our way. It has always been our way. Our challenges simply ensure the person's dedication and stability.

"Seeing his family grown, his sons strong and proud, Francis gave up the name of Peacekeeper when Agnes died. Cutting his bindings with beast affinities, he devoted the remainder of his life to God, trusting another Peacekeeper would rise in time.

"My father, Jude, was born to a beast affinity family in England within a decade of Francis's departure. He was recognized as Peacekeeper from the moment he was born and raised to fit our essential role.

"He was not religious and did not marry. To my knowledge, he had three meaningful relationships throughout his life. My mother died young in childbirth. I have no memory of her. Nathaniel's mother raised us as well as two other children before she died of natural causes.

"My father had one more partner who brought him daughters. I dared not ask, but I suspect Jude loved his daughters more than his sons. My sisters were lovely creatures who doted upon everyone within reach, including him.

"When his third partner died by suspicious circumstances, my father was entering his sixtieth year and tired. He was not long in following her to the grave.

"Take that to mean, neither of the more recent Peacekeepers was long-lived. Francis lived about fifteen years after cutting his bindings. Jude didn't live to see sixty-one. There have been longer-lived Peacekeepers, but not many. I've spent a lot of time over the last few days reading. I don't know of a Peacekeeper that was also of the Circle, Lucas. I don't know what to expect of your lifespan, but my father would have died from the injury you sustained last week, even with the help Sianna, Charlie, and I could offer. It's amazing you are alive."

Edgar fell silent, looking toward me but obviously seeing something else in his mind.

"Estrid?" Sianna breathed, shaking Edgar from his thoughts. "My mother?"

He sighed, the sound full of pain. "Yes, dear one. We'll get back to the point. Your mother was a daughter of Francis. She was a beast lord of six forms and nearly as quick in transforming as you. I believe your speed comes from her.

"'Beast Lord' did not suit her, though we've not had a feminine version of the title in any language I know. I've always appreciated that our empowered cousins differentiate their lords from ladies."

He blew out another gust of air then gulped down another drink. Sianna's alarm bells were ringing. I guessed Edgar wasn't much of a drinker.

"Even as a young man, I loved Estrid. She was the most beautiful creature I had ever seen. She was older than me by more than thirty years, but age didn't matter. We were beast lords, able to ignore the ticking of time.

"Eventually, I grew into a man with a strong affinity, courted her, and married her. Over six hundred eighty-three years of marriage, we had one hundred forty-seven children."

Sianna was so still next to me, I wasn't sure she was breathing.

"Our surviving children grew to adults and lived their lives with children of their own. Given the option to live long lives, most chose a shorter lifespan to match their spouses, children, or grandchildren. It's difficult to watch everyone you love in the world age and die, and true beast lords have always been rare—maybe a handful in each generation. There are a few long-lived in my family, but not many. We've always cherished quality of life over quantity of time.

"Today, our line remains strong throughout the world with beast masters and lords in every generation. Charlie is special with his knack for adopting forms, but not unique. There have been similar beast lords in our family tree."

"They speak of *your* line," Sianna said slowly. "They never speak of a wife. I had thought there were many."

"No, dear one. Just Estrid. It was always Estrid for me. The ones that know our story don't speak of her out of respect for me. And I think they mean to honor what we sacrificed. Love that spans centuries is rare."

His eyes drifted to me before landing on Sianna. "I know what I saw. I know that binding was there, beloved. I know it's my fault it is gone."

"No," Sam interjected. "Don't mourn for its loss. I needed it.

I needed it there to keep him alive and get him out of that arena. But it has to be gone for her to do what she should do. They're strong and brave, Edgar. Have patience. Don't waste energy mourning that love."

Edgar frowned. "I don't understand."

Sam met his eyes. "You worry for the wrong things. She sits beside him, holding on for dear life. The binding is gone, not the love."

Sianna's white-knuckle grip on my hand loosened before she tried to pull away from me. I held tight. "It's fine," I said softly. "I'm here. You're allowed comfort too, Sianna."

She grabbed her tumbler then, downing her double whiskey in a single swallow. Sam played bartender, refilling all three glasses.

"I really wouldn't be opposed to a drink," I muttered.

"No," Sam said. "Stop it. You're fine."

He drank his refill down and poured himself another drink, I think just to spite me. "You and Estrid had lots of kids and still have a lot of family. Go from there," he prodded Edgar.

Edgar glared as I bit back a smile.

"This is why he's a horrible storyteller," I explained. "All facts, sometimes in the wrong order, and absolutely no emotion."

Edgar glowered at Sam before continuing. "Together, we traveled where we were needed. She was not named a huntress, but we worked as a team. John led as Overlord for a long time, then asked Godwin to take the burden from him. None of the beast lords, your mother and me included, objected. It was a natural progression of leadership as John realized his energy was spiraling.

"When the title transitioned from John to Godwin, we gathered and 'challenged' Godwin to see who could come up with the best blended form. Godwin won on paper, but your mother dominated that game. She turned herself into something like a sphinx, cracking her older brothers up into rare fits of laughter. Have you ever heard John laugh? It's always been unsettling."

Sam smiled. "I like him. We're friends."

Edgar nodded. "He mentioned that yesterday. I've never known the empowered to walk in our dreams. The Peacekeeper was known for it, but not other empowered people.

"Anyway, there was drinking and laughter involved when Godwin became Overlord. By the time we were done, we were confident he was well balanced, in control of his energy and mind. There was no battle necessary.

"Godwin led for nearly two hundred years before his energy began to falter. Then, finally, he asked me to take the title from him.

"Understand, there is real energy involved in being Overlord. It is mentally and physically taxing to care for our people. I agreed to his request, hoping that taking the energy would keep him mentally fit to stay with us. John managed to stay. We hoped Godwin would survive as well. Estrid wanted her brothers to remain. By that time, many generations of our children had come and gone. We cherished the family who chose to stay among the living."

"We traveled to Rome for the transfer of power. Nathaniel challenged for the position. At the time, I thought it was a token challenge. He fought, but not well. Looking back now, I believe he meant the challenge in truth. He just had no idea how to fight. He has never had a heart of service. He never served as a hunter and never understood the value of protecting others. And I don't believe he understood there was actual weight and work involved in being Overlord. He saw the title and power without any of the responsibilities.

"But I took the title, not understanding he coveted it. Estrid and I stayed in Spain for many years, then moved near my ancestral home in England before moving to what is now America in the eighteenth century. John spent time in the Middle East and Asia. Godwin lived in Spain and traveled most of Europe. Other long-lived lords scattered throughout Africa. There was no one in the new world. So, Estrid and I came here, claiming a home for ourselves and a space for the next Peacekeeper.

"She and I shared the burdens of leadership. Many of our sects bonded to her rather than me. I did not mind, nor did she. She was brilliant, strong, and patient. By sharing the weight of leadership, we remained better balanced and healthy. Our people flourished, and always, we watched for the next Peacekeeper.

"It was during this time, Luke, that I invited a Peace pillar into our world. I wondered then if Lord Peace was just another name for the Peacekeeper. He had a limited circle and no Mistress or Walker. I thought he might be able to help us. I was dreadfully wrong, and he paid a terrible price for his willingness to try. I regret that to this day."

Sam made a little sound. "Don't regret that either. He was not long for this world. His Walker and Mistress were unfit. He could not remain as Peace without them. It was worth a try. Had it worked, you would have saved his life. As it was, you just accelerated the end."

"Huh," Edgar grunted. "How do you know this?"

Sam's eyes glowed as he turned to Edgar. "I am the Time

Walker. Your people lived well for many years until you went to Rome. Pick up from there."

Edgar blinked in confusion, staring at Sam. I wondered if the alcohol was starting to hit home. "He does this," I offered. "Especially on things that interest him."

Edgar shook his head, even as he began talking again. "I had traveled to Rome to settle a dispute toward the end of the nineteenth century. The agitator had been threatening the wellbeing of innocents around him if I didn't act, so I did. I believed he was unbalanced and looking for a quick death. I still think that's true. When I got there, I was challenged by the idiot and faced him in wolf form. He was dead within two minutes.

"When I released my energy to transform back to human, I realized I couldn't move the energy properly. It had knotted within me, leaving me stuck as you found me not two weeks ago, Peacekeeper. To this day, I have no idea how it happened. Now, I'm convinced the agitator set some form of trap for me. At the time, most believed I'd lost control of my energy. I'd believed that as well, except now the energy returns to me and seems as balanced as ever."

I shook my head. "There was a tie around your life energy. The night I met you, I broke a tie that was strangling your energy like a snake."

Sam's eyes narrowed. "His life energy? The tie was not in his mind?"

I nodded.

"Hmm," Sam said, then shrugged. "I don't know either, Edgar. Ties that affect life energy are more of a siphon thing, aren't they? I'll go back and look again, but I'm reasonably certain your brother set you up somehow."

"I figured as much when Nate reacted to the tie being

broken," Edgar admitted. "Until that moment, I wasn't confident he was part of my trapping. As it was, I became a cautionary tale among beast affinities. 'Listen to your power and know your limits. Don't end up like Edgar.' I didn't mind being an object lesson. I agreed with the advice.

"Estrid came to me in Rome and sought help. Unfortunately, there was no circle known to us. The siphons were unable or unwilling to help. The elementals and more nefarious elements of nature just didn't care. I was horrifically stuck and unable to properly access the affinity bindings that relied upon me for help. Stuck as I was, I could not be Overlord. I could not harness the energy appropriately.

"Godwin and John came, along with Nathaniel and a few other lords. Nathaniel was the next logical person to take the title. Godwin and John argued that Estrid was better prepared and already held some of the power. Some sects would not see a woman as a leader, though. We risked tearing our society apart by naming her. So, Nathaniel would take the title and lead with Estrid's assistance.

"After taking the title, Nathaniel began talking at length about his lack of a viable heir. There were other beast lords but none who could bear the title with ease.

"Nate has had many children by many women. He never sought or valued love in the way Estrid and I did. I don't think he understands the concept. Nate Jr. is physically strong but mentally weak. He can take five forms and hold his humanity, but just barely. Becoming Overlord would likely break his psyche. Daniel is his strongest son, but Daniel is strong in ways Nate does not value. I know of no other beast lord that can manifest fire or healing. Daniel has as much affinity as he does empowerment.

"Nate has other sons, but none with as much affinity as Junior or as much raw power as Daniel. I had other male descendants around the world. None of them wished to be Overlord. So, there was no clear successor to Nathaniel's reign.

"Within a year, he claimed Estrid as mate, saying the next Overlord would come from their line. There was no other beast lord woman with as much affinity. Godwin and John were horrified. Their sister was not a broodmare. I was… enraged. Betrayed. My wife. My lifelong companion. How could my brother demand such a thing?

"But he demanded it and kept demanding it. He had a large enough group of supporters to push us toward civil war among affinities. I thought then that a new Peacekeeper would rise. If ever there was a time for God to give us such a helping hand, it was then. I couldn't bear the thought of my beloved wife forced into coupling with my brother.

"I was not in a position to challenge. When Estrid challenged him, she was shouted down by the same people that would not see a woman lead. A woman had no right to challenge. A woman's role was to do as the men dictated."

Edgar paused, considering his words. "I do not believe Francis or Jude envisioned women as lesser beings. They loved their mates and their daughters. I believe they thought a woman should never *need* to challenge in our way. Our women are wise and strong. They should be honored and respected. They should not need to fight tooth and nail to be heard."

He shook his head. "Godwin and John intervened, trying to talk sense into Nate. He would not listen. John's gifts of mental compulsion were well known. He risked uprising by using them against Nate.

"Godwin sought to challenge in his sister's place. The

masses would not allow it. Godwin had surrendered his position as Overlord for lack of control. He could not stand a challenge and risk himself over a woman.

"In the end, we were stuck. Even if one of us challenged and killed him, there was no other to take the title of Overlord. We could not fault his analysis. There was no one. A woman as Overlord would tear our society apart, no matter how misguided and wrong we believed it to be."

"You are not my father?" Sianna asked, unblinking. "When you mentioned my mother as your wife, I thought this would be a tale of why you misled me. But, in truth, you are not my father?"

Edgar's lips tipped up even as he watched the tears race down her face. "It is a matter of perspective. I am your uncle as you are my brother's child. I am also your stepfather, as you are the daughter of my wife by another man."

"You brought me here and raised me," she argued. "Even as you were—trapped between forms—I believed you were my father."

"Estrid hated Nate. She had always hated him. She couldn't even look at him. In retrospect, she saw him more clearly than I ever did. She would give him the strong heir he desired and nothing more. She allowed a single child from a single partnering, then crawled back to my bed to sob through the night.

"You arrived and were not a boy. You held no value in Nate's eyes. He demanded another child once she was well. She refused, saying she'd rather die.

"Less than a week after your birth, she lay sleeping in our rooms, still recovering. I had bundled you in my arms for a walk through the Peacekeeper's Roman estate where we could both feel the sun on our skin… or fur, such as it was.

"I felt Estrid's bindings of love break from where you and I walked, probably a half-mile from her sleeping chamber. I ran to her, but it was too late. If she had the power to heal from that type of wound, it was diminished after giving birth."

"'Dispose of the babe. She is useless,' Nate said. Covered in my wife's blood, he stood before me and told me to dispose of the last bit of light Estrid gave to this world. I would not. You and I left Rome as soon as I could find passage with friends who would hide me in my odd form.

"No, dear one. You are not of my line, but you are my child." Edgar sat back, blinking at his empty glass. "And he is not yours to challenge. He will die by my hand."

Turning to meet Sam's gaze, he continued. "I will dance in the ashes left from Daniel's fire and watch my beloved wife's daughter take the title of Overlord. That is your intention, is it not, Walker?"

22

"Yes," Sam agreed. "I believe she will be Overlord. The best futures for your people are under her leadership. But explain why you cannot be Overlord again, Edgar."

Sianna was pulling the peace energy from me in giant waves, trying to calm her broken heart. *"My mother. My poor mother,"* she wailed in my mind. *"Poor Edgar."*

"Shh," I soothed, running my hand through her hair as I pulled her off the piano bench onto the floor. I wrapped my arms and legs around her, offering all the comfort I could manage.

"Dear one," Edgar breathed, climbing to his feet.

"Leave them be, Edgar. She had to know," Sam said, voice firm but kind. "There is no one better to help her. Let her process. And explain the custom. I don't understand why you cannot be Overlord again. I know it is true. There is not a single future I can find where you stand as anything but an elder."

Edgar sat back on the edge of the couch, watching Sianna and me. The alcohol was helping his pain, but I let the peace go to calm us all.

"I gave up the title, Walker. I gave it up when I couldn't control the power. I can't take it back now that I'm better. That's not how the energy works. Micah stands your circle. You know the titles and names have power in their own right. I cannot take it back."

Sam's mouth dropped open in surprise. "Your titles are like our names?"

"I don't know enough about your names to answer that. But there are real power and ability that come with the titles of Hunter and Overlord. They each bear a burden. The energy requires real work."

"Huh," Sam muttered. "We should ask Jen about that."

"I have a whole list of things to ask Jen and Micah," I said, even as I wiped tears from Sianna's cheeks. She was done crying now, lost in thought.

"Rajena? Are you connected to her? I sensed that on Wednesday but couldn't imagine why she would involve herself with you," Edgar said, eyes on Sam.

Sam nodded. "She is welcome among my family. We would welcome her within our circle, but she refuses to stand it."

"That is another story I would love to hear," Edgar admitted, back to watching Sianna. "How can I help, dearest one?"

Her voice was flat as she spoke into my chest, not looking at Edgar. "You have addressed me as such for my entire life. 'Dear one' or 'dearest one.' 'Darling child,' sometimes. I do not understand how you look upon me with such favor and love."

Edgar swallowed hard while blinking quickly as his emotions overwhelmed his thoughts.

It was Sam who answered, his tone gentle. "I told you. The day I met you, the first time I saw you. 'Outcome of sacrifice and a true love's final gift.' Those are names bestowed by Edgar's love. He has never seen you as anything but the final gift from his true love."

"Yes," Edgar choked out. "There is more of Estrid in you than in any of our children. Sometimes, you look at me just so, shoulders fixed, fire in your eyes, and my mind is fooled into thinking she is still here with me. You are, and have always been, glorious to behold, daughter of my heart, my dearest one. For you, and for her, I stayed. You needed to grow strong and powerful. I would not see you mistreated. I failed to protect your mother. I'd be damned before I failed you as well.

"We stayed here, out of Nate's reach. He didn't ask about you. Godwin, John, and I oversaw the hunters as best we could. That responsibility belongs to the Overlord, but Nate had no interest. He empowered us to do the work for him.

"As you grew and found your forms, we worried for your wellbeing. Nate had proven he held no respect for others. So, it didn't seem beyond reason that he would try coupling with his own daughter.

"You wanted to be a hunter, our Huntress. In that desire, we saw a way to bring a strong, capable woman into a role of leadership. It would also give you the authority to defend yourself.

"I worried that we were using you as a tool and overlooking you as a person. I had been blessed with so much love. I wanted that for you. I knew your mother would want that for you.

"I made you swear that oath. When you found love and a mate, you would set aside our politicking. You would no longer be the tool Godwin, John, and I used to move our culture forward. You would be free to live as you desired. You swore the oath, and we named you Huntress.

"Nathaniel was furious. So far removed from your life, in an age where communication was lacking, he had no idea how strong you were. He seized the power to name hunters back from us, saying we had abused his trust. He came to see you then. You remember?"

"I do," Sianna said, head resting on my shoulder. "I had not met him previously. I was eager to please my father. Now I realize I should have been eager to take his head."

Edgar pressed his lips together, unhappiness radiating from him.

Sianna turned to meet his eyes. "This is why no one spoke of my mother? You did not want me to strike against him?"

"I wanted you to grow healthy and strong, mentally sound in all ways. Picturing yourself at the center of a Greek tragedy would not help achieve those goals."

"I am long since grown," she snapped. "You could have told me!"

"To what end?" Edgar asked, calm as could be. "How would this knowledge have helped you before this moment? I disagree with the Walker's assessment. I don't believe you *ever* needed to know this."

"She did not believe she had the right to challenge," Sam mumbled. "Charlie has a plan. It's a good plan. But she has to accept a challenge for it to work."

"Charlie," Edgar snorted, smiling. "I love that one too. Strong, powerful, and determined. He would make a glorious Overlord, but he is an even better advocate. He brought us the Peacekeeper, the Circle, Lady Light, and maybe the next queen of the siphons too.

"Nate has been trying to groom Charlie for leadership since childhood. The affinities absolutely radiated from him, even as a baby. So, Nate came here more often after Charlie's arrival.

"Each visit, I was glad Sianna was gone, doing the work of a huntress. By then, the hunters had started dying out. I wasn't worried. I hoped Elias would come looking for Sianna's head. She is many times more powerful than any of her brothers ever thought of being. Daniel is the only one smart enough to see it."

"Daniel and Candy? He is Daniel, right?" Sam asked. "He was here yesterday? We didn't do formal introductions."

"Yes, that was Daniel," I said, loosening my hold on Sianna as she shifted to face the room. "Yes, he has feelings for Candy."

"She rejected him," Sianna said. "Daniel came here often while I was young. I think he wanted to escape our father as much as he wanted to know me."

Edgar gave a tsk of disapproval. "Nonsense. That brother loves you. He has never been anything but a kind, gentle soul. He should have been born to Estrid and me instead of Nathaniel. Your father has no tolerance for him."

"I know my brother loves me," Sianna said, frowning at Edgar. "I was not suggesting otherwise. I meant that he and I have always been the familial outcasts. I will never forgive the cat for hurting him as she did."

Edgar tsked again. "That's not fair. She was very young. Daniel nears his three hundredth birthday. He offered for her too quickly. They may find their way in time."

"She made a fool of him," Sianna said flatly, trying to end the conversation.

"He made a fool of himself," Edgar countered. "He put her in that position, dear one."

"Do I have this right?" I asked. "Daniel asked Candy to marry him. She said no. And now Sianna hates her."

Sam waved his head in a so-so gesture. "Mostly true. Daniel asked Candy in a very public way after they'd dated for a short time, not expecting that she would decline. But she said no, causing him embarrassment. He furthered his own humiliation by not forcing the issue.

"He is powerful in his own right as an affinity. I think he may also have a name in our circle. He could have demanded her cooperation. He didn't, which makes me like him more. I think that one belongs to Harbor, Luke."

"Huh," I grunted. "What name?"

Sam shrugged. "I didn't look."

He said it too casually. I didn't believe him.

"You got that last part wrong, though," Sam continued. "Sianna only partly hates Candy because of Daniel. You're the reason for the rest of that hate."

"Me?" I asked, starting to laugh even as Sianna's spine went straight. I poked her in the side. "Don't hate her because of me. I dumped her. She blew up my car."

"YOU CLAIMED HER!" Sianna roared, turning furious eyes on me. "She is under your protection forever unless you make her an outcast. And I know you won't do that! So, she may do as she pleases, trouncing over everyone else's desires. Of course, I hate her! She is a whiny, selfish, manipulative—"

"She also outranks our Huntress since you claimed her," Edgar interrupted, laughing at Sianna's outrage.

"I will not bow to that one," Sianna replied, voice low in warning.

"I would never suggest such a thing," Edgar said, still laughing.

Eventually, the laughter fell to silence. "That's what I needed her to hear," Sam confirmed, nodding to Edgar. "Thank you."

"Nathaniel is not yours to challenge, dearest one," Edgar said, looking at Sianna again. "I will face him when the time is right and clear the way for you. I agree with the Walker, with Charlie, Godwin, and John. You are the next Overlord and should make that challenge after your father is displaced. You will take that role and make your mother proud."

23

After Sam and Edgar left, Sianna and I stayed cuddled on my living room floor for a long time. Finally, the sky faded to true darkness. I didn't say the words to turn on the lights. I thought she'd leave if she realized we were lounging together.

She cried twice more, cathartic waves of cleansing more than sadness or remorse.

"He never yelled at me. I would ask about her often. He never answered me but also never scolded me over it. The others did. The family that lived with us to help him. Godwin. John. They forbade me from asking about her."

I could say nothing, so I continued running my hand up and down her back, offering comfort.

"Godwin and John are my uncles," she realized. "I used to call them 'Uncle' as a young one. It felt foolish as I got older. Edgar has always been Edgar, though."

Her eyes closed. I could feel her falling into a restful state.

"Let's not sleep on the floor," I murmured. "There are beds upstairs."

"I'm not really sleeping," she mumbled. "Just resting my eyes."

"I wonder what happened to Janie. She went to the store hours ago."

"I sent her to your parents. She will stay with them tonight. She pulled up shortly after the Walker returned with Edgar. I told her to go. We can stay here. Right here." Her voice was fading.

"Okay," I said quietly, recognizing that I was about to spend the night sleeping on the floor.

Our breathing evened out to match, slow and steady. Our heartbeats were aligning as my eyes drifted closed. "Sleep, love," I muttered.

Sianna was on her feet, screaming in outrage. "NO! YOU DID NOT DO… Oh. You didn't. How did you do that?"

I was not great at tracking conversations while falling asleep or waking up. She'd startled the fuck out of me.

"What?" I asked, alarmed by her horror and surprise. "What did I do?"

She blinked at me, confused by my confusion. "Did you say it and not mean it? There is no binding of love, but you said the word. You acknowledged it."

Realizing she was right, I opened my sight. My silver and amber bindings of familial love and friendship surrounded her entire being. Bindings of amber friendship and blue loyalty flowed from her to me. There was not a spec of radiant gold bindings anywhere.

"I don't know," I admitted. "But there's no binding."

"You love me in the same way you love Lady Loch?" she asked, sounding sad.

"No," I disagreed. "I love Tali like a sister. Can we not talk about this? I don't want to mess up and forge it again only to have to destroy it."

"It could reforge? You do not hate me?" she asked.

"No, I don't hate you. Not by a long shot. I'm still not particularly happy that I could have left it alone without you hating me, but it is what it is. You will be Overlord."

She stayed silent as she curled up next to me on the floor again.

"We could go upstairs and go to sleep," I suggested.

"It is early. Not yet seven o'clock."

"Hungry?" I asked.

She shook her head. "I would like to stay here and whisper secrets in the dark."

I grinned. It had been a terrible evening. If she wanted to be playful, I was happy to oblige. I turned on my side to face her. "What are we telling secrets about?" I whispered.

Her smile turned solemn as she ran a hand down the side of my face. "I would rather be the Peacekeeper's mate than the Overlord. I do not want to face the ugliness ahead. I would rather stay here with you, make love and babies, eat Sunday dinner with your family… torment the Walker and apologize to your sister. I know I must face what comes. But I would much rather be happy with you."

My power roared forward, swallowing the rage before I even recognized it. My body tingled as my mind went numb. I sat up, realizing I wasn't myself.

"Luke?" Sianna asked, sitting up beside me.

"Lights on," she called, turning on the lamps in the room. "Oh. I've lost you to the power."

"No," I disagreed. "Still me."

"Your eyes are glowing. Your face has changed."

I jumped up, running for the bathroom mirror. My eyes were glowing turquoise fire. My face had turned all hard angles like skin stretched over my skull with no other flesh to soften my features.

Sianna walked in behind me. "You will not remember this when you come out of it."

"I will," I disagreed. "I should go spar with William."

I was already turning to go when she grabbed my arm. "What will sparring do?"

I stared at her hand.

"Peacekeeper, what will sparring do?"

I met her eyes again. There was no fear, just curiosity.

And then we were moving. I dodged as her fist flew at my face, shoving her back into the wall to gain space.

An eye blink later, I faced a wolf. I didn't know how to fight a wolf, so I took the energy from her, forcing her back to her human self—Sianna in truth, with no mask to hide behind.

I dodged again, grabbing at the leg that tried to kick me. I missed, and she tossed my ass down the hallway and back into the living room.

"You have gotten better at this," she noted. "What happened?"

I studied her, looking for a weakness, only then noticing she was naked. My focus shifted from sparring to another form of wrestling.

"No," she said, voice cold. "I am not convinced you are you. Tell me what happened."

I stalked toward her as she backed away. "Numb. Cold. Indifferent." I bit out the words, mirroring her movements. The binding had not returned with an admission of feelings. I could take Sianna to bed.

"More words," she demanded. "I do not understand."

"We will go to bed."

"Not those words," she said. "Explain the numb. This is different than when Peace stole time before."

"You just finished telling me you longed for my bed. Now you refuse?" She moved too quickly for me to follow, suddenly behind me.

"No," she disagreed, grabbing my ear and twisting as she kicked my feet out from under me and planted her knee in my back. "Tell me of the numb and the sparring."

I screamed in pain as the numbness finally faded. "Stop! It's gone!"

She let go of my ear, moving quickly off my back to send energy through me to heal injuries. There was nothing to heal. No damage was done.

"Tell me of the numb," she said again. "What is this? Do you remember?"

I nodded, panting. "We sat up from the floor. I looked in the mirror, dodged a punch. You went wolf. I pulled the energy. I remember it all. It's all there."

"The numb?" she asked again, expression concerned.

"The binding. Breaking the binding can affect how I process emotions. When I get truly angry, the peaceful energy drains the anger and leaves me with… nothing. William says it will happen at odd times. Sparring, or maybe pain, seems to chase the numb away."

Her expression turned puzzled, then wounded.

"What?" I asked.

Her spine was straight and chin high as she went in search of her dress. "Peacekeeper, I apologize for burdening you with my… feelings. I will not do so again."

"Whoa!" I yelled, grabbing her arm as she made for the door. I was surprised I'd managed to catch her. "Back up the crazy train. What just happened?"

"I did not expect my… confession… to anger you. Again, I apologize for my insolence." She tried to yank her arm away.

"What the fuck are you talking about?" I demanded.

She stared at me while I thought back over what happened.

"Okay," I allowed. "I acknowledge that it made me mad, but not at you. Not really. I was mad at the circumstance. Mad that we can't just be left alone. And extremely pissed off that you think you'll face it all alone. You are not alone anymore. Stop thinking like you are."

I let go of her arm so she could leave.

She didn't move, just stared at me.

I stared back.

She squirmed a bit, looking at her feet before peeking back up at me through her lashes.

I lifted my eyebrows. "Are you thinking food or sex? I can't tell."

"Yes," she said as her lips met mine. "Sex and then food, man-wife?"

"Sex and then food and then more sex?" I countered, already pulling her dress off as she pulled my shirt over my head.

"Missed you." She groaned as I kissed down her neck and cupped her breasts, pulling her with me back toward the stairs.

"This house needs a main floor bedroom," I complained, trying to go up the stairs backward. Things were further complicated when Sianna tugged my jeans down. "Shit!" I fell on my bare ass on the stairs.

"No more playing. Enough playing," Sianna said, sliding herself down my body. I rolled on the stairs, trying to avoid giving her rug burns as our bodies moved together.

And that's how Sianna and I ended up in flagrante on the stairs when Noah opened my front door.

"You know that's going to leave rug burns, right?" he asked, laughing. Then, I heard his phone camera shutter.

"What the fuck! Get out!" I yelled.

"Mom sent you pity fudge, but now I'm keeping it. You don't need pity fudge; you're having pity sex."

He closed the door.

"Damn," I muttered, kissing Sianna even as she laughed.

"I—" she started.

I covered her mouth, knowing what was coming. "No. No words. The binding is horrible to destroy. I don't think I could do it again."

She nodded, her smile sad as I moved my hand.

We were moving together again, slower and more gently, kissing, nipping, and teasing as the sensations built.

When I couldn't take it anymore, when Sianna was beyond words and near frustrated tears, I let my power roam free, felt her return it in kind, and shoved us both over the edge.

But not off the stairs.

"Dinner?" she asked a few minutes later.

"Grilled cheese?" I suggested.

"Bacon?"

"Of course."

24

Someone smacked my ass.

"Get up, stud," Janie said. "You have to sign for the car. Is it my car? Please say it's for me! It's such a pretty blue!"

I groaned.

"Get up! The Huntress went to check on everyone. The car guy says you have to sign. I understand his point. It's a fifty-thousand-dollar car."

I groaned again, throwing my legs over the edge of the bed to sit up.

"I love this," Janie breathed, eyeing me.

I pulled the covers over my waist. "Would you please go find my pants?"

Her eyes narrowed. "There are pants in your closet. You'll be dressed before I'm back."

"It's true," I agreed.

"First, no sex. Now, no show. What the fuck, Luke?"

"Please?" I asked.

"Fine." She flounced out of the room, humming to herself. I couldn't pick out the song.

I pulled on clothes and ran down the stairs.

"Holy shit, man. I'd still be in bed, too, if she was bouncing around my house. She's gotta be related to Marilyn Monroe, right?" the car guy breathed.

"I don't think so," I said, smiling. "Thanks for bringing the car. I signed for your tip. Happy new year."

"Happy new year to you, too!" he said cheerily, walking away as I closed the door.

I knew he'd looked at the paper with his tip when he yelled, "Ten thousand dollars!"

It was a new day. I was feeling good about life. A twenty percent tip felt right.

"Please let me drive it. Please! It's so pretty," Janie said, bouncing with joy. "I have to get Missy and Tammy from the airport today. Can I drive it? Please?"

I tossed the keys to her. "It's all yours. I need it tomorrow to go to the arena. Otherwise, have fun. Why do you all have the names of exotic dancers?"

"What?" she asked, confused.

"Candy, Janie, Missy, Tammy… There's not a 'Jen' among you," I muttered.

She frowned. "You don't like my name?" Her tone was actually… offended.

"I love your name. It suits you great. I just wonder why you all have similar names of… a certain type." I realized I'd backed myself into a corner over something stupid.

Her eyes narrowed. "You don't even know my girls."

"I'm sure they're great. Sianna said they were fine to come here. I'm glad for the help. I just... wondered."

"We're beast affinity women, Peacekeeper," she said coldly. "Our sole purpose in life is to find a man, get married, and make beastly babies."

My mouth dropped open, "Janie, I'm sorry. That's not what I was...." My words trailed off as she grinned.

"I know. I'm not mad. It's fun to mess with you, though. Missy is a stripper. You'll love her. Great muscle control. And don't lump Candy in with us. I'll scratch her eyes out if I get the chance."

"Wow," I murmured. "That was actual anger. I felt it."

"There's history with her," Janie said, the frown sitting unnaturally on her face.

"I heard about the thing with Daniel," I acknowledged.

"Daniel is a kind person in a bad position. He was very clear in his intentions. She just let him carry on, not signaling in any way that she wasn't interested. It was cold, and wrong on many levels. He's too good for her, and you're too good for her too. How could you claim her?"

"We're friends," I said defensively.

"You've given her a rather high standing with your claim. She's the *only* person you've claimed. That irritates the crap out of me."

"I don't know the significance of claiming someone," I admitted. "Would you explain while I make breakfast?"

"There's not much to explain, Luke," Janie said snottily. "It's exactly what it sounds like. You've claimed her as part of your role. People won't mess with her for fear of messing with you, and no one wants an unhappy Peacekeeper."

"That's it?"

"Pretty much. If you were anyone else, you'd be somewhat responsible for her actions and for punishing her misdeeds. But you're Peacekeeper. You can do whatever you want, and so can she. The rules don't apply to you, and they don't apply to her by extension."

"Huh," I said, thinking. "What if I claimed every beast affinity woman on the planet and declared them all free of the ridiculous rules?"

Janie's eyebrows shot up. "I hadn't considered that." She paused. "I don't think it'd work. Someone would test that, Peacekeeper or not. You'd have to make good on defending your claim. If someone disregarded it, you'd have to challenge them."

"Huh," I said again, still thinking. "What's on your agenda for today?"

"Well, first, you're making me breakfast. Then, I pick the girls up at O'Hare at noon. How about you?"

"After I make us all some breakfast, I need to talk to my dad about starting a non-profit, and I want to talk to Matthew."

Her nose scrunched up. "He's the Chaos one? Does he hate us?"

"Yes, he's the Chaos one. But, no, he would not be able to hate you," I tweaked her nose as I walked by on the way to the kitchen. "He's harmless."

25

"No, I'm not sorry," Matthew said, meeting my glare with his own. "I will snap their minds like toothpicks. I have enough control over my energy to do it, and you know it. You felt it on Sunday. I will call the wild things out and set them free if they hurt you again."

"It was my fault," I said, flabbergasted by his anger.

"I'm not claiming otherwise. You're a moron. Did you have to wait until the very last second to form the binding? I keep wondering if you actually formed it in time, or if Sam saved your ass by freezing us all like he did when he broke the tie in Tali's mind."

I rocked back on my heels, the air whooshing out of my lungs. "I'd not considered that. What does he call it when he does that? Does he call it in-between?"

"I don't know," he ground out. "I don't speak 'Sam.' Ask him. I doubt he'll answer, though. Even worse, I doubt you want to know the answer. The fact remains: if they swing for your neck again, I'm going to bend their minds to my will. I know I can do it too. I tested it."

"What? Tested it how?"

"Why do you think that guy freaked out on Sunday? I absolutely started bending his mind."

"Holy shit, Matthew! Don't do that!"

"They needed to understand exactly what they're playing with," he argued, staring at me. "And so do you. Don't put yourself in another situation you can't get out of. You think Beth is ruthless? Ha!"

I didn't know what to say. "I'm so sorry. I'm sorry, Matthew. I didn't think it would go the way it went."

"You know what I'm sorry for, Luke?" he asked, voice laced with sarcasm.

I waited, knowing he wasn't done with the verbal thrashing.

"I'm sorry it took you most of a fucking week to turn up. You spent the night at William's house over the weekend. You couldn't stop by?"

I made a fish face, my mouth opening and closing without words.

"I've had your back your entire life. I blew up part of the garage so you'd have an easy out on Wednesday. I was there on Wednesday night to see your neck sliced most of the way through and to try to heal you. I sat with you on Thursday when you were unconscious, just to make sure you kept breathing. There wasn't even a 'Hey man, I'm on the mend' from you. I know you have shit going on, but you fucking suck, Luke."

I blinked quickly, lost. Matthew and I didn't argue.

"Oh, for fuck's sake, I will beat your ass if you start crying," he threatened. "Stop it. I had my rant. What changed with the circle?"

"What?" I asked, confused.

Matthew sighed. I bit back a relieved laugh. The sigh was so familiar and welcome. It was Matthew's *'why are you so slow?'* sigh.

"You torched the binding Friday night?" he asked.

I nodded.

"The connection to the circle was fixed on Saturday? Or was the circle working on Friday? The wound looked bad on Thursday. By the time I saw you on Friday, it was a thin scar."

"No, the circle started working on Saturday. Adaline and Sianna figured out how to heal me together on Friday, making the wound better. I didn't do that. They did it."

"So, torching the binding to Sianna fixed the circle connection. Maybe. Did anything else happen before the circle started to work?"

"I don't think so."

"Can Sianna still heal you? Do you still cycle energy with her? Noah said you were bumping uglies on the stairs last night."

I winced. I'd refused to look at the family text thread.

"She can still heal me. The energy still cycles."

"Huh." Matthew went quiet, thinking.

"I really am sorry," I muttered.

"I know. Shut up. I'm thinking."

I stared at the wall, trying not to laugh.

"Don't hum," he complained.

"Sorry," I said again.

"Did you even realize you were humming?"

"No."

"Did you play some kind of music today?"

"No, not yet."

He glared. "You need to do that. You get grumpy when you don't. Now the blonde is there too. You'll upset your harem."

I threw a couch pillow at his head.

"Can Other-Luke make with the sex energy again? I kinda miss a randy Randa."

I threw the other couch pillow at his head.

"Think back," Matthew said, serious again. "Did you try to heal from the circle before you met Candy?"

"I don't think so," I said after a minute. "Not intentionally, at least. Maybe after Talise and I broke the axle on my car. I was sore until we got to the lake house. But I also drank a lot of beer that weekend."

"The night you met Candy, when your energy went nuts... was that the first time Other-Luke came out to play?"

"I don't think so. I remember that clearly. I don't think my lack of circle connection had to do with Candy or Charlie, Matthew. I felt the power slide through my body on Friday night. I was just in so much pain I didn't care. I think by forcing the binding to break, I also let the energy truly go. When Sam broke the tie in my brain, I wanted to die. It was horrible. Breaking that tie had nothing, and I mean absolutely nothing, on breaking that love binding."

"Did you bleed from your ears and nose?" Matthew asked.

"No. No blood. Just pain. Like my brain was on fire."

"I didn't feel your energy that night. I was in the next room. I didn't hear you or feel it."

"I know. There was no sense in trying to calm the pain. I had already accepted the reasons why the binding had to go." I shrugged, feeling sick to my stomach. "I guess I didn't want to dilute the experience. Using my power would have been like hiding behind the energy to numb the pain. I'm trying this new thing where I'm not a coward."

"How's that working out for you?" Matthew asked, smiling.

"There's something to be said for being a coward." I laughed.

Matthew shook his head. "I was a coward when I ran from Miranda. I meant it as a kindness. I meant for her to go on to bigger and better things. But I should have told her. I should have let her choose. Then, when that came back around, when she and I got together and balanced each other, I got some control over the energy."

I nodded in agreement. Matthew's energy was chaos. There was no control or direction until he had balance.

"You faced the hard shit without running from it. You got control. Maybe that's it." He didn't sound convinced.

"Uh, Luke?" he asked a moment later.

"Yeah," I answered, still thinking things through.

"Why are there three women bouncing around in front of your house? And don't take this the wrong way, but are they exotic dancers?"

I turned to look out the window behind me. "Oh, shit."

"I thought you weren't doing the harem thing?" Matthew asked, shaking with laughter as he reached for his phone.

"Do not take pictures!" I scolded.

"Are you kidding? We're chronicling this shit. Who are these women?"

"Janie, the blonde, is my assistant."

"And the other two?"

My voice came out stoic. "They're also going to be my assistants. They'll keep Janie company since I'm not interested in a relationship at this time."

Matthew froze, processing my words. "That seems like a lot of women for you to manage."

"I think they're self-entertaining," I mumbled, looking at the fascinating pattern of Matthew's living room rug. "Did Miranda pick the rug? I like it."

"These women are all staying with you? So, you'll have a harem of bisexual women traipsing around your house?"

I didn't bother answering. I just stared at the rug. It was a lovely rug.

"We need to get you a better doormat. 'Welcome' doesn't cover it."

"I hate you," I said.

"Can we paint your house?"

"Please don't tell them," I begged, even as Matthew typed on his phone.

"And… send. There. That's done."

My phone dinged in my coat pocket.

I sighed.

Matthew's phone dinged like mad in time with mine.

"You know, I have access to at least one estate that's not here. So, I could go live there."

"Is there more space? It seems like you're going to need it!" Matthew patted my shoulder in a show of support. "Go get 'em, Luke!"

WHILE I WAS hell-bent on facing reality and avoiding cowardice, I had no trouble with procrastination. I went out Matthew's back door, hopped his fence, and walked around the walking trail between the fence line and the wall to our gated community.

I wondered at the walking path. I was pretty sure my fence was the only one with a back gate on it. Did Sam plan this walking trail into our family compound so I'd have an easy way to avoid my harem? Hopping fences was easy after all of William's bodybuilding and training. Did this walking trail exist for my convenience? I thought about asking, then decided I didn't want to know.

I hopped the fence into my parents' backyard, startling Roscoe and Glinda. They each gave a startled bark and then shot me a look that clearly said, *Oh, it's just the stupid one.*

"Don't you judge me," I murmured to the dogs, even as I scratched their ears.

As I approached the house, I was surprised to realize Dennis was still there, hanging out in the kitchen with my mom. Coming through the back door, I took my wet shoes off in the mudroom.

"Hi Luke," my mom called. "You can't live here. Don't ask."

Well, there goes that idea, I thought. There was no way my siblings would let me live with them. They'd think the harem thing was too funny to allow me to avoid it.

"Sianna and Janie ate all my fudge," I said, trying for a second round of pity.

"I sent more fudge with Noah last night. Why sex on the stairs? That could not have been comfortable. If you're going to have a harem of women, you need to work on your patience," Darla said, choking back laughter as my uncle shook with silent mirth.

"Ha ha. No harem," I said again, ignoring the fact that my house was slowly filling with women.

Darla snorted. "I know. You'd have no idea what to do with that many women bossing you around. But it's hilarious. Janie is so sweet. I just love her."

"Yeah, I got that part when you taught her how to make the fudge." I scowled at Darla.

"I still won't teach you how to make the fudge. No. If you know how to make it, you'll make it every week, and then it won't be special anymore."

"I'm surprised you're still here, Dennis," I said, changing the subject.

He shrugged. "Ain't much happening at home right now. My girls are takin' care of my dogs. Your momma asked if I wanted to stay, so I did."

"We're having a nice visit," Darla said, patting her brother's arm. "He's an excellent cribbage player."

Something in her voice was ringing my alarm bells. I lifted my eyebrows at her.

She shook her head. *Not now,* her expression said.

"Is Dad home? He's usually home on Tuesdays, right?" I figured I'd find out what was going on with my uncle at some point. I had a purpose for this visit aside from avoiding the women taking over my house.

"He's downstairs, honey." My mom stomped her feet as she walked over to the basement door. "Luke's here," she called.

"What's he building?" I asked. When left to his own devices, my dad enjoyed building models. But he didn't like anyone to look at his work until he was finished with it.

Darla shrugged. "He hasn't talked about it yet. But he's paranoid about your brother spying on him."

"Ah, I didn't think about that. Dad did seem awfully upset when Sam went looking around the houses without his body."

"Your father called Jen yesterday to ask how to keep Sam out. She yelled at him. 'He's your son. Tell him no peeking.' He looked shamefaced after he hung up with her." Darla grinned.

"I thought we weren't supposed to talk about that," I muttered, eyeing Dennis.

"Meh." Darla shrugged again.

I could hear my dad's feet on the basement stairs.

"Lord Peace," he greeted me facetiously, "how are your ladies?"

I glared as everyone in the room laughed at me. "Can we talk about business things? I think I need a non-profit."

The teasing stopped immediately as my dad gestured toward the big room. "What's wrong?"

I explained about the people standing watch as well as Janie and her friends. I mentioned the other beast affinities too off to hold a nine-to-five job and the resulting financial strain on the overall community.

"Yes, absolutely," Hank said, reaching for his phone as we talked. "We'll form a business. But let's include Hennessy in this."

"Hennessy?" I asked, surprised.

"Yes, Lucas. Hennessy, who runs a multi-million-dollar security and private investigation firm."

"Wow! I had no idea it'd grown so big."

Hank nodded. "He hires and trains a lot of displaced veterans. He might need people attuned to security, even if they're not typical communicators. He's made a bit of an empire from working with people the world has mistreated. The first year or two, his operations were primarily based on us. He ran in the red as an expense center for Sam. Once he figured out how to make it work, he scaled it well—even more so since Beth joined the mix."

The front door slammed. A minute later, Hennessy turned the corner into the big room. "Are we turning your house into a strip club? I'm not a fan of that sort of traffic coming through here."

"Hennessy!" My dad barked, frowning.

"One of those women is a stripper, Hank. I ain't bein' a pig."

My dad turned to me. "No harem!"

"I agree!" I said, hands raised.

"What's with Sianna? I thought that wasn't happening. But, based on Noah's picture last night, that's still happening." My dad was glaring at me.

"I don't deserve that glare. There was a whole thing yesterday. I don't know if it's happening or not happening to be honest."

"What do you want?" Hank asked. "Do you know what you want? Once you decide that, everything is easier."

"I don't think I can have what I want, Dad. I don't think she can allow it."

Hank nodded in understanding. "Time, then. You'll figure it out. Patience. All you boys went from zero prospects to effectively married in no time at all. Give it some time for things to settle."

I snorted. "It took Jake most of two years!"

My dad rolled his eyes. "Jake was a goner from day one. It took him a while to get his act together, much like Hennessy."

Hennessy grinned. "I don't deny it. So why am I here?"

26

Wednesday morning started with an argument.

"No!" Sam yelled. "Absolutely not. Go take down the wards, then Adaline will help."

"We will take down the wards together when we arrive," Adaline murmured. "It will be fine."

"I can't Walk there, Addy! No. If something goes wrong before it's supposed to, I can't get to you."

I hesitated at the '*before it's supposed to.*' "Uh, Sam?"

"No," he yelled again, working himself into a fit. "Take Micah and Sianna, drive there, and take down the wards that prevent Adaline and me from Walking there. That happens first. Then, Adaline, Talise, and Matilda will join you."

"Does Matilda know she's going?" I asked, surprised.

"No," Sam barked. "I'll tell her. It's fine. She'll go. She must go. Then we'll all circle later, no more secrets between us."

"I don't know how to take down wards, Sam," I said, my words quiet and calm.

"Micah does. He'll show you. You might need Edgar to do it. I'm not sure how the wards work. Anyway, the wards have to come down first. We can't count on the bindings this time."

"Am I walking into danger again? Should I *not* go, Sam?"

"What? Stop it. I thought you got over this cowardly shit. You're going. You're just driving. You're not in immediate danger. Things are moving faster than Edgar realizes. That challenge will come before tomorrow's nightfall."

"Nate is in Rome," I disagreed. "John did something to make him stay away."

Sam's face lost all expression as his eyes lit with power. "How many times must I prove this power to you, Peace? How many times will we do this? I am not wrong."

"I'm not suggesting you're wrong," I said immediately, not wanting to tangle with Spooky Samuel.

His eyes continued to glow. "If his mental compulsions held against the Overlord's power, don't you think John would have saved his baby sister? He believes the stopgap will hold long enough, and he's correct. All the pieces are in play. Charlie and Ellie remain out of position but will move quickly. By nightfall tomorrow, we will be at war."

"What?" I demanded as the light left Sam's eyes. "War?"

"War," Sam agreed. "Those wards need to come down."

I GOT into the back seat of my new car. "I don't mind driving," I said again.

"No," Sianna disagreed.

"Is there an address?" Micah asked from his shotgun position, pulling up the navigation on his phone.

"I know where we are going," Sianna said. "No need to navigate."

"Yes, but I would like to know where we're going," Micah countered.

Sianna glanced at me in the rear-view mirror. I shrugged.

She spouted an address for Micah as she backed out of the driveway.

"Ah," Micah said under his breath. "I haven't spent much time in the area. There's not much out there."

Sianna nodded. "More now than in the past, but still fairly remote."

"I would've been glad to visit Edgar if I'd known where he was," Micah said. "He's a good man."

"The very best," Sianna muttered under her breath, her sadness radiating to me. My peace energy reached to soothe her hurt without my conscious effort.

"Sorry," I whispered, too low for Micah's ears.

"Did you push the energy intentionally?" she asked in my mind.

"No," I whispered again.

"Then there is nothing to apologize for, Peacekeeper. It is your nature to offer comfort. I do not fault you for it."

"Did your ladies really pack us a lunch?" Micah asked, grinning to himself.

I groaned, looking at the giant cooler bag next to me. "It appears so."

"There is fudge in that bag," Sianna said. "I can smell it."

"Really?" I perked up, reaching for the bag.

There was fudge, three different notes wishing me a good day, and an unmentionable that I hoped had been recently washed.

"The panties are clean," Sianna confirmed, laughing. "They are making fun of you."

"There are roast turkey sandwiches in here," I said, picking through the mound of food.

Micah stuck a hand back, mutely accepting a sandwich.

"Sianna?" I asked.

"No. I am still full. The girls made a wonderful breakfast." And they had. Pancakes, bacon, eggs, and fresh orange juice. "You will adapt to their silly and be glad they are there in time."

"They had already fed everyone and sorted through the shift schedule for the week before I was even awake," I admitted.

"Lazy Luke," Sianna said, smiling. "Not bright in the morning."

"Not bright before seven o'clock," I agreed. "I'm typically awake by then."

"Unless you've had an all-night sex marathon," Micah muttered, laughing. "That was fun for everyone. Explain again why the harem won't work?"

"Hey!" I objected to Sianna's laughter. "You're not supposed to laugh at that! Can you at least fake a bit of jealousy?"

"No," she said, still laughing. "You would not know what to do with such energetic women. Perhaps they will teach you over time."

"That's cold, Huntress," Micah scolded. "You could pretend to pine for him."

"Bah," she said, still laughing. "He may look at the young ones and enjoy their silly. It does not affect what we are."

"Too close," I muttered in warning, all traces of humor gone as I felt the bindings of familial love, friendship, and loyalty quaver between us. "Don't do that. I can actually feel it now."

She nodded in acknowledgment. "Sorry."

We were all quiet for a few minutes as we watched the empty fields pass around us.

"Did they send new pictures?" Sianna asked, laughing again.

"I don't know," I admitted.

"You did not check?" she asked.

"I took a hammer to my phone this morning. There are a lot of texts I don't want to read."

Micah exploded with laughter again. "I don't think that will work, Peace. This is why your brothers call you Pollyanna."

"Pollyanna?" Sianna asked, nose crinkled.

"What do you call him when he's behaving particularly naive and wholesome?" Micah asked, bemused.

"Huh," she murmured, thinking about it. "I do not like calling him a woman's name. It is a slight to women."

"Hey!" I yelled.

"You call him man-wife, though," Micah objected.

"Yes, but that is truth. He is caretaker and heart, the very center of his home."

Micah's lips tipped up. "I don't need to feel the bindings to know you dance close to that edge, Huntress." He took the hand Sianna had rested on the console between them and kissed it. "I'm glad. May they collect all of us, lonely and worthy, and give us a purpose."

We were silent for the remainder of the car ride.

"HOW DO WE TAKE THEM DOWN?" I asked Micah. Each ward was small, but they overlapped. We stood at the property gate as I stared at the hundreds of connected rings of wards before us.

"I have no idea," Micah admitted. "I would not even consider these wards."

"They are protections," Sianna offered. "We call them protections. They feel like your wards, just a little different."

"A lot different," Micah disagreed. "They don't use power. No one holds or controls them. They are like void spaces where specific power is not allowed."

"Sam said they have to come down." I looked at Sianna. "Where's Edgar? I've never been here during the day. This place is massive, and there are affinities everywhere. Hundreds of people. Am I about to sit on a throne again? Because I won't do that."

Her lips quirked. "He is coming. The people are families, Peacekeeper. Families who are eager for your help. They will do as you ask."

From where we stood outside the gate, I saw three men moving quickly in our direction.

"Micah! I did not expect you today. Peacekeeper, Sianna, why do you wait at the gate?" Godwin called.

I could feel Sianna's emotions roll unsteadily and offered my hand. She took it without a word.

"Uncle. He is my uncle," she said in my mind. *"How many knew and did not tell me? I am a fool. I was made a fool after all I have given."*

I gently squeezed her fingers, shaking my head in disagreement. I needed to practice mental communication so I could answer her.

"The wards must come down, Edgar," Micah called. "How do we remove the protections so the Mistress and Walker may be here?"

Less than ten yards from us, the men slowed in their walk.

"I hadn't considered that," Edgar admitted. "They come from my father's power. I brought them here from England."

"They're older than that," Godwin disagreed. "My father brought them to Rome from the Peacekeeper before him. The Circle has never been welcomed among affinities. Legend says Walkers of old have tried to subvert the Peacekeeper."

"What do you mean you brought them here?" I asked. "Wards are drawn, not carried."

All three men shook their heads in unison, now joining us at the gate.

"No," Edgar disagreed. "It's more like a stamp than a drawing. I memorized the nature of the protection and then imprinted it here with an act of will."

"Huh," Micah grunted. "They are like our markers then—the markers we use for travel. It's an imprint of will rather than energy. Break the will that made them, Luke."

I stared at him, confused.

"Focus your will and break the ring in front of you. I think it will work if this is a Peacekeeper thing."

Out of the corner of my eye, I saw John wrap his arms around Sianna, holding her close and whispering something to her. Sianna nodded, eyes on the ground as she accepted a similar hug from Godwin.

"Try it," Micah prodded again, watching the exchange but having enough decency to keep his questions to himself.

Opening my sight, I watched the rings of glowing hunter-green power undulate throughout the estate. They were a giant web of protections, covering every bit of land in sight. "Holy shit, Edgar. How long did it take you to do this?"

I felt his amusement without looking at him. "More focus than time, Peacekeeper."

As Micah suggested, I applied my will, trying to snap the protection circle directly in front of me. It broke, only to be repaired immediately by the connected rings.

"Are you able to move them?" Micah asked Edgar.

"No, I wouldn't even know where to start."

"Can you still make them?" I asked. "Can you make one while I watch?"

Edgar frowned but walked outside the gates where no protections existed. With my sight, I saw his will force the shape of the circle around him and then watched as he infused it with a touch of peaceful energy.

"Ah," I said, finally understanding the color of the protection rings. "I understand."

Without another word, I sucked the power from Edgar's newly drawn protection. It folded immediately. I turned back to the estate, realizing I was about to hoover up a tremendous amount of energy. "Well, I guess we need the energy for the kids anyway," I mumbled to myself.

Twenty minutes later, the protection circles were gone, and my entire body glowed with energy. It was a new level of overload for me.

"So, this doesn't feel great," I admitted, turning to Sianna. "Can we have sex?"

"Peacekeeper," John whispered, ignoring me. "Do you feel the bindings? You should have bindings to all of us—all affinities—can you find them?"

I hesitated, looking for what he suggested. "No," I said. "I think that would be very apparent, and I don't feel anything like it."

"Push it out like you did last week," Edgar suggested. "Push it through the land, as far as you can make it go. It won't hurt anyone, Luke. It's Peace. Let it go."

I tried to let the energy go. Nothing happened.

"You did this last Wednesday, Peacekeeper. You can do this," Sianna said quietly. "You did it with enough precision and control to exclude me from it. How did you do it last week?"

"I thought of the world turning and admitted to myself that the world would keep turning whether I lived or died," I said, feeling stupid. "I don't know. I wanted to push it out and share it so they would understand what I was, so we wouldn't have problems."

She nodded. "Share it now because you want to help those that are here."

"Is this going to turn the arena into an orgy? Are they all going to get overloaded with sexy energy?" I stared at Sianna.

"It did not happen last week. I do not think today would be different. I think that aspect may dwindle when you share the energy with more people," she offered.

Somehow, that made sense to me. Like pieces of a puzzle clicking together in my brain, I found all the affinities within the range of my senses and pushed the energy to them.

"Better. Much better," I breathed, relieved.

I looked around, surprised by the absolute silence. Godwin, John, and Edgar stood before me, heads bowed in respect. Micah stood on one side, mouth hanging open. Sianna stood on the other side of me, holding my hand, pleasure and pride shining in her eyes.

"Peacekeeper," she breathed, stretching on her toes to kiss my stubbly cheek. "Well done."

I narrowed my eyes. "I swear you were the curvy blonde a minute ago. Don't be this version, now!" I complained, looking at the short brunette form she assumed when hanging out with her dad.

She smirked. “I told you. Most recognize me in this shape.”

“Let them see you as you are, Sianna. No more hiding,” I suggested, squeezing her fingers again. I watched as her form elongated and the planes of her face grew sharper.

“As the Peacekeeper demands,” she said, quirking a small smile at me.

“Sure, now she listens,” I mumbled.

27

I could feel the children as we approached the arena. My stomach churned with dread, knowing I was about to witness the suffering of hundreds of people between the children and their families.

It didn't occur to me that I should warn big, tough Micah.

He gasped as the children came into view. "Dear God," he choked out. "I had no idea. I would have helped. Edgar, you should have told me!"

"I don't know what you would have done, Micah," Edgar responded. "Hate would not help these souls. Even your newest incantation of energy would be a stretch—there was no wrongdoing for them to repent. But give your Lord Peace the credit he deserves. They are already improved. Already calmer."

Edgar turned to me. "None are medicated. We thought it might be easier in here with space, but if you are uncomfortable here—"

"No," I cut him off, already sinking into my power. "I'm fine,

Edgar. But Micah, will you ask her to bring my guitar? It's in my living room."

I could feel Micah's dread radiating from him. He was adamantly opposed to these people knowing Mistress Life shared the ability to move through space like the Walker. I turned to meet his eyes. "Do you believe anyone in this building would harm her knowing she helped to bring relief?"

He nodded in acknowledgment of the truth before turning to leave. "I will await the Ladies outside. They should be warned before entering."

I walked out into the arena proper, taking in the crowds of people. There had to be at least as many people in the stands as there were the week before. Some wept. Others breathed silent prayers. Most looked on, vacant-eyed and afraid to hope.

There were probably a hundred children on the floor of the arena with me. They ranged in age from infancy to about ten years old, and they were all restrained in some way. They were a danger to themselves and those around them without the restraints.

Edgar sighed, coming to stand beside me. "This first group is primarily from the Midwest. We could organize them the fastest. I thought we'd see how this went and then adjust with future groups."

"How many?" I breathed, horrified.

"I believe there are roughly seventeen hundred people that need some form of assistance," Edgar said, voice low. "There are varying degrees of damage, and not all the damage is related to energy."

I nodded in understanding, decidedly ignoring his embarrassment. It wasn't his fault people thought inbreeding was a good idea. Edgar, of all people, should not be forced to apologize for that sort of ugliness.

I felt Adaline's power slam through the arena and knew she'd encircled the whole building. I turned back toward the entryway, awaiting her arrival.

"Did Mistress Life just—" Edgar started, mouth hanging open.

"You have no idea, my friend. None at all. We will see this done. Wherever we need to go, whoever needs the help, it will be done," I assured him while trying not to notice the startled, appalled looks on John and Godwin's faces.

"Luke," Edgar said urgently. "She closed the circle without him. These people are *inside* the circle. It will not hold."

I scrunched up my face. "As I told you, I think you have that part wrong. They use the circle differently. But, for what it's worth, I'm guessing Micah will hold the circle with Light and Water outside. There might be fire. Matilda doesn't like to be cold. Don't let it alarm you."

Adaline made an entrance then, glowing with the white fire of life energy. She walked directly toward me, holding out her hand. I took it without question. "Share your energy, Peace."

At her prompting, I felt the energy slide around within me, spreading throughout my body and then exploding outward to the circle.

"Light," Adaline demanded, sharing the mental command with everyone in the circle. Matilda's energy burned through the circle, lighting up the knotted energy in each child as I watched.

"Water," Adaline projected in time with Talise's energy rolling through the room.

"Well, that's kind of nice," I said aloud. "I don't need to do them separately. I can see them all. Can you?"

Adaline nodded, tears dripping down her cheeks. "I cannot do the net. We should do your net."

"Where's the guitar?" I asked.

She blinked at me.

"I told Micah to tell you to bring the guitar," I said, annoyed.

"*Micah!*" Adaline mentally yelled.

"I forgot that part!" he yelled back, using his voice. "I was thrown by the mass of suffering children!"

"Go get the guitar!" Adaline yelled back to him. "I know you have a marker inside those wards!"

"I don't have one here," he yelled back, obviously annoyed to be bickering at high volumes in front of hundreds of people. "Do it without the guitar!"

"I believe there is a keyboard in the house," Edgar offered.

"Ach!" I yelled. "Gross. Never mind. Addy, the net comes with the natural life rhythms. First, you align breathing and heartbeats, then thoughts, and then you pull yourself out of the pattern while leaving everyone else in it."

She blinked. "You want to listen to the breath and heartbeats of a hundred tortured children?"

"That's how I do it. It's not hard."

"I don't think I can do that, Lord Peace," she admitted, biting back a smile. "So, I will leave you to it."

I sighed before I started walking among the children, touching each one for a brief moment, just long enough to sense their patterns and braid them with all the others.

About a third of the way through the crowd of kids, I stopped at one of the boys. His rhythms were so far out of whack, I wondered if he was having some sort of seizure. "Addy!"

"Oh," she said, making an unhappy little noise. "Go, Luke. I will help this one."

"Be careful," I warned, watching her unbind his arms. "The children do not always know reality."

"No, this one does not know reality. Only pain," she said aloud. Her words continued in my head. *"He knows torture. His family has been cruel, trying to beat the 'demon' out of him. We will tell John."*

I nodded in agreement even if her preference for telling John, of all the elders, surprised me. I continued on, finding two more children beyond the help of my net.

After touching the last child, I sat where I was and closed my eyes. Then, rotating my head, I released my energy, holding the healthy bindings safe from those that were knotted. In one swift motion, I willed the other bindings free.

It was good that I sat. I would have fallen over from exhaustion if I had been standing. Even as that realization dawned, the circle's energy rushed into me, filling me with life and fire. I let go of the mental webbing, noticing the children were still wide awake, turned to focus on me.

"It's done," I called to Edgar. "I think the circle made it easier on everyone. They're fine, though."

The kids started looking around in confusion, the meanings behind their expressions obvious: *Where the heck am I? Where's my family? Why'd that weird dude touch my hand? Why is that lady glowing with white fire?*

There was murmuring in the stands mixed with sounds of disbelief.

"Really," I yelled for the whole arena to hear. "It's done. Come get your kids. They're confused. Addy, break the circle?"

"John," her voice snapped like a whip. "I require your

attention."

I didn't ask what happened with those three kids, but I was confident they'd know joy in the future. At Adaline's whispered words, a look of pure rage settled over John's features. I had no doubt he would see them safely to a home of love.

As families reunited with the children they thought they'd lost, I made my way out of the arena with Sianna, Edgar, Godwin, and John. Adaline walked with us until she reached Micah.

"The guitar?" she prodded.

"I was distracted. Sorry," Micah said, clearly displeased with Adaline's admonishment.

"He might have been able to help quicker," she said, laying it on thick.

"It took fifteen minutes," I argued. "I'm not even sure the guitar would have worked."

Adaline turned to me with a straight face. "Don't ruin this for me. He is forever coaching and needling me. It's nice to have a turn."

Micah sighed, watching as Talise walked toward us. "Can we go home?"

"Where's Matty?" Talise asked, just as a fireball erupted on the other side of the building, followed by mad, cackling laughter.

"Did Jake come?" I asked, wondering at the male sound of it.

"No, he went to work today," Talise said as we walked in Matilda's direction.

Rounding the corner, we found Matty and Daniel laughing

hysterically, playing games... with fireballs.

"That can't be safe," I yelled.

"I'm not sorry!" Matty yelled back. "He's like me! He does this better than Sam!" As we watched, she tossed Daniel a fireball and laughed as he kicked it around like a ball. "I'm not that coordinated," she admitted. "I'd fall on my ass."

"You're Lady Light!" Daniel argued as if that explained everything.

"What the hell?" I whispered, glancing at Sianna.

She was smiling, but her eyes were full of tears. "Leave him," she whispered back. "He deserves a friend."

"He'll have a lot of friends if he joins our circle," I countered.

"Ah!" Adaline exclaimed, turning to John with slitted eyes. "You await Samuel's invitation to our circle? My invitation is not good enough?"

Eyes huge, John looked to me for help.

I shrugged.

"Mistress, I think he did not want to assume his welcome," Godwin said, speaking for John.

"You are welcome. You are all welcome. You will come to my circle. Tonight. It must be done. Sam and I have discussed it. Luke, the farmhouse. Bring them with you tonight. Matilda! Now!" Adaline snapped.

"Addy? Why are you mad at me?" I asked. I could feel it radiating off her. She was epically pissed at me and taking it out on everyone else.

Eyes burning with white fire, she turned on me. Words echoing with power, the world shook around us. "You will find them all. It was nothing. No work at all for you. The suffering and pain took nothing but a moment to resolve. Around the world, I feel them, Lucas Peacekeeper. I cannot do what you did. They have suffered while awaiting your presence. No more. No more hiding yourself. You will fix them all."

"Yes, Addy. I agree. I absolutely agree. I knew I needed to do this!" I said, trying to calm her.

The fire left her eyes. "I did not," she said, voice full of shame. "I thought I could do this. I thought I could help life and keep you safely and selfishly within our circle. I argued against you. But you were right to do this."

I nodded in acknowledgment of her unspoken apology. "It will be done, Mistress Life."

"I'll take you wherever we are needed, as Edgar guides us. We'll stand this circle to make it easier."

I nodded again in agreement.

"I'll see you all tonight," she said, smiling at the others and then disappearing with Talise, Micah, and Matilda.

"What?" Daniel asked, extinguishing the fireball he held. "Where did they go? I didn't see the Walker."

"I'm extremely thirsty," I admitted, staggering in place a bit. "It's to do with the energy, I think. Hungry and thirsty. Is there a faucet somewhere nearby I can drink a couple gallons of water from?"

SIANNA and the elders watched in morbid fascination as I guzzled water as quickly as they could hand it to me.

"It was not like this before," Sianna said, concerned.

"More. More children. More power," I offered between gulps.

"Less time, though. Not even a quarter of the time you

spent with the children in the church basement. That was amazing. My father could not have done it," Edgar said.

"Did he get thirsty?" I asked.

"Hungry," Edgar and Godwin said together.

"A bottomless pit and always a skinny stick of a man," Godwin continued, smiling.

I shrugged. "Food wouldn't make me sad, but I'm so thirsty."

"You were thirsty after the injury. I thought it was the blood loss," Sianna said, obviously sorting through her memories. "Were you thirsty going into the arena that night? After you used the power?"

"No. Not thirsty like this. Matthew gets thirsty like this," I said, thinking aloud.

"Lord Chaos?" Godwin asked, voice tentative.

"It is worse than that," Sianna countered. "Lord Pandemonium. Why did he take that name? Why that name specifically? Has he always intended us harm?"

"What?" I scowled at her. "No. Matthew doesn't mean you harm. He was pissed off at me. Sorry he screwed with your mind, Godwin. He wasn't sure he could affect you and was testing."

"That is terrifying," Godwin admitted. "I felt him and could not stop it from happening."

"Yeah. For what it's worth, he's more scared of his power than you are. He's spent his entire life trying to contain it. He would not harm an innocent. He studied Ancient Greek mythology in school. Being Lord Pan was more entertaining for him than being Lord Chaos. It was not intentional. We didn't even know about beast affinities when we took the names."

"Was his power tied? Did they tie him like they tied you?"

Sianna asked.

"Tied?" Edgar roared, suddenly furious.

"They tied him. The circle he stood as a child tied his power because he lacked control. The Walker destroyed the tie shortly before they took the names," Sianna explained to the outraged elders.

"That's barbaric," Daniel muttered, horrified. "Not even Nathaniel would suggest such a thing."

"Sianna and I have been through this. My energy was out of control. They couldn't close the circle with me in it—"

"You're telling me that Mistress Life, who closed a circle with nearly a thousand people *in the center* today, could not stand a circle with you?" Edgar interrupted.

"No, that's not what I'm saying. Back it up and try to remember that my family did not know what we were. Until this past summer, we had no idea...."

I spent the next hour outlining how my family came into our powers, how Matilda found Jake, and how Jen came to be among us. I left out the details of the pool table, knowing Matty wouldn't appreciate me sharing that little tidbit.

I decided to save it for a special occasion.

"They are unshadowed. There is no corruption at all within the circle. *Micah* is the most corrupt among them—righteous, avenging Micah." Godwin scratched his cheek before continuing. "What is it that Mistress Life wants?"

"She wants you all to stand a circle with us," I said, unsure how there could be any confusion. "She was pretty clear about that."

"I understand that part." Godwin smiled. "What is it she intends to gain? What does she want in exchange for helping John and maybe Daniel?"

My eyes darted between them. "I'm not sure you understand how our circles work."

"There is a price for everything, Luke. What is it the Mistress wants? Is there some portion of power or control she desires from us?" Edgar asked. "Before we stand a circle, I would know the cost."

I stared at them, dumbstruck.

"If you don't know," Edgar offered, "we could negotiate with the Walker."

"Edgar," I said, voice cold. "What have I asked of you? What have I demanded from you in exchange for my assistance?"

"Peacekeeper, please don't misunderstand—" he started.

I cut him off with a jerk of my hand. "She came here today and closed a circle to help. Micah, Lady Water, and Lady Light came to help. What did they ask of you in return?"

He sat silently before me, eyes downcast.

"My family wants nothing but to help," I said, tone gentler. "Samuel believes Daniel belongs to our circle. Adaline thinks she can help John cycle energy. Is the thought of uniting the Empowered and the Affinities so disgusting? It is all the same energy."

We sat in silence for most of a minute before I spoke again. "If you won't do it for yourselves, would you do it for me? My power has grown. They won't let me stand our regular circle until we know that I won't unbalance it and hurt the less empowered. I love my circle. I miss it. I'd like to know if I still belong to it."

"We will go," John croaked, nodding in agreement. "I do not believe your brother means to harm us so long as no harm comes to those who belong to him."

I nodded. "Thank you."

28

I drove to the farmhouse where my family held circles. Sianna sat stiff and silent next to me while the beast affinity elders followed in the car behind us.

"How are you?" I asked. I couldn't get a read on her emotions or thoughts. She was either doing her best to hide from me or was just completely zoned out next to me.

"Tired," she admitted. "More tired than I can ever remember being. I will sleep tonight and trust that your family will keep you safe."

"There are roughly a hundred other people standing guard."

"They are alarm bells, not warriors," she countered, yawning. "What are the girls making for dinner?"

"I have no idea."

"Can you ask Janie? Do you have that control yet?"

"No." I changed lanes in traffic, watching to be sure the other car followed us. They had navigation, but Chicago evening traffic was annoying. "We should practice sharing thoughts. I tried to respond to you today and realized I couldn't."

"Lazy Luke," she teased, smiling. "We do not stand this circle in the fields near home. Where are we going?"

There was a slight sound of unhappiness. "Near your home," she corrected herself before I could speak. "I apologize."

My mind exploded with possible responses, all of which walked the dangerous line of admitting to real, deep feelings again. I swallowed them down. "No offense taken."

"Where are we going?" she asked again, her emotions twisting unhappily within her.

"My family's larger circle is known as Harbor. We stand the circle in a more rural area, outside of DeKalb, at the farmhouse of one of the elders. You'll probably meet some of the circle tonight, including those vicious elders that tied my power when I was a teenager. They're not the monsters you believe them to be, Sianna. I probably would have died without their help."

"You did not need a circle," she said again. "You needed affinities to share your energy."

"Maybe," I allowed. "But I found a circle, not an affinity. They did everything they could to help me."

Thirty minutes of silence later, I turned into the farmhouse driveway, surprised to recognize only a few cars that didn't belong to my family. This was going to be a small circle.

"Huh," I muttered, pulling into one of the paved spots.

Sianna went from dozing to high alert. "What is wrong?"

"Nothing. There are just not many people here besides family. I thought it would be the wider circle."

"How big is the circle?"

"Just over a hundred people usually, plus my family."

Sianna stared at me.

I lifted my eyebrows, asking a question without words.

"Your normal circle is a hundred people? No wonder the Mistress closed the arena without effort today."

"Harbor was a large circle, even before we came into our powers. Greggory held the center with more than seventy people."

"Harbor. Greggory of Harbor," Sianna said, the pieces clicking together in her mind. "I know of this circle. I did not put it together. I assumed your family founded your own circle rather than taking over another."

"Nope, I've been in Harbor since I was fourteen. Greggory held the center with Ben, Jared, and Nora at the corners. When my family took the names, Jared left the circle and the other elders made way for us, opting to stay and help us learn. If you think we're clueless now, you should have seen us six months ago.

"Gregg, Ben, and Nora are here along with Talise's parents, Mike and Monica. Claire is also here. She's married to Hank's best friend. She introduced me to the circle.

"Sianna, I swear none of these people intended me harm. None of them. There is no reason to lash out at them. It's funny when you make William contemplate the meaning of life, and it's hilarious when you make Sam squeal like a pig, but these are good people."

She smiled a bit. "I will not punish them for ignorance. Do not worry so much."

I nodded, opening my door to get out of the car.

Nora walked out onto the farmhouse porch as we approached. "Lucas," she chided. "What have you done to yourself?" Then she was hugging me, sobbing into my coat.

"I'm okay, Nora. I'm all better. All healed," I soothed, shuffling into the house with her.

"Take off your coat. Let me see. Did they really…" Her words trailed off as she touched the faint line around my neck. It was only noticeable if you looked for it.

"I think it'll be gone soon," I offered. "It becomes a little less noticeable every day, and it's only been a week."

"Oh, my God," she sobbed, hugging me again. "We almost lost you!"

"Lucas," Greggory breathed, joining the hug as he kissed my forehead. "I cannot stand the thought of losing another son. What were you thinking?"

"I swear I'm okay. All healed up. Sam's planning worked out. Things are just a little whacky now."

The third Harbor elder, Ben, shook my hand as he joined us in the entryway. "Everyone scoot," he admonished. "Our guests are waiting behind you. Lucas, would you do introductions, please?"

"HOLY HELL," Matilda complained as we walked out into the field behind the farmhouse. "Too cold! Too much snow! I just melted this shit on Monday!" Then, in a flash of light and heat, one hundred yards of snow melted. "Lucy. Knock it off with the wind!"

"It's natural wind, Matty. Not my fault," Lucy objected. "It's winter. Why do you live in Chicago if you hate the cold?"

Matilda glared at Lucy even as she surrounded the open ground in the field with a ring of fire.

Behind Sianna and me, I could hear Daniel laughing. "I love her," he muttered. "I love everything about this."

"Go stand by her," Sam said, lips turned up in his little Sam smile. "I'm not sure where you go yet, but we'll start there. John and Godwin, stand together anywhere you'd like. Edgar to one side of Luke, Sianna on the other."

"I don't need the circle, Walker," Edgar objected. "I will just watch."

Sam frowned in confusion. "Why?"

"Edgar," I barked, annoyed. "Come here. Stop it."

"What's wrong?" Sam asked. "You don't want to do this? You don't have to if you don't want to, but it's worth trying."

Edgar's eyes darted around the circle before landing on me.

"He doesn't trust us," Adaline realized, voice sad. "He doesn't know or trust us. He thinks someone empowered trapped him as he was for centuries."

"Oh." Sam sighed, the sound conveying his hurt. "No harm, Edgar. No harm to you or yours. There is no cost and no demand. You are welcome here. Thank you for helping to save my brother."

Edgar's expression relaxed, and I knew he'd made some sort of false equivalency in his mind, in which he'd already paid the price for participation by helping me.

"Other than my circle today, have any of you stood a circle before?" Adaline asked as she walked around us.

Sianna was the only one to nod.

That threw the other affinity elders.

"When did you stand a circle?" Daniel asked, jealous.

"Last week. With them," Sianna said. "The Walker demanded it. It helped balance the Peacekeeper before Wednesday. I am not sure he could have withstood the tithe of power if we had not done the circles."

There was a pause before she spoke again, obviously answering something asked telepathically. "No, Edgar. They took nothing from me and asked for nothing but my help pulling energy from him."

I was running out of patience with Edgar's distrust. "Where are Mom and Dad?" I asked.

"They stayed home with Dennis," Jake replied. "His mind's still too jacked up to do this."

"He's so strange to look at now," Jess added. "Under my sight, there are holes where his emotions and personality should be. It's getting better, but he was seriously fucked up before."

"Ah, that's why he's still with the parents?" I asked.

"Yeah," Jake agreed. "Plus, I think Mom likes the company. They seem to get along well now despite the fact that he was a fucking asshole when they were younger."

I felt John's anger spike from where he stood with Godwin.

"He lives?" Godwin asked, surprised. "Your mother's brother lives?"

My annoyance ratcheted up a few more notches. "Yeah, I told you. I don't have a vengeful turn to me."

"He was a monster," Godwin argued. "He tormented her. By his own admission, he enjoyed seeing those weaker than himself in pain."

Micah sighed. "And I used to fill the world with hate, Godwin. He found his way to being a decent human being."

"I will close the circle in a moment. You will feel it close. You might see it. Be warned, it might fall," Adaline said, eyes on me. "I don't know if Luke can stand where he is anymore."

I tried not to feel dread, but it was there as I closed my eyes. Harbor was made up of my second family. I loved the flow of energy in a circle. It was damn near addictive.

As it closed, I felt Adaline's energy flicker around me and then explode upward.

"Well, that's different," Jess drawled. "Puking Peace is taking over things. The circle's up, though, Addy."

I looked around. The field was glowing with Matilda's fire. The line of our circle was clear as could be. The circle shone with the pure white light of Adaline's life energy. Then, overlaying it like a secondary circle, my forest green peace energy radiated upward. "It's like two circles," I muttered.

Sam gasped. "Yes! YES! Let's do that. Addy, break the circle."

She stared at him in confusion.

"I saw it. It was different but similar. I saw it years ago. Let's try it. Break this circle so they can leave it." Sam was shouting in his excitement.

We all watched as Adaline dispersed the circle she'd just made, then turned, as one, to stare at Sam.

"Okay! Okay! I think this is even better. It's going to be better! I didn't get it. But maybe now I do. It might be great. Wildflowers, Addy! We're going to make circles of wildflowers! Not right now, but eventually. When we're all together. It'll be like flowers. I get it now. But not now. Now it'll just be two circles. But two circles together. Joined circles! I think this will work. He doesn't stand our circle. He stands *his* circle," Sam babbled, talking too quickly to easily follow.

"Uh, Adaline?" Will asked, looking for a translation.

She shrugged.

"No, listen. It's going to work. I know it will. Lüke, get out.

Out of my circle. Go be your own circle. You go to his circle, Sianna. Edgar, Godwin, and John, you go with Luke. No. No, Daniel. You stay. You go where Luke was. You're in both circles."

"Sam," Greggory said, already shaking his head.

"No, it'll work, Gregg. We're going to try it. Just wait. Let me try! I didn't think this was us, but it might be us! Luke, make Daniel the northern point of your circle, and he'll be the southern point of mine. Everyone rotate! I'm serious. We're going to try this!"

There was a lot of sighing as everyone moved. We knew it was easier to try what Sam wanted than to argue with him.

Sianna stared at me, waiting for instructions.

I shrugged. "Stand opposite Daniel. Godwin and John stand opposite Edgar, I guess."

"Perfect. It's perfect!" Sam cheered. "Addy, start at Daniel and go clockwise. Luke, start at Daniel and go the other way around your circle."

"You want me to close the circle?" I asked. "Then what?"

"You stand the center of your circle, and we'll stand the center of ours, but it's one thing. You'll see. It works. I know it'll work."

I shrugged again, doing as I was told.

"Don't close it. Wait for Addy to get back. Then, close the circles at the same time," Sam instructed, almost bouncing in excitement.

Adaline rolled her eyes, grinning at me as she rounded the circle. I laughed with her, sharing her amusement at Sam's buoyancy. When we closed our circles, I swung her up into a hug, making her laugh before we each turned to the centers of our circles.

It wasn't until I stopped moving that I noticed the dead silence around me.

I looked at my circle, glowing bright green in the winter grass, and then looked at Adaline's circle, glowing blindingly white. The two circles met, crossing energy between them, where I'd hugged Adaline—where Daniel stood.

Sam exhaled, dumping glowing purple love, glittering with excitement in his circle. I watched as his energy washed through my circle.

"It works," he grinned. "Do the peace thing."

I pulled my power all the way forward, shoving peace into my circle and watched as the tension left Edgar's shoulders.

"Okay?" I asked Sianna, wondering if the field was about to turn into a strange beacon of lust.

"Just peace," she said, smiling.

Things got a little silly after that, as our family circles were prone to do. The speed at which the energy traveled through the joined circles seemed to fluctuate, but neither circle gave any sign of faltering.

"Daniel," Samuel called in his booming Walker voice. "What is your name?"

"Uh, Daniel?" Daniel asked, confused.

"Why does everyone get this wrong?" Sam complained. "Everyone. Miranda is the only person that truly understood what she was before I asked. You belong to our circle, Daniel. You have a name like I am Walker, Addy is Mistress, Matilda is Light, and Luke is Peace. What is *your* name?"

He looked at me, lost.

I shook my head. "It's fine if you don't know. It'll come in time."

"You really think I'm of your circle?" Daniel asked Sam, sounding a bit awestruck.

"Yes," Sam and Adaline said together.

"Whether Luke stands our circle or his," Adaline added, "you belong among us. It feels better, right?"

"Yes." Daniel's quiet word was almost a groan of relief. "Yes."

Then, without warning, Adaline walked from her circle right into mine… without breaking either circle. She grinned. "I thought that would work."

"Oh, hello," I said, laughing as she stood in the center of my little circle.

She kissed my cheek before heading over to John. "Let's sit," she said, pulling him down with her. "May I help?"

After John gave a slow nod of acceptance, she smiled as she touched the sides of his head. "I don't believe it will hurt but tell me if it does."

Slowly but surely, pulses of dark green energy flowed from John.

"You see?" she asked. "That is how you let the energy go in a circle."

The pulses came faster and lasted longer until John eventually laid back on the ground. "Dizzy," he muttered. "Better, though. Hungry and dizzy."

"Stay there," Adaline whispered, standing again to come back to me. "Can you pull the energy from the circles?"

My brow furrowed, confused. "Why?"

"I can find the children, Luke. Between Godwin, John, and Edgar, the origins of most affinity family lines stand here. We can try to help."

"Oh." I gasped, dropping to the ground immediately. "Let's try."

It took Adaline and me a while to figure out how to share her mental connections to the lives that needed attention. It was exhausting work, more difficult from afar. We eventually had to stop from fatigue, and we lost count somewhere along the way. But Adaline estimated that we'd helped roughly a third of the children trapped within their own life energy before calling it a night.

DANIEL ENDED up driving us to the cornfield houses. My family had been bickering over who was driving which car home, knowing neither Sianna nor I were capable of safe driving on the dark winter roads.

"I'll drive them," Daniel interjected quietly.

Will shook his head. "Sorry, we're just arguing to argue. You don't need to do that. We'll get them back. You can go home."

Daniel hesitated. "I don't have a home, and I would like some time with my sister if you don't mind me within your wards. I'll find my way back to the Peacekeeper's estate after they are home safe."

"Stay tonight," Sianna muttered. "Please stay and watch tonight. I would like to sleep."

Daniel nodded. "Then I'll stay and watch. I'll leave before daybreak and disturb nothing. I swear it."

Adaline was glowering at him. "If you are welcome in our circle, you are welcome in our space, Daniel. No oaths are necessary. There are no enemies here. You felt who we are in that circle as much as we felt who you are."

It was the truth. Daniel had fed the circle wonder and joy. Afterward, the circle took loneliness, longing, and heartache from him.

I tossed him the car keys without another word.

"Janie's girlfriends are here," Sianna mumbled from the backseat as we turned past the guardhouse. "I do not know if I told you that. Missy and Tammy are here."

After he turned into the driveway, Daniel looked at me, eyebrows raised.

"No harem!" I objected. "She asked if her friends could help. I didn't realize there was more to it."

"She's a rabbit," Daniel countered, laughing.

"We're back," I called, pushing open the front door.

They'd rearranged my living room furniture while we were gone. A week and a half ago, I would have lost my mind over it. Now I rather liked the new layout. My piano was more of a centerpiece.

"Daniel!" Missy squealed, jumping up and wrapping her legs around his waist as she kissed his face. "How are you here?"

"I'm visiting," he said, grinning at her. "I'll watch tonight while the Huntress rests."

She squealed again. "We'll put on a show!"

"Not that kind of watch." He spun her in place as she dropped her feet to the ground. "You look well. No forms, though?"

"No," Missy said, mouth pursed into a pout. "Maybe here, though."

"Maybe," Daniel agreed, greeting Tammy and then Janie in turn.

"What happened?" Janie asked me. "You look terrible."

"Hard work," I slurred. "Food?"

"Food." She agreed. "Sit. We'll bring food. What were you doing?"

"Tonight, our Peacekeeper and the Mistress freed roughly five hundred children from being trapped within their affinities," Daniel said, his tone proud. "It was the most amazing thing I have ever seen. I don't think the Empowered and Affinities have ever worked together with such incredible results."

"Wow, Edgar moved people fast!" Janie said, surprised.

"No," Daniel disagreed. "They did the work from within a circle. They helped a group of children in the arena this afternoon. But, tonight, they worked from afar, through the circle."

"You stood a circle?" Janie asked, smiling in delight. "How do you feel?"

"Better." He grinned again. "Your uncle literally cried tears of joy. He said he might try retaking a form when things settle."

Janie gasped. "Godwin is going to take a form? How many *hundreds* of years has it been?"

"It was amazing for all of us. John looks... different. Less tense. It was not an experience to forget," Daniel said, still smiling. "But food and a copious number of beverages for our Peacekeeper and Huntress would be most welcome. They are exhausted."

Janie jumped, realizing she had forgotten about me. I didn't mind. On the couch, Sianna had curled up beside me and was already resting.

29

I don't remember going to bed that night, but when Daniel woke me, Sianna was asleep in bed next to me.

"You must wake. Both of you. Sianna, you must wake," his voice was an urgent pleading.

"Time is it?" I asked, fighting to open my eyes.

"Shortly before sunrise. Peacekeeper, you must wake now. Sianna, I can feel our father coming. He is here. Not here at the compound, but back in the states."

She sat up immediately and then flopped back down. "I am sick," she mumbled.

"Do you feel him?" Daniel asked. "I feel him. He's not within range to talk to me, but I feel him trying to reach through."

She groaned, rolling out of bed to crawl to the bathroom. I heard her being violently ill.

She groaned again. "Peacekeeper. Luke. Please. Check my mind—my bindings."

She was sick again as I tumbled out of bed, tripping over the blankets and landing flat on my face. "I'm coming," I muttered, climbing back to my feet.

I didn't even have to touch her to feel the wrongness. I passed peace through her and ripped out the poisoned binding.

I wasn't gentle. It was trying to do her harm.

She lay panting on the bedroom floor, nose bleeding, while I tried to make sense of what had happened. It was early. I wasn't awake yet.

"How would that have happened?" I grumbled.

"What happened?" Daniel asked. "I don't follow."

"One of her bindings… went bad. It made her sick."

"Was it the binding to our father? Peacekeeper, you need to pull mine out as well. It needs to go. He can command things mentally that we cannot ignore." He dropped to the bathroom floor beside me.

"Oh, shit," I mumbled. "I forgot about that. I wouldn't know which binding to sever, Daniel. Unless he's trying to hurt you or cause you a lack of peace, I don't know how to sort through what's there. I can't break it."

"Then break them all!" he yelled, starting to panic. "Please. I will reforge the ones that I need."

"Daniel, it's excruciating. The pain… It will incapacitate you. I destroyed one single binding and wanted to die. All of them? I can't even imagine."

"Peacekeeper—Luke—please. You don't understand. He hates me. He has always hated me. I've never been anything but a tool for him to use. Please. I have never had what you have here. I have never had this sort of place to belong. Please.

If he knows I am here, he will use me again. I know it. Cut them all."

I touched Daniel's hand to make it easier. I could feel a binding of friendship between us. But this way I didn't have to look for it.

"Daniel," I said, infusing my telepathic words with energy, *"I forbid you from accepting or following mental commands that do not align with your own wishes."*

I grunted in surprise. The mental communication worked just fine when I wasn't thinking about it.

He blinked as the words settled in his mind. "I don't know if that will work, but you are Peacekeeper. It should."

"Hop around on your right foot," I commanded through our binding.

"Why?" he asked, frowning.

"I don't know. I figured it was worth a shot. You're not compelled to follow my command. Either I don't know how to command people to do shit or my original command held tight. I guess we'll find out."

I grabbed Sianna's hand and repeated the command.

"Can your dad affect Edgar, Godwin, and John?" I asked.

Daniel was shaking his head. "I don't believe so. They are all mentally stronger than my father."

"So, I need to find Charlie," I murmured. "And Gary. And Candy."

"Charlie cannot be compelled," Sianna said, rolling onto her back. "I feel so... strange."

"I'm sorry. I wasn't gentle," I admitted.

"It hurts but not like being sick," she said. "I will be fine. Will you help Janie and the others?"

I swore, angry that I'd forgotten about them.

It turns out I shouldn't have worried. They were asleep in a tangle of limbs in Janie's room, none the wiser to anything that had happened. Then, gently touching each of the women's available arms or legs, I laid a similar compulsion, not even waking them.

"WE WILL BRING HIM NOW," Sianna was saying into her phone. "Maybe an hour."

I looked at Daniel. "She called Edgar rather than doing it the other way. No sense in confusing things. Edgar also feels Nathaniel. They want you at the compound."

Sianna hung up the phone, looking at me. "Put on actual clothes. We must go."

I looked down at my pajama pants and t-shirt. "I'm not going without telling everyone."

On cue, there was a banging on the front door as Sam let himself in. "Nathaniel's coming with his best people. I told you. By nightfall, it will be done. We'll be at war, one way or another. William, Micah, and Jake are ready when you are. You'll ride together in Will's Suburban. Daniel, I know you don't want to go, but you must. You have to go. You will be a lever for him if you're not there. He'll declare any challenge invalid because not all elders are present."

Daniel sighed, nodding. "I understand."

"Why are we going by car? Why aren't you going?" I asked.

Sam's answering smile spoke of… Otherness. "I would rather he not know I can Walk onto the estate. Adaline and I will join when the time is right."

"Why is Jake going? Why not Matthew?" I asked, surprised

that Sam's power was so controlled. I would not have guessed that his energy was hanging out around the edges.

"The beast affinities fear Matthew. It's not his time yet. Soon, but not yet.

"Jake is going because I'd like him to be there. He can be very distracting if the need arises. I don't know if you'll need him, but I want him there. Hennessy, Beth, and Adrian will stay here with the others to ensure Mom and Dad are safe."

I frowned. "Nathaniel's coming for me? He's going to try to kill me again? Should I say my pre-emptive goodbyes?"

"No, he will not touch you," Sam said. "He's coming at you sideways. It will not work because Edgar has spoken his truth, John is balanced, and Godwin wants to be friends. All the pieces are in play, except for Charlie and Ellie. I don't know where they are. But I have no doubt they will find their way. It's Charlie's plan, after all."

I didn't bother asking for more detail. Instead, I headed upstairs to change clothes, wishing I had not destroyed my phone the previous day. I had no way to message the people I loved in the event Sam got this one wrong.

"I don't have it wrong!" Sam yelled after me, guessing at my thoughts. "I'm just not sure what kind of war is coming."

SIANNA and I sat in the far back seat of William's oversized SUV. Daniel and Jake sat together in the center row with William driving and Micah sitting shotgun.

"The estate is large," Micah said, breaking up the silence. "It has some strange wards that may or may not work since Luke destroyed the ones that blocked Sam and Addy. I saw the main house and four outbuildings yesterday."

"Six outbuildings," Daniel corrected. "There's also a tornado-bomb shelter. There are four entrances to the estate. Does anyone have a piece of paper? I have a pen. I can draw a map."

Will nodded to the glove box in front of Micah. "There's a pad of paper in there. There might even be graph paper in there if he can draw it to scale."

I zoned out while Daniel was outlining the property for Will and Micah. Jake obviously didn't care; he was almost asleep. Sianna sat next to me, white-knuckling my hand.

"I do not know what binding you severed," she breathed, her voice so low I just barely caught the words. "I do not think it was the binding to my father. He is talking to me, telling me to meet him at the estate later today. He and my brothers will 'rescue' me from the mess I have landed in. He's saying he does not fault me for your survival and will not see me mated against my will."

I frowned. "Who else would want you sick like that?"

"I do not know," she admitted. "I do not know who would want me ill and have the power to force it. None of my brothers have that gift as far as I know."

"Do your sisters?" I asked.

Her eyes narrowed, considering. "One, maybe. She is not more powerful than me, but she has a gift for mental connection. I do not believe she would wish me ill, though. And my father's words make me think he is not aware that I was ill."

I shrugged. "He might be aware it failed and be trying to heal the breach now. I was not gentle. I hurt whoever held the other end of that binding."

She nodded in acknowledgment, not agreement. "Daniel, you are well?"

"Fine," he said. "He's talking to me as well. He has not demanded anything. He is just talking, explaining why he has returned against the elders' wishes."

"What's his reasoning?" I asked, curious.

"He wishes to be tested to prove he can continue as Overlord," Daniel answered.

"Wow." My mouth hung open in shock. "Wouldn't he have to transform and stand a challenge for that?"

"Yes," Daniel confirmed. "I have not seen him take another form since before he came into the title. If he could hold the energy steady, he would not choose to look as he does. Regardless, he intends to present himself at the estate this afternoon."

"If he's not showing up until this afternoon, why are we in this fucking car before seven in the morning?" Jake grunted.

"Is he lying?" I asked. "Can he lie telepathically?"

"It's a good question for Edgar or John," Daniel replied. "I don't know. I've experienced him intentionally misleading others, but not outright lying. He's certainly not required to tell the whole truth."

Sianna stared out the window, ignoring my question. I got the feeling I didn't want to know the history.

30

Hours later, I was pacing a hole in the carpet in the estate library. Jake and William were playing billiards in the corner. Sianna was resting in one of the bedrooms, still not herself. Godwin and John were playing the world's longest game of chess.

"Please sit," Edgar said from the couch, where he and Daniel watched me pace. "I'm tired just looking at you. You are the physical embodiment of peace, Lucas. Calm down."

My lips twitched into a small smile. "I don't want to pull the power forward to soothe myself. I'm fine, Edgar."

"I know you are. It's me I'm worried about," he replied, smiling.

Daniel's head tilted. "He's about ten minutes away."

Edgar nodded. "Pace down the hall and wake her, Luke."

I nodded in response, returning a minute later with Sianna. I admired her ability to be immediately awake with no slow wake-up process.

"Are you better, dear one?" Edgar asked, standing to kiss her forehead.

"Better," she agreed, forcing a smile for him. "Has Charlie called back?"

"No," I swallowed my anxiety over Charlie skipping out on this.

"I still cannot mentally connect to him." She frowned with worry.

"Nathaniel is pulling up." Daniel stood to pace my opposite path.

A few minutes later, there was a knock on the door. "The Overlord has honored us with his presence," Edgar's assistant said without a trace of irony to his voice.

"Thank you," Edgar murmured, standing to greet his brother.

"You look... well," Nate said, eyes on Edgar as he came into the room.

He had not noticed the rest of us, but I was staring in horror as Jen followed in his wake along with three more men, obviously Nathaniel's sons.

"Gentlemen, children," Jen said, greeting us all with a nod. "We will not drag this out. I question Nathaniel's ability to lead. He holds too much mental control over a large swath of people to let things lie as they are. Nathaniel, you know Lucas Peacekeeper as well as Lord Micah. William, Lord Fear stands in the corner, playing pool with Jacob, the Anchor. Of course, pool." Jen rolled her eyes.

"It's billiards," Jake corrected automatically.

She glared at him before continuing. "Nathaniel will face a challenge to prove his stability. If he stands the challenge successfully, fine. If not, another Overlord will be chosen."

"You overstep your place," Nathaniel growled at Jen, hatred toward her radiating from him.

I guessed it wasn't the first time he'd said the words because Jen just waved them away.

"I told you I have done this on four other occasions. The mind is *my* domain. I will not have you affecting others if you are unfit. If you are unwilling to stand the challenge, you fail by default, and your life is mine to take."

"Wow," I breathed, surprised. I'd never mistook Jen as someone to be trifled with, even when she was the family administrative assistant. But her no-nonsense attitude when dealing with terrifyingly powerful beings was a step beyond her usual level of impressive.

"Understand this, Nathaniel Overlord, lesser son of Jude." She paused long enough to drop one of Nate's sons to the ground when he raised a hand to strike her. "Those of the Circle belong to me. I will be displeased if you strike against your Peacekeeper again. I will utterly destroy you if you target Lord Fear. I will let the Anchor destroy you all by himself if you're fool enough to strike at him. Good luck with that one."

She turned to Edgar. "I offer you first right of challenge."

"I accept," Edgar said, glaring at his brother. "I have many grievances to air."

Jen's eyes shot to Sianna, eyebrows raised. Then, after a moment, she nodded. "Excellent. We will go to the arena. Lucas, stay here."

"What? No!" I yelled. "There's no way I'm staying here."

"Your energy cannot be involved in the challenge. You cannot help either of them. It must be a fair and proper challenge. They must transform and maintain their forms under their own power."

"Then I won't share my energy. Fine."

She looked at Sianna before looking at me. "If you wish to be present, I will lightly tie your power."

"No," Sianna said immediately. "Now, you overstep your bounds."

"I don't think he can watch you fail in a challenge, Huntress. He must either stay out or be tied so I will know if he uses the energy."

"I don't mind," I said under my breath to Sianna. "She's probably right. If you end up in a challenge, I won't sit idly by."

"I will not tie the energy such that he cannot use it. He will not be defenseless. I will tie it just enough to know *if* he uses it. I would not like him hurt any more than you would, Huntress," Jen said quietly.

Sianna stared at me. *"You trust her with your life?"* she mentally asked.

"I would already be dead, twice over, without her help," I responded aloud, earning a sad smile from Jen.

"Bend down," she muttered to me, "you're too tall for me to reach."

A second later, I was standing straight again, shaking my head. "Well, that feels strange."

"You can break it at any time with a touch of will. Try not to do it until the challenges are done," Jen explained. Turning toward the rest of the room, she said, "Let's go."

Edgar was the last from the room, pausing long enough to pick something up off a bookshelf.

SILLY ME. I had expected the arena to be empty. But, as we left the house, I felt the wash of affinity minds against mine. There were hundreds of people in the arena. Again.

"Who the hell is in there?" I asked Sianna.

"There were some families still here from yesterday," Sianna whispered. "Maybe some of them, though I believe most decided to clear out in a hurry. Likely my father's supporters."

"Correct," Jen said, not hiding her contempt. "He kept whining about being unwelcome and demanded support. That's why we didn't arrive until this afternoon. He had to round up his posse of morons. It doesn't matter, Luke. They can't interfere in an issued challenge, nor can they help him transform. When Nate loses the challenge—"

Nate cut her words off with a growl of pure rage.

"When Nate loses the challenge," Jen taunted, not at all impressed, "they may have a say in the next Overlord. We'll see how it plays out."

Edgar led the way into the arena, not acknowledging the crowd. I went where directed as Sianna pointed me to a ground floor bench.

"Nathaniel Overlord and brother, I name you unfit for leadership, shown by acts against our Peacekeeper and the death of my wife. Face me in a challenge or die now by my hand."

Edgar tossed a sheathed dagger onto the arena floor. "You'll die by the same blade that took her life."

The arena was utterly silent. I had nothing to do with it. I couldn't offer energy or accept it, tied as I was. Whatever the crowd had expected, it wasn't this. I could feel the anticipation building. This particular challenge had been centuries in the making.

"Ten paces from center," Edgar continued. "We battle until death separates us."

Nathaniel stared at his brother, stiff and stoic. There was no expression on his face. "I do not desire your death, brother. I will stand this challenge without the requirement of death."

"I will not," Edgar replied immediately. There was no hesitation. He intended to kill Nate.

"So be it," Nathaniel said levelly.

Starting from the dagger on the floor, both men marked off ten steps.

"Begin," Jen said. Eyes on Nathaniel, she sighed, "Fool."

"Hold her, Luke. Don't let her enter this challenge," Jen said in my mind.

As Edgar quickly stripped his clothes, Nathaniel pulled a gun from a leg holster, took aim, and fired four shots at his brother.

The arena erupted in chaos. Sianna was off the bench and trying to pull free of me before the sound even registered.

One shot missed, hitting someone in the stands. White light flashed. I knew Adaline was with us even as Sam appeared at the other end of the oval arena.

Edgar had taken two shots to the torso and one shot to the leg. He didn't even pause, dropping immediately into a charging cheetah form, sprinting for his brother.

Nathaniel tried to shoot the cat but missed, again hitting his crowd of supporters. I felt Adaline's power flare a second time.

Edgar landed on Nate as a lion, roaring in outrage as he closed his jaws around his brother's head.

It was already over. If Nathaniel could have transformed, he would have done so at that moment. Edgar shook his head, flinging his brother's body back and forth like a rag doll.

I could hear Nathaniel's muffled screams of terror and pain.

Edgar shifted again, taking a wolf form to savage Nathaniel's midsection, shaking intestines free.

Intestines are not meant to see daylight, but I didn't begrudge Edgar his revenge. I felt my stomach turn and wondered if I would puke as Nathaniel screamed in mindless pain.

An eternity later, the screaming stopped. The arena was perfectly silent again.

Back in human form, Edgar had the dagger in hand, freeing his brother's head from its associated body.

"Daniel," he growled, dropping the human remains into a heap on the floor and walking calmly toward his clothes.

Nathaniel's body was a blazing inferno before Edgar was fully dressed.

The crowd was screaming and cheering, chanting Edgar's name, chanting for Edgar as Overlord.

I recognized the echoing words, but they were lost on me. A bat had dropped from the ceiling, landing on human legs.

Charlie waited in his Adonis form, utterly naked. Once the crowd quieted, he pointed to Sianna.

"Sianna Huntress," he bellowed, "I call you to challenge!"

31

"He means to take the title," Nathaniel Junior yelled in joy. "The Prodigy will take his place among us!"

If he was right, he'd just been bumped down the line of succession and seemed awfully happy about it. I thought about Edgar and his talk of the title bearing real weight and responsibilities. Maybe Nate Jr. realized he wasn't fit for leadership?

Sianna's eyes were huge with shock and hurt. "On what grounds?" she asked Charlie. "How have I wronged you?"

"In your defense of the Peacekeeper, you have abandoned your duties as Huntress. You will meet me now in challenge to defend your honor."

I looked among the elders. They were baffled. But Sam was smiling at the other end of the arena, so it couldn't be all bad.

Sianna rose to her feet. "I do not wish to fight you, Charlie. I will not oppose you as Overlord. I believed you did not want the role."

"You are called to challenge," Charlie said again.

"If you do not wish me as a huntress, I will give up the role to your leadership. You do not need to challenge for it."

Charlie didn't bother answering her. He just stood, waiting.

"What are your stakes?" Sianna asked

"Do you deny my right to challenge? Do you refuse to meet me?" he demanded, prodding her.

"I can't feel your mind. Our binding is gone. The binding that made me sick this morning was yours," Sianna muttered, frowning. "Of course, I do not deny your right to challenge. I will stand to meet you if you desire. But there is no need. I will submit to your leadership."

"Does anyone here deny Sianna Huntress's right to defend herself in a challenge?" Charlie demanded, eyes on Nathaniel's sons first, then circling the crowd.

"He means to strip her of her position and power," Nate Jr. yelled, eagerness and joy radiating from him. "He will see her shamed before he takes the title of Overlord. I do not oppose this!"

There was a lot of muttering and whispering going on, but the crowd was unsure how to react. The moment passed without anyone voicing an objection, though I could feel that a large portion of the crowd did not want to see Sianna shamed.

For the life of me, I couldn't imagine why Charlie would do this. Edgar took the seat next to me, his brow furrowed in confusion.

"Name your challenge, Charlie," Sianna said, near tears.

"You will match me, form for form. When you fail, I claim from you the title of Hunter, protector of our ways."

"I cannot win that challenge," Sianna said, distraught. "You will be the final hunter, Charlie. You don't need to do this. I will give you my role once you are Overlord."

"I know," he said, smiling at last. "Accept the challenge, Sianna."

She sighed. "I accept the challenge in defense of my honor and concede the loss. Charles Hapner, I hand you the rights and responsibilities of the final hunter. Protect us by tooth and nail, as our laws demand."

Charlie responded, voice booming through the arena with power. "I accept the role of a hunter from Sianna, Nathaniel's daughter. I will protect as our laws demand."

He hugged Sianna then, smiling at her as he wiped at her tears. Stepping back from her, Charlie's voice boomed through the arena one final time. "Sianna, Nathaniel's daughter, I raise your name in praise as Overlord. Let those who dispute your worth meet you in challenge!"

"I object," John's voice boomed through the rampant chaos in the arena.

Half the crowd was cheering at the turn of events. The other half was split between confusion and rage. Nate Jr. was obviously part of the confused crowd. His mouth hung open in shock.

"I object," John roared again, bringing silence to the crowd. "I object to the naming."

Charlie and Sianna both turned to him.

"We talked about this," Charlie said to John, eyes narrowed.

John turned to Edgar, waiting.

Exhaling hard, Edgar rose to his feet again. "Sianna, Estrid's daughter, former Huntress and beast lord of more than one hundred forms, I name you worthy of the title of Overlord. Let those who dispute your worth meet you in challenge."

"Niece," John's voice boomed. "Most worthy child, I second

your naming. Take the title as it is offered and give way to a new era of affinities!"

I only saw it because I was watching him. I was waiting for the challenge. But there would be no fair challenge. Nate Jr. wasn't equipped to match Sianna, so he would cheat. Just like his father.

I saw him pull the gun and take aim at his sister's profile, where she stood in the center of the arena, focused elsewhere.

Rage exploded through me again. My peace energy answered in kind, breaking Jen's tie without any effort. But, as the rage and peace mixed into that dangerous wave of numbness, the tithe of energy from the collected affinities washed through me. I roared in surprise and pain, belatedly realizing that the sound came out of my throat in a howl—a wolf's howl.

The arena had dropped to muted colors of grey. The sound was deafening, and I could smell the drying blood on Edgar next to me.

Baffled, I tried to look down at myself. I had paws.

Holy shit! I'm a wolf, I thought, just before the bindings of a million beast affinities slammed into my brain.

32

WILLIAM

I was watching for it. Sam had told me there would be firearms in play. So, my sole reason for being present was to take the guns away so they couldn't shoot Luke while he was doing something.

When Nathaniel had pulled the gun on Edgar, I'd worried I'd missed my window. Then Sam had appeared, and Adaline's power had flared. After that, I'd figured it was fine. I was supposed to keep *Luke* from getting shot while he was busy, not Edgar.

It would have been helpful if Sam had told me Luke would be shifting into an animal, though. As it was, I was torn between disarming the asshole with the gun and taking a picture of Luke as a fully clothed wolf.

I wasn't worried. Jake was there for a reason too. Surely,

he'd take a picture. Between the stair sex and the wolf-in-clothes stupidity, Luke's holiday card would be epic this year.

Even as Sianna's brother bent to his ankle, I was moving. Running the length of the bench, I was in front of Nate Jr. before he could get a shot off.

Amateur, I thought, taking the gun right out of his shitty handhold and dislodging the clip in one motion. Then, I punched him, just for fun. He was an asshole. He'd had it coming.

I looked over the other assholes in Nathaniel's would-be entourage. They stared back, horrified. "Play by the rules," I scolded.

"A woman cannot be Overlord," Nate Jr. called out. Unfortunately for him, the effect was somewhat ruined by the fact that he was holding his bleeding nose closed.

"Stand in challenge then," Charlie replied, voice calm.

"A woman cannot stand a challenge," Nate Jr. squeaked.

"She has already stood a challenge," Charlie argued. "You had no objection to her meeting my challenge. There is precedent. She may stand a challenge."

Half the crowd was on their feet cheering, overjoyed by the way this had played out. They called to Sianna Overlord, praising her strength and bravery.

Another part of the crowd meant Charlie harm. I could feel it radiating toward him. The remaining part of the crowd was just flat-out confused. Things had happened too quickly. They weren't sure how to feel about a woman as Overlord.

Now would be a good time to do your peace shit, Luke, I thought, glancing toward my youngest brother.

He was still in wolf form, laying on his side, panting hard.

Did he get injured after all? Oh, shit.

I dropped to my knees beside the wolf, trying to find any sign of injury.

"He's not injured," Edgar assured me. "I think the bindings hit him."

"What bindings?"

"To beast affinities. To all beast affinities. I can feel his energy in my brain," Edgar said.

I frowned, not understanding.

"It's fine," Sam said, appearing from nowhere. "He's functionally overloaded. He's processing something like a million new bindings. Give it a few minutes, and then Jake can help pull some of Luke's energy."

"Oh. I thought Jake was here for the picture."

Sam's lips twitched. "That too."

I looked around. "This is a shitshow, Sam."

"Yeah, it's going to be war. We can't avoid it," he muttered. "Well, we could, but the ways to avoid it are worse than the war."

"Micah!" Sam yelled.

Already on his feet, Micah stood in the arena between Nate Jr. and Sianna. When he finally spoke, his words radiated with his own blend of power—strength, courage, spitefulness, and something like hope mixed with faith. Micah and Sam called it Redemption. It was good enough for me.

"You have a choice now," Micah's voice echoed through the building. He was looking at Nate Jr., but the words couldn't be missed by anyone. "The ways of the past are best left to the past. You may move forward in strength or fight against change, knowing it is a losing battle. Recognize your sister as your rightful leader and watch your people prosper under her care."

Nate Jr. blinked a few times as Micah's words hit home in

his brain. But then I saw his expression change and knew it was no good.

"I will never bow to a woman. Our kind will never see her as a leader in truth, no matter how the Circle interferes."

"Uh, Sam?" I asked.

"Yeah?"

"We're just going to let him walk out of here?"

"Yep," Sam said easily. "It goes better like this. He'll leave with the remainder of his father's entourage, regroup, and come at us directly."

"Us? They're coming at us?" I asked. "Not Sianna?"

"Well, her too. But us to start. They'll blame me for this. It's fine. We're ready."

"I could just go finish them now. It'd end this whole thing before it gets started," I said, watching as a portion of the crowd followed the misogynistic assholes out of the building.

"No, don't do that. It'll weaken Sianna's position if we do that. We play defense on this and let her put it down. If we start making martyrs of them, someone with intelligence might take over leadership of their group. It's easier this way. Let them go."

"You could have told me he was going to change into an animal," I complained. "That shit is funny."

"Bah. If I'd told you, you'd have told him. Then he'd have thought too hard about it and fucked it up. I can't tell you people anything. You get all freaked out. He's starting to wake up."

33

I could feel the symphony rolling through my mind. All the lives, the thought patterns… breathing lungs, beating hearts, mumbled words. The cacophony of sound played through my brain, the harmony I'd been searching for my entire life.

Some part of me recognized this new internal music as bindings—a lot of bindings.

My children. The sound of my children, Other-me whispered. *They belong to you now, Lucas Peacekeeper.*

I lay still for a while, lost in my mind, processing the music. It was loud and overwhelming but also natural. It took over the blank space I'd created when I had destroyed the binding to Sianna.

Sianna! I realized I'd zoned out right as I'd seen her brother reach for a gun.

But, at the thought of her, I felt that new music shift inside my brain, making way for one specific sound to rise among many. My brain had sorted through the bindings, finding the one to Sianna.

As I lay there, I knew she was focused elsewhere. Standing with Charlie. Becoming Overlord in truth. Sianna would be Overlord. She was no longer Huntress.

I wondered what that meant for us. Then I felt her love pouring into me. The true, unfiltered, passionate love that could burn for eternity. It was there in her binding. I knew if I looked for it, the binding would shine with gold.

I nearly cried with relief, only then realizing I was still a wolf.

How had that happened? I wondered.

"Wakey, wakey," Sam cooed. "Time to get up."

I turned my head.

"Alright, Jake," Sam said. "He's with us. Do your thing."

"What am I doing?" Jake asked, sounding as confused as I felt.

"Help him pull the energy," Sam prodded.

"How?"

"Like you pull energy from Matty."

"I don't want to be a wolf, Sam. No." Jake refused. "Luke, get up or I'll light your fur on fire."

"He'll come back to himself, Walker," Godwin said. "He won't need help. The first time is just a little rough. It took Jude a few days."

I stared. *"I can transform?"*

"Yes," Godwin replied, nodding and smiling. "It's the beasts' gift to you. You can also communicate through mental bindings now. I heard you loud and clear. Be careful of that, Luke. Commands given mentally cannot be disregarded."

"Always wolf?" I asked.

He shrugged. "I have no idea. It depends on the Peacekeeper and how often it's used."

"She is glorious," Edgar murmured, wiping tears from his eyes. "So like her mother."

I turned then, watching Charlie hold Sianna's hand as the bindings joined her brain, just as they'd joined mine. They weren't the same type of bindings I held to affinities, and there weren't as many of them. But, somehow, her bindings seemed more patient than mine.

I gave a wolf snort of jealousy.

Edgar walked out to her then, the remaining crowd screaming in worshipful delight. He extended his own hand to her, offering the binding of a father to his daughter. "Lead in glory, dear one," he said, the words barely audible amidst all the noise.

Godwin and John followed, each kissing her forehead, bestowing a blessing that was visible to my sight.

Sam poked me. "Go. The binding can stay now. Go match her binding in kind."

I stared at him, processing his words.

Will yanked my ear, gaining a whimpering yip from me. "Don't be a fucking sissy. Go out there and offer her your love in truth. Be overjoyed if she accepts it. You look like a moron. Next time take the clothes off before shifting, Pollyanna."

If Matthew or Ethan had been there, they'd have helped me out of the stupid clothes. Instead, I'd been left with the brothers who just laughed at my expense. I glared at Micah for joining them. I expected better from him.

"Adaline," I mentally whined. *"Please? I don't want to wander out there looking like an idiot."*

She appeared then, an angel of mercy, to pull me free of my shirt while I shook off my pants, underwear, and socks.

As I trotted my way out to the center of the arena, I heard Sam say, "Quick, hide the clothes!" But I didn't stop to worry about it. Undoubtedly, I'd end up bare ass naked in front of hundreds of people. *Oh well.*

I made my way through the people surrounding Sianna and brushed against her leg.

Smiling, she crouched down to meet my eyes. "Well, you figured that part out." She laughed at me, joy radiating from her. I'd never felt her so centered and calm.

I found the shining gold binding that belonged to her so I could get the words through.

"Sianna Overlord."

She grinned, nodding her head. "Lucas Peacekeeper," she greeted me in kind, saying the words aloud.

"I love you. I don't like being parted from you. Your joy brings me joy. Fierce, beautiful Sianna, I love you."

She sighed, feeling my binding of love settle between us, meeting and twisting with her own. "I love you," she breathed into my ear. "But enough of the wolf. I would like my lazy, lavish Luke back now. Pull the energy back in line."

She stood straight, looking down at me, waiting.

I had no idea how to do what she asked, but I tried.

Sianna's lips tipped up into a smile.

"Rise, Lucas Peacekeeper," she said, words ringing with her power, calling my peaceful energy forward.

"Rise, Peacekeeper," she asked of me again, the edges of her body glowing.

I could feel the wolf form giving way, answering the call of a stronger affinity. The beastly bindings were shifting into the background of my mind as my body came slowly back to me.

"Rise," she commanded one last time. "We have work to do, Peacekeeper."

Luke & Sianna's journey to leadership and love concludes in

Rise, Peacekeeper's Harmony, Book Three

THANKS FOR READING!

As always, if you enjoyed this story, your Amazon rating and/or review would be appreciated. As a new author, reviews are imperative to attracting readers.

For updates on my releases as well as **bonus content,** please subscribe to my newsletter at https://maggielilybooks.com/sign-up/.

You can find me on Facebook, Instagram, and Bookbub.

Want to chat? My Facebook reader group is cozy and fun with next to no smarmy sales pushes. Otherwise, you're welcome to email at maggie@maggiemlily.com.

BUILDING THE CIRCLE SERIES

To follow the Trellis family as they uncover their unique psychic, empathic powers, check out the *Building the Circle* series. The events in this series happen before the *Peacekeeper's Harmony* series.

The Call

The Power

The Center

The Corners

The Pillars

The Close

Volume 1 - The Call, The Power, & The Center

Volume 2 - The Corners, The Pillars, & The Close

Becoming Hank - The story how Hank & Darla fell in love, got married, and ended up with NINE children.

ALSO BY MAGGIE M LILY

Peacekeeper's Harmony Series

Ransom

Reaping

Rise (Sep 3, 2021)

A Lovely Twist of Fae Series - Fall 2021

Ainsley

Aurora

Arbor

CHARACTER INDEX

Adaline — The Mistress Life who holds power over all living things and balances the Time Walker (Samuel Trellis)

Adrian Trellis — Lord Rage and partner to Lady Wind (Lucinda (Lucy)), second eldest Trellis brother

Ava — Mother to Adaline and Jess

Bethany Trellis — Lady Hope, partner to Lord Loyalty (Hennessy). Youngest Trellis sibling

Candace (Candy) Hapner — Cat beast master, Charlie's sister, and Luke's ex-girlfriend

Charlie Hapner — Beast lord prodigy, Candy's brother, Ellie's husband, Matilda's friend

Daniel — Beast lord elder who also possesses some empowerment for fire and life

Darla Trellis — Mother to the Trellis kids; respect her table

Dennis — Darla's brother

Edgar — Beast Affinity elder, Sianna's uncle

Eleanor (Ellie) Hapner — Matilda's best friend, Charlie's wife, energy siphon

Emma Gracen — Lady Love, wife of Lord Fear (William Trellis)

Eric — Mental guide, Matilda and Ellie's BFF

Ethan Trellis — Lord Joy, partner to Lord Hate & Redemption (Micah), fourth Trellis sibling

Gary — Beast affinity fox, Adrian Trellis's best friend

Godwin — Beast Affinity elder, Sianna's uncle

Hank Trellis — Father to the Trellis kids

Jacob Trellis — The Anchor, partner Lady Light (Matilda), third Trellis sibling

Janie — Beast affinity rabbit, Luke's assistant, Godwin's great-niece many times removed

Jess — Adaline's sister, gifted with all-sight

Hennessy (Jessup Garland) — Lord Loyalty, partner to Lady Hope (Bethany), William's best friend, Darla's (claimed) ninth son

John — Beast Affinity elder, Sianna's uncle

Linda Wright— Lady Perseverance, Lucy's sister, Ree's mother

Lucas Trellis — Lord Peace, the Peacekeeper, eighth Trellis sibling

Lucinda (Lucy) Wallace — Lady Wind, partner to Lord Rage (Adrian), Linda's sister, Ree's aunt

Matilda Trellis — Lady Light, partner to the Anchor (Jacob Trellis), dear friend to Ellie, Charlie, and Eric

Matthew Trellis — Lord Pan, Pandemonium, Capitan Fucking Chaos, partner to Lady Earth (Miranda), seventh Trellis son.

Micah — Lord Redemption & Hate, partner to Lord Joy (Ethan); also known as Micah the Aged and Micah the Desolate

Miranda — Lady Earth, partner to Lord Pan (Matthew Trellis)

Nathaniel — Beast Affinity Overlord, Sianna's father

Nate Jr. — Beast lord and Nathaniel's eldest son, the heir apparent to the Overlord title if Charlie refuses

Noah Trellis — Lord Passion, partner to Lady Loch/Lady Water (Talise), sixth Trellis sibling

Rajena (Jen) Meeli — Queen of the Mind, also the former Trellis family administrative assistant

Samuel Trellis — The Walker who holds power over time, space, and the elements; partner to Mistress Life Adaline); the middle Trellis child

Sianna Huntress — The Huntress, a beast lord of great power, daughter of Nathaniel, Luke's primary love interest

Talise Ayers — Lady Loch/Lady Water, partner to Lord Passion (Noah); she's a little edgy

William Trellis — Lord Fear, Lady Love's (Emma) husband, and eldest Trellis sibling; considering a new career in relationship counseling

Made in the USA
Columbia, SC
08 August 2021